**For the first time in more ce
remember, he desired a woman**

He sat next to her and set the wineglass on the table by the couch. The warmth of her body reached his skin, and another deep convulsion of need shuddered through him. He held very still. He should smoke. But he wanted to *feel*. This desire was the deepest emotion left to him, and he'd kept it at bay for so long. He wanted to let it take him over just for a time. Long enough to experience it, but not to act upon it.

She turned to look at him. He blinked as her eyes measured his. She sensed his desire—somehow he knew that. More, she shared it—he saw it in the darkening of her blue-blue eyes. Her body shifted toward him, her breath brushed his lips even as his fangs slid into place behind them.

Feel it, he thought as his body became a flame of hunger. *Feel it, because it's the only thing you* can *feel, because it's the closest you'll ever get to love—*

The smell again, brittle and invasive, as if a knife had cut through the air made soft by the scent of her skin. The smell of bloodied breath. Then a sharp, violent pain at the base of his skull, and then nothing.

To Mom and Dad, for endless support and encouragement.
I couldn't have done it without you.

Other Books by Katriena Knights

Time and Time Again
The Haunting of Rory Campbell
The Vampire Apocalypse Book Two: Apotheosis
(Coming in 2003)

The Vampire Apocalypse
BOOK ONE: REVELATIONS

***

Katriena Knights

The sale of this book without its cover is unauthorized. If you purchased this book without a cover, you should be aware that it was reported to the publisher as "unsold and destroyed." Neither the author nor the publisher has received payment for the sale of this "stripped book."

The Vampire Apocalypse
Book One: Revelations
Published by ImaJinn Books, a division of ImaJinn

Copyright ©2002 by Katriena Knights
Printed and bound in the United States of America. All rights reserved. No part of this book may be reproduced in any form or by any means (electronic, mechanical, photocopying, recording, or otherwise) without prior written permission of both the copyright holder and the above publisher of this book, except by a reviewer, who may quote brief passages in a review. For information, address: ImaJinn Books, a division of ImaJinn, P.O. Box 162, Hickory Corners, MI 49060-0162; or call toll free 1-877-625-3592.

ISBN: 1-893896-09-9

10 9 8 7 6 5 4 3 2 1

PUBLISHER'S NOTE:
This book is a work of fiction. Names, characters, places and incidents are products of the author's imagination or are used fictitiously. Any resemblance to actual events or locales or persons, living or dead, is entirely coincidental.

Books are available at quantity discounts when used to promote products or services. For information please write to: Marketing Division, ImaJinn Books, P.O. Box 162, Hickory Corners, MI 49060-0162, or call toll free 1-877-625-3592.

Cover design by Rickey Mallory

ImaJinn Books, a division of ImaJinn
P.O. Box 162, Hickory Corners, MI 49060-0162
Toll Free: 1-877-625-3592
http://www.imajinnbooks.com

JULIAN

Apocalypse: Gr. *apokalypsis*, an uncovering, revelation.

The Nephilim were on the earth in those days—and also afterward—when the sons of God went to the daughters of men and had children by them.
—*Genesis 6:4*

The Creatures of Dark Light came among the Children of Men. Thus was born Ruha and Belial, Ialdaboth and Samis, and they moved upon the Earth and showed unto the Children of Men the Ways of the Blood Gods.
—The Book of Changing Blood

PRELUDE

Beautiful. It had been a long time since he had seen such beauty.

She lay sleeping on a small bed where she was supposed to be safe, her black hair spread over a pink flowered pillowcase, black lashes against ivory cheeks. Six years old, he thought. She might remember. He wished he could have found her earlier, so all that happened tonight would be forgotten.

He knelt beside the bed. She'd dropped her teddy bear onto the pink carpet. He picked it up and held it a moment, looking into the empty gaze of its plastic eyes. Gently, he laid it aside.

His fingers touched her throat, just below her ear, feeling her pulse. It pattered beneath his touch, a child's heartbeat. If there had been any doubt she was the one, it disappeared as her blood moved beneath his fingers. A soft tingle passed over his skin.

Three, perhaps four humans out of nearly six billion, and he'd found one. He couldn't help smiling at the wonder of it.

She opened her eyes. His smile faded as fear touched her face.

"Shh," he said. "It's all right." The compulsion in his voice quieted her, and she lay still, looking at him in wonderment. "Don't be afraid."

He touched her face, then bent to her, and put his teeth in her throat.

ONE

Lorelei Fletcher was in over her head. She should have followed her instincts from the beginning. Too late for that now—she just hoped she could get the hell out of here somehow.

On any other night but Halloween she never would have followed Dina east of Tompkins Square Park, dance club or no dance club. But Halloween and her vampire costume made her feel invincible, so she'd agreed.

They'd never made it to the dance club. Instead, following directions given Dina by her latest boyfriend, they'd ended up here, in a bizarre tenement building where all the rooms seemed to be connected, and where no hallway seemed to be the same shape from moment to moment. Lorelei was beginning to wonder if the weird smell in the place was some kind of hallucinogen.

It would, at least, be a logical explanation for why everyone was so weird.

Everybody in the place was dressed like a vampire. It hadn't seemed strange at first. It was Halloween, after all. Lorelei herself made a stunning vampiress, or so she thought, with her black hair and naturally milky complexion. But, unlike the weirdoes at this party, she only played vampire one day a year.

She had to admit the image of the vampire intrigued her, sometimes to the point of obsession. She could spend days watching every vampire movie she could find, tracing dim, elusive memories. In twenty years, she hadn't found a mirror to the scene she remembered from childhood.

But compared to these nuts, she was a paragon of sanity.

She'd been accosted half a dozen times by guys with razor blades, and, looking for the bathroom, she'd stumbled into a couple of leather-clad women sucking each other's wrists with an enthusiasm Lorelei reserved for sex or good chocolate. She'd heard about things like this, but she'd never really believed people could be so freaky. So much for unbridled optimism.

She wished she knew where Dina was. Lorelei had lost track of her about an hour ago, when they'd split up to find the front door. They were supposed to meet at a designated bathroom fifteen minutes later, but Lorelei hadn't seen Dina since. Nor had she seen the front door.

Somewhere a clock began to strike. Lorelei looked at her watch. Midnight. A woman in a bright red cape brushed by her, a coppery smell of blood drifting in her wake.

"Excuse me," Lorelei said, but the woman only cast a grin over her shoulder and kept walking.

"Thank you so much." Lorelei came to a halt and crossed her arms. This was ridiculous. She could swear she'd been down this stretch of hallway at least twice. Where the hell had the front door gone? She thought a minute. If she went this way, she should end up back at the bathroom...

"No!"

The voice, faint but frantic, seemed to come from around a bend in the hall. Lorelei froze. Had it been—?

"No! Stop it, Nicky!"

"Dina!" Lorelei broke into a run.

"Get your hands off me, you bastard!"

"Dina!" Lorelei ran full-tilt into the closed door. She was certain it was the bathroom—or *a* bathroom—and behind it Dina's voice rose, frantic.

"No! Nicky, no!" The voice sobbed now in terror.

Lorelei slammed herself into the door. "Dina! Dina, hang on!"

Hang on to what? Lorelei had no idea what was going on. Her breath tore in her throat, heaving toward panic. Visions of razor blades and blood swam in her mind. She smashed herself again and again into the door until she thought her shoulder would shatter. Suddenly the door came open with the sickening sound of splintering wood.

There was Dina. There were no razor blades, but there was blood.

A big, dark-haired man had her pinned against the wall, face buried in the bend of her throat. Of course, Lorelei thought fleetingly. If they thought they were vampires, of course they'd go for the throat. Shallow cuts, probably, like the wrist cuts.

"Get away from her, you freak!" Lorelei grabbed the man

by the shoulder and dragged at him, trying to haul him off Dina. But he was heavy, and stronger than she could have imagined...

Panic clawed up her throat. This wasn't like the wrist-sucking girls in the bathroom. Something more was going on here. The room reeked of blood. From this angle, Lorelei could see it, winding in a thick, red line down Dina's bare shoulder, down the length of her arm, dripping steadily from the end of her index finger. Dina's head was thrown back, the man's mouth fastened to her throat...

He was killing her.

Lorelei struck him again, fruitlessly. Then, so deep into panic she had no awareness of it anymore, she grabbed a handful of his silky black hair and jerked as hard as she could.

The man's head snapped back. Blood sprayed everywhere. He turned toward Lorelei as Dina's body slumped down to the floor, filling the small room with a rhythmic spray of blood that suddenly subsided.

The man grabbed Lorelei's hair on either side of her face, holding her riveted. She'd thought the paleness of his skin was makeup, skillfully applied. Now she saw it was only his skin, smooth, seamless, painfully white. He opened his blood-filled mouth and she saw white again, slender fangs.

He struck.

***

Julian Cavanaugh had been sitting in the alley for hours, chain smoking and smelling blood. He came here every Halloween, to remind himself of what he'd been, and what he'd become.

Sometimes he wondered why he did it. With the blood-smell in his nostrils the craving became almost unbearable even with the aid of the cigarettes, which weren't exactly over-the-counter Marlboros. But if he could sit here from dusk until dawn, smelling the blood and not giving in to the need, he knew he could make it another year.

As of tonight, it would be two hundred and thirty-six.

Sometimes he thought it was a waste of time, namely the hours he invested every week making the cigarettes. The tobacco he could buy at the mall, nicely dried and prepared, but three of the other ingredients were herbs which, as far as he knew, had been extinct on this planet for a millennium. Except for the few plants preserved by a Native American shaman, given to him by a god of blood then passed on to Julian two hundred and thirty-six years ago.

Deep, throaty laughter came from a second-story window. Julian recognized the voice. Nicholas had been made a vampire three years ago tonight, during the annual Halloween bloodbash. Vivian had made him. As Julian recalled, she'd found him in a bar and brought him home for the party. It was strange to Julian how many humans were willing to come, to slash their wrists and lap each others' blood, pretending to be something they couldn't begin to imagine.

Julian lit another cigarette from the tip of the butt in his mouth and listened to Nicholas' voice. A woman answered him, first laughing seductively, then, suddenly, in fear.

"No. Stop it, Nicky." He heard scuffling. "Get your hands off me, you bastard!" Then she screamed, "No!"

Julian closed his eyes tight and sucked hard on the cigarette. He'd promised himself a long time ago to stay out of the business of other vampires. But he hated to hear the taking of an unwilling victim.

He should get up and walk away. Inside, the voices rose. Another woman's voice screamed from the other side of the door. Julian snubbed the cigarette against the brick wall and put the butt in his jacket pocket. Gathering himself, he leapt, catching the sill and levering himself up on it. The cigarettes had stilled the need for blood, but hadn't affected his strength.

The victim's head lolled against the partly-open window. All Julian could see was a mass of gold-brown hair and Nicholas' face pressed into her neck. Julian grabbed the window and shoved upward. He should have moved faster. Now it was too late to save her.

Suddenly the bathroom door burst inward and another woman half-fell into the room. With an astonishing show of strength, she tore Nicholas away from the dying blonde woman. And Nicholas, predictably, turned on her.

Julian launched himself through the window and onto

Nicholas' back, breaking him loose from his victim and knocking him to the floor. The woman fell in a heap to the ground, all pale skin and black hair, unconscious, not from blood loss, but from the beginning of the vampire's trance. Her throat had been pricked, but not penetrated.

Nicholas, interrupted at the beginning of a new feed, stumbled. Julian grabbed his shoulder and shoved him down. The younger vampire glared up at him, eyes glinting black.

"You," he said, his voice still wet with blood from the first girl.

"How observant," said Julian dryly.

Nicholas leaped at him. Julian hadn't expected that and he threw up an arm to ward Nicholas off, but he landed hard against him, threw a punch that smashed Julian's lip against his teeth. The taste of his own blood made Julian momentarily dizzy.

"Stop," he said, his voice pitched low and deep.

Nicholas stopped. He was young, his three years no match for Julian's eight centuries. He gaped at Julian, then struggled to formed words. "There's a Call out for you, man."

Julian stared. There had been no Call put out for a vampire for nearly two centuries. But under the compulsion, Nicholas had no choice but to tell the truth.

"Sleep," Julian said finally, and Nicholas slumped to the floor.

Julian turned to the dark-haired woman. She was alive. He could still help her. It was far too late for the other woman. All he could do was get away from the smell of her blood as quickly as possible. Gently, he lifted the living woman from the floor.

***

At home in the deep darkness of the early morning, Julian put the woman in one of the spare bedrooms and tucked the blankets around her. She'd be safe here until daybreak, if he could protect her from himself.

Not that he was much of a threat at the moment. His head ached from the effort of holding a compulsion over the cab driver who'd brought them here. It was the only way he could get the unconscious woman from the fringes of the vampire colony to his house in Connecticut without awkward questions.

The pain faded slowly as he knelt next to the bed to watch her.

Her soft breathing and the slight movement of her eyes under closed lids reassured him. The vampire trance seemed not to have damaged her, seemed to be wearing off and weakening in the usual manner. He touched her face, telling himself he was checking her temperature, the texture of her skin, to judge her recovery. In truth, he only wanted to touch her. Blood pulsed just below her skin, a tickle of sensation under his fingers.

Leave her. Leave her before you kill her.

It was the best advice he'd heard all day. He forced himself away from her bedside. She'd be safe alone. Safer, even. He went downstairs, out onto the porch, and lit a cigarette.

"You have no idea."

Startled, Julian dropped the cigarette he'd just lit.

"Show yourself," he said, putting as much force into the compulsion as he could while fumbling for the cigarette. The last thing he needed was attention from his neighbors, and setting his lawn on fire would definitely bring that. Not to mention each butt represented a half-hour of labor.

The voice came closer, laughing now, as a dark, hulking shadow came into view. A human figure, yet not human, face shadowed by the long, dark cloak that obscured the outlines of the rest of his body.

"Your voice tricks won't work on me," he went on. "You're far too young."

He was right. Julian could feel it now, the age rolling off the other vampire in waves, the power behind it. Julian had only felt such a thing in the presence of the Senior. There was no vampire older or more powerful than the Senior.

But this one was, and this one was not the Senior.

"Who are you?" Julian took a deep drag on the cigarette. The appearance of the stranger had driven most of his thoughts about the woman out of his head. The blast of smoke did the rest.

The stranger turned. Moonlight touched part of his face, illuminating his jaw, one corner of his mouth. He smiled. "I think the greater question is, 'Who are *you?*' Or, more precisely, who are you becoming?"

The smoke had eased him, but the other vampire's presence tingled over his skin and through his blood like an electric shock. Julian could barely hear over the drone of it. Still, the outrageous words penetrated.

"I don't understand."

The other vampire reached toward Julian, plucked the smoldering cigarette from his lips.

"How does it work, do you think?" He held the cigarette up. Julian stared at the waning spark on the end of it, then at the vampire's big, long fingers. They tilted the cigarette back to Julian. "Take it."

Julian had it back between his lips before he realized the order had been spoken as compulsion, so practiced and delicate, Julian had barely felt the manipulation.

The other vampire shifted a little, seeming to come closer, though in truth he'd barely moved at all.

"Have you thought about it at all? Why a vampire must feed, and how you've been able to go so many years without?"

"How do you know me?"

"I make it my business to know. Answer."

Julian opened his mouth, then closed it. He'd expected the compulsion again, but there was none this time. The vampire had merely spoken, in his deep voice with its odd, undefinable accent. So Julian took a moment to think.

"The blood is alive. It's the only thing within us that is. When it dies, it must be replenished." He paused to take a long drag on the cigarette, feeling the nicotine and herb-smoke rush through him—throat, lungs, blood—tingling to the tips of his fingers. "The nicotine, the smoke, the herbs, whatever they are—the stimulation keeps the blood alive, I think."

The other vampire smiled again. "Ironic, isn't it, that something that would kill a living human sustains the undead."

"Fitting, though." Julian couldn't restrain his sarcasm. This stranger tried his patience. "Somehow I think there's more to it than that."

This time the other vampire did step forward, a long, powerful step. The movement brought his face partly out of shadow, showing the bridge of a long, slightly misshapen nose and the piercing gray of eyes so old even Julian couldn't comprehend it.

"Yes, there's more to it. More than you can possibly understand." He fell silent, his stillness like that of stone. "I watch you. Always."

And he disappeared.

Julian stared at the place where he'd been and sucked the last bit of life out of his cigarette.

"Great," he muttered. "That's just what I need."

TWO

She dreamed a dream she hadn't had in years. A scene from one of those long-ago movies she'd watched as a girl. A scene she'd never been able to find on film, no matter how many late-night horror classics she watched.

A man, broad and shadowed, in a brown cloak. He came into her bedroom, silent. She couldn't see his face. She was a little girl, and she should have been frightened.

She wasn't, though. The man told her not to be afraid, and she believed him. He sat on the bed next to her and touched her face. His hands were big, the ends of his fingers rough.

"Don't be afraid," he said again.

"I'm not," she told him. "Who are you?"

She thought perhaps he smiled, but the hood of the cloak obscured his face, so she couldn't be sure. He didn't answer her question, but bent his head to her throat and kissed her, right on top of her pulse.

"That tickles," she told him.

He straightened, and slid his hand gently over her dark hair. "That's good," he said.

She laughed a little, and again she thought he smiled.

"Close your eyes," he said.

She did. When she opened them, he was gone.

***

She floated in an odor. A strange one—spicy, coppery, smoky. Then came a sound—shifting movement. Slowly, Lorelei opened her eyes.

She lay in a wide, white bed. The sheets felt stiff, like hotel sheets. The smell wasn't a hotel smell, though. It was too rich, too natural. The room was dim.

Carefully, she sat up. Her head felt spongy, and her arms wouldn't quite move the way she wanted them to. Her neck hurt just below her ear. She laid her hand on it, pressing against the pain.

"Good morning."

Lorelei jumped. A man stood near the door. She hadn't seen or heard him come in, and wondered if he'd been there the whole time. The thought made her shiver. Had he been watching her sleep?

"Who . . . who are you?" Her voice felt thick, and the wound on her throat hurt when she spoke. "Where am I?"

He smiled and took a few steps closer. She could see him now as he stepped closer to the circle of light from the bedside lamp. "My name is Julian." His deep voice held a strange accent, brittle and unfamiliar. "You're in my house. I rescued you from the party last night."

Memory flooded back—the blood, Dina's screams. "Dina—"

The man's face gentled. "I'm sorry."

Lorelei swallowed tears. She didn't know this man, couldn't afford to let herself be vulnerable right now. If she broke down, she'd have no way to defend herself.

"I won't hurt you," he said.

Lorelei believed him. If he'd wanted to hurt her, he could have done it a hundred times already. But she knew instinctively he hadn't.

Still, he looked dangerous, too much like the creepy-freaks from last night, with his pale skin and jet-black hair. His features were strangely cut, with an almost Asian cast that disappeared when you looked a little away. Strange. Certainly his name didn't sound Asian. Neither did his accent.

He dropped his hands into his pockets and took a step back towards the door. "Dawn is two hours past. I need to sleep. You're welcome to stay as long as you like. Help yourself to anything you might need. The kitchen is downstairs."

"You sleep during the day?"

He smiled a little. "I work nights. Someone has to."

With that, he slipped quietly out of the room.

Lorelei stared at the closed door for a long time, waiting for her emotions to settle. She couldn't think about Dina, not yet. Instinct told her she was safe for the moment, but she wasn't quite ready to trust it.

Finally, she swung out of bed. The single window in the

room was covered by drawn drapes. She threw them back. The sight of the sun, the sensation of light on her skin, brought a strange surge of relief. It looked like late morning, though—she was definitely late for work.

Not much she could do about that. She still wore her costume from last night—white shirt, black leather miniskirt, thigh-high black boots and a short, black cape. And she had no idea where she was, or how she could get home from here. Her only source of information was snoozing somewhere in the house, completely useless and, given the company he apparently kept, far from trustworthy.

Oh, well. It wasn't the first time she'd been on her own.

Outside in the hallway, the house was silent. Lorelei had expected to at least hear Julian somewhere, but the house was utterly silent. Maybe his room was soundproofed. Probably a good idea for someone who worked at night.

Whatever the case, she didn't feel she should rummage around his house. He had, after all, saved her life.

Unlike the vampire house, this house was fairly straightforward. Lorelei went down the stairs and found herself in the living room. Resisting the urge to sift through the collection of books on the big, antique-looking bookcases, she went straight to the phone.

"Castle Boutique."

"Randy? It's Lorelei."

"Thank God! Where are you?"

"I'm not sure. Look, I got caught in a really bad scene last night." She stopped, listening to the sounds of the boutique in the background. Randy waited her out. "Randy, Dina's dead."

Randy hadn't known Dina, not really. "Shit. I'm sorry, Lorelei. Are you all right?"

"Yes. No—I don't know." The tears she'd swallowed before had come back with a vengeance, building hard behind her eyes. "Look, Randy, I have to go—"

"It's okay, Boss. I'll hold down the fort. Just call me when you get home."

"All right, I will."

She hung up the phone and let herself cry. It went on far

longer than she wanted, but she kept it silent.

She hadn't known Dina that well, but she knew Dina hadn't deserved to die. No one deserved to die like that, the victim of some weirdo's fetish. It just wasn't right.

Finally, Lorelei regained control of herself. She needed to talk to the police, she thought. They'd want information about the murder. But first she had to figure out where she was, and how to get home.

Carrying the cordless handset with her, Lorelei went into the kitchen. The refrigerator was surprisingly empty, but there was milk in an unmarked jug. She poured a glass and drank it slowly. It tasted strange, but not spoiled. Swallowing made her neck ache. She left the glass half-empty.

She could call a cab to get home, she thought, but she didn't know where she was, so she couldn't tell them where to come to get her. Scanning the kitchen, she found a pile of mail neatly stacked on the counter. Jackpot. *Julian Cavanaugh*, said his electric bill, with a nice, mundane address under it.

Connecticut. She looked out a window. Middle-of-freaking-nowhere Connecticut. This cab ride was going to cost her a mint.

***

As always, Julian woke slowly. His system had been shutting down later and later over the past decade, sometimes not sending him to sleep until two hours past dawn. He saw sunlight in the evenings now, too, his body awakening more often than not in time to watch the sunset from a carefully shaded distance. In the winter, after the clocks fell back, it gave him a substantial period of time to interact with the world of humanity.

He lay still for a time, waiting for sensation to return to his extremities, then sat up. The clock on the table next to the bed said 4:15 p.m. Earlier than yesterday. He didn't know why it was happening, wondered if someday, centuries down the road, he'd meet himself in the middle and not have to sleep at all.

Then the hunger hit, and he could think of nothing else.

Blood craving ripped through him like a wave of nausea. He scrambled for the cigarettes on the nightstand, managed to get one into his mouth and lit.

The first rush of smoke quieted the need. In spite of the theories he'd offered the ancient vampire, he had no idea how the cigarettes worked. He only knew how he'd found them.

He'd been a long way from home in those years, having traveled through most of the known world and a good portion of the unknown. He wasn't even sure where he was when a stumble into a fast-flowing river had carried him for miles, eventually dumping his temporarily dead body on the banks of a human settlement. The tribe was some brand of Sioux, he'd decided a century later, based on the blood-drenched ceremonies.

They called him a Blood God there, gave him prisoners from another tribe to feed on. And the tribe's shaman told Julian of another Blood God, who'd come generations before with a bag of herbs. Julian had smoked the herbs for the first time sitting cross-legged in the shaman's tipi. He hadn't tasted human blood since.

Over two centuries later, he smoked three cigarettes in a row and rolled out of bed.

His bedroom was in the basement, behind a metal door with six deadbolts. It was as safe as he could make himself. He'd considered installing an alarm on the door, but no matter how loud the alarm, it wouldn't wake him, and he certainly didn't want the police showing up if his resting place was disturbed. So a mechanism on the door would deliver a lethal shock to anyone who jimmied the locks. He disconnected that, opened the deadbolts, closed everything behind him, and headed upstairs.

He hadn't expected the woman to still be there, and she wasn't. She'd left nothing behind except her smell. That was all Julian needed.

It was said dogs could smell a single drop of blood in a gallon of water. A vampire's sense of smell was keener. With the smell of her skin in his nostrils, Julian could track the woman down, even through the steaming odors of the City.

He ate first. As his body had begun to adjust to sunlight, as he had gone longer and longer without human blood, his stomach had begun to tolerate other foods. He'd started with animal blood—big animals at first, cows or deer. Eventually he'd found he could eat the meat as well as the blood. Lately, he'd been able to stomach unpasteurized milk, which he acquired from a dairy upstate. It was far from a human diet, but it kept him nourished.

He threw frozen chicken breasts into the microwave, defrosted them and ate the meat raw. His hunger subsided as he finished the meat and smoked another cigarette while he called a cab. He stuffed a supply of smokes into his jacket pockets and went out into the growing dark.

What was left of the sun tingled on his skin. A century ago, he would have gone up in flames. On the sidewalk, he paused to enjoy a moment of the sunset.

He was changing, he was certain. He was also certain the changes were connected to his weaning himself from human blood. Stories had circulated in the Family of vampires who had abstained a few years before the blood hunger had sent them back to the streets. Julian had never heard of anyone who'd gone as long as he had. He had no idea what the consequences might be.

He told the driver to take him to the East Village. Sure enough, as they approached New York, the smell drifted to him, sweet and ripe, like a peach. When the smell became overwhelming, he told the driver to let him out. 9th Street, he noted, near 2nd Avenue.

Nostrils flared, he stood for a time. Then, smiling, he lit another cigarette and set off down the sidewalk.

"Castle Boutique," said the sign in the window above a display of antique jewelry and knickknacks. A classy place, he thought. He opened the door and a little bell tinkled to announce his presence.

There were two people in the shop, and neither of them looked up as Julian came in. One was a slight, dark-haired man in dark suit pants and a white shirt. The other was his quarry.

Julian stopped abruptly only a step inside the doorway. Her smell was strong here, overpowering. To his surprise, he felt the tips of his fangs prick his bottom lip. That hadn't happened in a long time. He stood still and breathed, waiting for them to retract and silently cursing the prominently placed "No Smoking" sign on the wall.

By the counter, the man nodded soberly while the woman spoke, her voice rapid, hitching from time to time.

". . . the cops said no one was reported missing. They didn't even want to listen to me—" She turned her head a little, and he lost the sense of the words.

She'd changed clothes, Julian saw, no longer the caped vampiress but a plain woman in faded jeans and a forest green silk shirt.

No, not plain, he corrected. Her milky skin and midnight hair made her extraordinary. Her hands fluttered uncertainly as she spoke, the nails, still blood red, dancing patterns in the air. Her friend had died, Julian remembered suddenly. Her name had been Dina, and Nicholas had killed her.

He felt a soft prick against his lower lip and closed his eyes as desire slid hot through his system. Desire for blood, and for other things. He could remember the last time he'd had a woman, but not how long ago it had been. She'd been another vampire, and it had gone as well as such things could go. To be truly satisfied, he needed a human woman. To be truly satisfied, he needed to take her blood afterwards. Or during.

His fangs slipped back where they belonged. Julian took a step forward, and suddenly the woman looked up. She stared at him, schooling her pale features to smooth expressionlessness.

"Julian," she said.

The man with her touched her arm. "You need me to get rid of him, Lorelei?"

Julian smiled at the thought. The slim man would be no match for him. But Julian approved of the fierce loyalty in the man's expression. He also approved, very much, of the woman's name.

"No, it's okay, Randy," said Lorelei. "This is Julian. He saved my life last night."

"Too bad he couldn't save Dina's," Randy said darkly.

"No. No, it wasn't his fault. There was nothing he could have done."

In spite of her defense, Lorelei still looked suspicious and wary as she turned to Julian. "How did you find me?"

Julian shrugged. "It doesn't matter."

Lorelei's eyes flashed. Blue, sapphire, striking in her pale face beneath the black hair. "Then why are you here?"

"I wanted to be sure you were all right." He paused. Lorelei regarded him from under a dark fringe of bangs. "Are you all right?"

"I suppose. Is there anything else I can do for you?"

"Have dinner with me." The words surprised him. Perhaps they shouldn't have. He wasn't even certain why he'd sought her out in the first place.

Lorelei looked at Randy, then back at Julian. "Yeah, all right. I could use some free food." She pushed away from the counter and came to join him.

"Who said I was paying?"

Lorelei's mouth quirked into a smile. She hooked her arm through Julian's and let him lead her out of the boutique.

***

He was dangerous. Lorelei was certain of it. But for whatever reason, she felt safe walking down the sidewalk with him, her arm hooked through his. He was dangerous, but not to her.

She watched as he paused to light a cigarette, cupping his hand around the flame until it took. He drew a long drag and released a breath of strange-smelling smoke. He smiled at her then, a twinkle in those odd, almost-Asian eyes. She smiled back.

"Did I thank you for saving my life?" she said.

He offered his arm again and they continued up the sidewalk. "I don't remember."

"Thank you."

He acknowledged it with a tilt of his head.

"So, Julian, what do you do that you have to sleep all day?"

"I work at night."

"Yeah, I caught that," Lorelei replied dryly.

"I work at a television station."

That piqued Lorelei's interest. "On air?"

"No. Very much behind the scenes. Somebody has to keep those late-night reruns re-running."

"Which station?"

"One of the independents."

"Fascinating." She couldn't identify the smell of his cigarettes. Not quite tobacco, certainly not marijuana. Strange, spicy. And, she noticed, hand-rolled. An odd man, this Julian. Odd and dangerous.

She followed him with complete confidence to a high-priced Japanese restaurant she'd always wanted to try. He ordered a monster tray of sashimi, and she indulged herself with sushi.

"This is wonderful," she said, thoroughly enjoying a spicy tuna roll.

"I'm glad you like it. I quite like this restaurant, myself." Then his gaze darted about the room.

"What is it?"

"Nothing." His careful smile didn't convince her. "Nothing at all."

***

To Julian, the meal seemed to go on forever. He'd had every intention of treating Lorelei to a leisurely dinner, a walk in the dark, a few stolen touches and perhaps a kiss. But a smell had drifted to him across the restaurant. Steely, coppery. Blood on the breath of a vampire.

Nicholas' words echoed in Julian's head. *There's a Call out for you, man.* Julian knew why. The Senior knew of Julian's change. He wondered if the Senior also knew what Julian was becoming. The Call could be for Julian's audience, or for his blood. Not to be consumed—it was anathema for a vampire to feed on one of his own kind—but certainly to be shed.

He could see no evidence to support either possibility, though. Only a smell, a sense, a flickering of shadow in the corners of his vision. Nothing he could hold, nothing he could be certain was more than his imagination.

They finished dinner, he holding up his end of the conversation with the easy web of fabrications he'd perfected over the years about his non-existent job at an imaginary TV station. He barely had to pay attention to what he was saying, which gave him the opportunity to concentrate on Lorelei.

She was beautiful. Brilliant, wonderfully alive, achingly mortal. Forbidden. He shouldn't have come, Julian could see that now. But he couldn't not. This kind of compulsion struck him rarely—three, perhaps four times in his eight hundred years. At that moment, watching the light shift on her black hair, the movement of emotion in her sapphire eyes, he chose not to recall that it had always ended in pain.

By the end of the meal, the coppery smell had faded, barely leaving a memory behind. And when Lorelei, much to his surprise, asked him if he wanted to walk back to her place for a nightcap, he agreed before taking time to evaluate the foolishness of it.

"I live above the boutique," she said. "I own the building, in fact."

"Ah. An entrepreneur."

"That's me." She flicked him a coy blue look. "The bank helped me get started, but it's all mine now. All debts paid in full, and we've been in the black for the last two years."

"Impressive."

"I think so."

She watched him as he pulled out a cigarette. He lit it and dragged deep, feeling his fangs retract again. They'd been insistent tonight, stabbing the back of his lip at the most inopportune moments. The raw fish had dulled the need a bit, but not as much as red meat would have—certainly not as much as blood would have.

"You smoke an awful lot," Lorelei commented.

"I'm sorry," Julian said. "Does it bother you?"

She shrugged. "If you mean the smoke, no, not really." She gave him an odd look. "Somehow it doesn't smell as bad on you."

He smiled, charmed. He thought of another girl, a Pictish warrior woman who'd worn her red hair in braids and painted her breasts and her face blue with woad after the manner of her people. They could have been the same soul. Maybe they were.

Her apartment above the boutique brought back similar

memories. A reproduction of a Celtic stone cross hung above her couch, and similar trinkets adorned a knickknack shelf in a corner. She took small glasses from a cabinet and filled them with wine. Julian didn't notice what kind. It didn't matter—he couldn't drink it.

"It's a very nice apartment," he said.

"Thank you. It serves its purpose."

She drank from her glass. He tipped his up so the wine touched his lips, but he didn't drink. A deep warmth moved through him anyway, the way wine had felt in his blood when he'd been mortal. But the smell brought the feeling to him now. The wine smell, her smell and the soft sound of her pulse vibrating in the air. In his pocket, he fingered another cigarette, feeling the length of it, turning it between his fingers. He didn't take it out. Desire rose in his throat, and his fangs pricked at the inside of his lip. He wanted her.

She sat on the couch and turned on the TV. "There. Is this your station? What time do you have to be at work?"

"No, and later."

He sat next to her and set the wineglass on the table by the couch. The warmth of her body reached his skin, and another deep convulsion of need shuddered through him. He held very still. He should smoke. But he wanted to *feel*. This desire was the deepest emotion left to him, and he'd kept it at bay for so long. He wanted to let it take him over just for a time. Long enough to experience it, but not to act upon it.

She turned to look at him. He blinked as her eyes measured his. She sensed his desire—somehow he knew that. More, she shared it—he saw it in the darkening of her blue-blue eyes. Her body shifted toward him, her breath brushed his lips even as his fangs slid into place behind them.

Feel it, he thought as his body became a flame of hunger. *Feel it, because it's the only thing you* can *feel, because it's the closest you'll ever get to love—*

The smell again, brittle and invasive, as if a knife had cut through the air made soft by the scent of her skin. The smell of bloodied breath. Then a sharp, violent pain at the base of his skull, and then nothing.

THREE

Lorelei didn't have time to scream. The black shadow appeared so quickly she barely realized it was there before Julian jerked and went limp against her. An arm closed around her from behind, pulling her away from Julian's slumped body.

"Hold still and maybe I won't hurt you." The voice was hot against her ear, the breath strange, metallic. Lorelei nodded emphatically. Afraid to move, afraid to speak, she watched as the other man lowered Julian's body to the floor.

"The Senior said we could kill him."

"No," Lorelei breathed.

The man holding her laughed. "You can do nothing for him, little girl. He sealed his own fate a very long time ago."

Silver flashed above Julian's face. Lorelei sucked in a breath as the knife descended.

"No!" she screamed. The man behind her jerked her closer and clamped a hand over her mouth. She brought her heel down hard on his instep. He howled in pain and let her go.

Blind now with fear and fury, Lorelei grabbed the first thing she perceived as a weapon. The fireplace poker flew up in her hand, pointed toward her attacker, who flung himself at her. Too late, he saw the weapon. Too late, as the force of his movement, combined with the force of Lorelei's, drove the sharp-ended metal straight through his chest.

"Oh, my God," said Lorelei. Purely on instinct, she yanked the poker free. Blood spurted everywhere as the man staggered backwards, utter bewilderment on his face.

A choking sound came from behind her. Lorelei whirled, poker at the ready. A second man knelt over Julian, hacking with the knife.

Lorelei was simply too shocked to think. On an intellectual level, she knew she should be gibbering in pure fear. Her stomach as well as her mind should have rebelled at the sight of this strange, dark man slicing Julian's throat open, again and again, with the long-bladed silver knife. Slicing it again and again because, with each fountaining spray of blood, the gaping, bubbling wound healed itself.

Lorelei swung with the poker. It struck the intruder's head with a sick thud. He sank, unconscious or maybe dead, to the floor next to Julian's blood-soaked body.

Julian's throat was open, sliced so deep the spine showed white. The flow of blood had become sluggish. Lorelei stared as the horrible wound knit itself shut, until his throat was whole again, smooth and unbroken, but covered with thick, blackening blood.

His eyes opened. They were dull and glassy. Lorelei had seen that look before—in Dina's eyes as she'd slumped bloodless against her killer.

"Blood," he whispered. "I need blood."

"I know." She wanted to comfort him, but her intellect was functioning again and the blood repulsed her. She found his hand and held it. "I'll call an ambulance."

"No," he said.

She nodded. There wasn't much a paramedic could do, anyway, she thought. And how could she explain this to the police? But she had to call. She started to move toward the phone, but his hand tightened on hers, stopping her.

She looked back at him, and saw, but didn't believe.

***

He was dying. His body shutting down by degrees, starved of blood. Helpless to prevent it as his semi-conscious mind, rattled by the blow to the back of his head, had felt each slash of the knife, the bursting forth of blood, the knitting together of the open wound. He'd felt this way only once before, when he'd been Made.

"Blood," he whispered. "I need blood."

He smelled it everywhere. His own, others'. The intruders who'd come to kill him. He thought he smelled death, too, but not his own. But the blood he smelled was vampiric. He couldn't take that—it was wrong, the most basic taboo of the vampire. There was Lorelei—but Lorelei was human, and that was his own taboo.

He closed his eyes. It was over, then. After eight hundred-odd years, it was over.

His mind drifted away, his body left behind. Some vague piece of awareness remained, to sense what happened next, but not enough to stop it.

He'd been drained to the most basic instinct—survival. His body, dead once, didn't want to repeat the experience. His hands found a living body. His fangs came forward, locked, sank into a throat, and blood flowed.

***

Burning. Fire, like the sensation of sunlight on his skin, but devouring him from the inside. The hot, fresh blood pumped through him, refilling him where he had been emptied. But it had never felt like this before—like liquid cauterization, the fire of a kiln, remaking him, changing him, healing him.

After a long time, the flow of blood slowed, then stopped. Julian slept.

***

He woke slowly, his body sluggish as it always was when waking. His chest felt hot and compressed, as if a heavy weight lay on it. When he opened his eyes, though, he lay in a bed, pale pink sheets drawn up to his chin. He was naked. Something smelled like lavender.

He remembered. He had fed last night.

Lorelei.

He bolted from the bed. What had he done when reason had left him?

The bedroom door was closed. He flung it open and stared into the living room.

Lorelei knelt on the floor with rubber gloves and a sponge, scrubbing blood off the wooden floors. Her brilliant blue eyes were bloodshot, puffy underneath, mascara streaked down her cheeks.

She looked up at him with a disconcerting calmness.

"Go get some clothes on," she said. "I brought some up from the boutique. They're on the bed. Maybe not your style, but they'll keep you decent."

Baffled, he went back into the bedroom. She'd laid out black cotton pants, a black T-shirt. He put them on and came

back out to her.
She was scrubbing again, frowning at the blood on her floor. There was a great deal of it still. A big job, Julian thought. He should help. There were no other sponges.
"I didn't kill you," he said, because the fact amazed him. He couldn't get his brain around it.
"No," she said matter-of-factly. "I think you wanted to, though."
He stared at her, at the smooth, white line of her neck. Her skin, pale and unbroken except for the marks, still red, from the Halloween party.
"Then what ... who ... What happened?"
"The guy who tried to kill you. He was lying next to you. You did it to him."
Julian sat down. Right on the floor in a spot which, luckily, had no blood on it. The man who'd slit his throat had been a vampire.
She looked at him quizzically. "Are you all right?"
"No. No, really, I'm not."
"Good. Because I'm sure as hell not." She pushed hair away from her face with the back of her wrist. "Now, get up off your ass and help me get this goddamn blood off my floor."
He went into the kitchen, looking for a sponge. He found one under the sink. The room was decorated in bright yellows and greens, and sun streamed in through a small window above the sink.
Julian stood gaping at the golden window. He reached out his hands slowly, letting the wash of sunlight touch his skin. A faint tingle, no more, but as he held them there, it grew stronger until the sensation approached pain. He watched, fascinated, as a soft pink invaded the paleness of his skin. The beginnings of a burn, but it was taking a good long time.
"Julian?" Lorelei's voice broke his reverie. He jerked his hands back, as if what he'd done was forbidden. "Did you find a sponge? They should be under the sink."
He looked at her as she stood in the doorway, a question on her face.
"What did you see last night?" Had it been last night? It

must have been. And now was today. To*day*. He wondered if he could go outside and walk in the full sun. Eight hundred years ago, he'd enjoyed the sun.

"Too damn much," Lorelei replied bitterly. She started to turn away from him, then turned back. "How much of it was real?"

He met her gaze squarely. "Probably all of it."

She shook her head. "I never should have gone to that fucking party."

He followed her into the living room and sat next to her, dipped his sponge in the bucket and helped her scrub. "What happened to the bodies?"

"I dumped them out the window into the alley, then I called the cops and reported a disturbance. They came and took them away."

"Why didn't you tell them what happened?"

"Because they were *vampires*, you idiot!" She turned on him, eyes sparking blue flame. "They had fangs. Real ones. I looked. And you—" She broke off, some of the fire leaving her. "You're one of them, aren't you?"

He looked at the floor, at the blood where it had soaked into the grain of the wood. "I honestly don't know what I am anymore." The pink had faded from the backs of his hands. "But whatever I am, I'm not one of them."

***

It was a hard job, scrubbing the blood off the wood floors, working the brown flakes out of the grain. She'd tossed two gorgeous Oriental rugs out the window with the bodies—it had broken her heart but there was no way she could get them clean. Now she was left with the job of cleaning up the blood.

It was a hard job, but not as hard as sitting there looking at Julian, understanding what he was, trying to deny it and accept it at the same time. She wanted only to put it out of her mind.

Except he wouldn't shut up about it.

"Over two hundred years without human blood, and now this. Something's changed. I was changing before, but this is different, and I don't know what it is."

Lorelei tossed her sponge down in exasperation and glared

at him. "Then find out."

Julian blinked. "Find out? How?"

"This Senior Vampire—person—has this Call out for you. He must have some idea about what's happening to you, or he wouldn't perceive it as a threat."

Julian was silent for a moment, scrubbing thoughtfully at the stained floor. "You're right." He'd had the same thought himself. Did he want to look for the answer?

"Of course I'm right. Just because you come in here and go off with all this vampire shit doesn't mean I can't figure it out even though it doesn't make any sense, and everybody knows there's no such thing as vampires except those crazy razor-freaks at the party. But you had real fangs, and those people—my God, he cut your throat seven times. My God, a lot of this blood is probably yours—"

She stopped. Her hands were shaking so hard she dropped the sponge. Julian stared at her. Aware of his gaze, Lorelei fought the gabbling panic trying to drag its way up her throat.

"Lorelei?" he said gently. "Are you all right?"

She threw the sponge at him. It hit him in the face. He caught it as it fell.

"No, I'm not all right! Why in God's name would I be all right?"

"I should go."

"Don't you dare go. This is your goddamn blood, and you're damn well going to clean it up!"

He laughed. He laughed and she wanted to hit him, then suddenly she laughed, too. It was a hysterical laugh, though, and she brought up a hand to cover it.

"It's too much," she said.

"I know." He reached out to her, cupped her elbows in his hands and drew her gently to her feet. "Go sit down and have some tea. I've cleaned up more than my share of blood in my time. I'll take care of it."

***

She sat in the kitchen for an hour, sipping tea and listening to Julian splash in the other room. Finally he came into the kitchen carrying the sponge, which he put in the sink. He looked out the window at the daylight, held his hand out to the sunlight and kept it there for a moment while his skin turned pink.

"How did it happen?" Lorelei asked quietly.

"The usual way," he said, a bit dryly.

"Why did you stop feeding on humans?" An ordinary kitchen, an ordinary cup of tea—it couldn't balance the conversation.

"I'd loved three women and killed them all." He shook his head as he turned to her. "I couldn't take it anymore."

"Do I need to buy you a carton of cigarettes to keep you from ripping my throat out?"

He smiled. She noted again the slight cant to his eyes and wondered where he'd been born. "Since I took the other vampire's blood, I haven't felt a need to feed."

"Maybe that's why you're not supposed to feed on other vampires. Because it changes you."

Julian nodded. He stood in silence for a long minute, then finally said, "You're right about finding the answer. If there's a Call out for me, I'll answer it myself, and find out what's happening to me, and why the Senior doesn't want it to happen."

"You'll go see him, then?"

"I see no other choice." Except to run, and he could only run so long.

In his dark eyes she saw something warm, something human, if she dared think that way. He was right—whatever he was, he wasn't one of the killers who'd invaded her apartment.

What he was, she thought, was compelling. Something in her stirred when she looked at him, listened to his voice. Had her late-night TV viewing really corrupted her so much she could sit here and feel lust for a vampire? The thought made her smile.

"I'll go with you."

FOUR

They couldn't go anywhere until nightfall. The deepest levels of the vampire city were closed off during the day, so thoroughly sealed not even a fly could get through.

"How do they do it?" Lorelei asked. No lock, no barricade, could be completely unbreachable.

"Human servants, dogs, electricity." Julian rubbed his eyes. He looked tired, she thought, and wondered if he might need to sleep before night fell. "I don't really know. I've never been during the day."

"But you've been?"

"Once. A long time ago. The Senior called for me when I first came to the City, and I went." He stood, walked to the window where he watched the light outside with a frown on his face. "It's not exactly as I remember it," he said after a time.

"What?"

"The light." He sounded disappointed. He stepped back again, and Lorelei watched as the pink on his face slowly faded. He pressed his fingers to his face.

"Does it hurt?" she asked.

"A little."

She stepped up to him and laid a hand on his face, feeling the heat leave his skin.

He looked at her, surprise in his eyes, and she suddenly realized she stood there with her hand on a vampire. As the sun-heat faded, his skin cooled, but didn't feel strange. She let her fingers shift, matching the contours of his face.

"You're not afraid," he said, the breath of his voice brushing the edge of her hand.

"Should I be?"

He turned his head against her palm, his lips touching her skin, then parting. Fangs pricked against her skin.

She shuddered, but held still, the warm breath and the cold fangs branded on the curve of her palm. After a moment, he kissed her again, then turned his head back and closed his eyes, his face nestled against her hand.

"No," he said.

She stepped closer to him then, letting her hand slide from his face to his chest, feeling the lines of his body under his shirt. Human, she thought. No reason to think otherwise except for the slight difference in his skin temperature, and even that was barely discernable.

She felt drawn to him suddenly, aware of her pulse against his face, in the tips of her fingers where they touched him. Something drew her in, wanting her to be closer than she was. A memory surfaced—the dream, the prick of fangs against her throat. Had it been a dream the first time? Was it only a memory of a story, or a movie?

"Have you seen me before?" she said suddenly, impulsively. "Did you ever come to me, a long time ago?"

His forehead creased into a frown, dark brows drawing together over the dark, vaguely Asian eyes. "No..." He drew the word out, paused, then said it again with more certainty. "No. I would have remembered you."

"I wonder who it was then," Lorelei murmured. Because she was nearly certain now it hadn't been a dream.

"Who what was?" he said, then his eyes fell closed and he sagged, pulled himself up again. "Time to sleep."

She led him to her bedroom and watched as he stretched out on the bed, then fell into a deep, daylight sleep in her room where sunlight slanted in through the partly open window.

***

He woke just before dusk. He could tell by the quality of the light in the room. Lorelei had drawn the curtain, but it still slanted in—dusty gray light that two centuries ago would have turned him to ashes.

Lorelei. Suddenly he realized she was there, nestled against him, her warmth a small miracle curled against his body. Long, slow breaths told him she slept. Her sleep told him she trusted.

How could she? How could she abandon herself to sleep, knowing what he was? Knowing he was likely to wake hungry.

He *was* hungry. But the hunger had lost its edge, its uncontrollable eagerness. Carefully, trying not to disturb Lorelei, he found a cigarette on the nightstand and lit it, breathing its spicy clove-smoke, feeling it do its work.

She shifted against him, turning to rest her face against his chest. Her breath warmed him, her body soft and warm as he cupped her closer with his arm. He took a long breath of the cigarette and set it aside, then turned to fold his arms around her.

She lifted her head, looking up at him with a bleary smile. "Good evening," she said. "You didn't sleep very long."

"I didn't need it." That surprised him, as did the lack of urgency to his waking hunger. Perhaps the vampire blood still lingered in his system, unlike human blood which died so quickly and needed to be replaced. And the changes continued within him, a subtle, constant hum in his blood.

"So is it time to go yet?"

He looked at her, studying the deep sapphire of her eyes, then gently brushed black hair back from her pale face.

"No," he said, and bent toward her, seeking the softness of her mouth.

Her face rose to his without hesitation. He took his time, exploring her mouth, letting his fingers trace the lines of her cheekbones and chin. It had been a long time since he'd wanted a woman like this. Her response surprised him, made him hope for more as her mouth answered his with gentle enthusiasm and rising passion.

He couldn't press the issue, though, couldn't even ask. He could only hold her, take what she offered as a gift, hope she might offer more.

It was hard, though, to hold back, when her hands and her mouth told him there was little reason to, when her movement against him brought a compulsion different from hunger but nearly as powerful. He tasted her mouth, the heat and the mortality of it, the pulsing life. He felt her body, the curves and softness, the heat as his hands found their way under her shirt. She melted into him, her hand sliding down his body. When her fingers cupped between his legs, he jumped.

His eyes met hers in surprise, hers shining with mischief as her hand continued to explore.

"I didn't know—" she started, but broke off, biting her lip in sudden embarrassment as her cream-pale skin flushed pink.

"Didn't know what?"

"If you could."

He smiled, thinking of all the vampire stories that had gotten it wrong. Her clever hands aroused him in ways that made his eyes water.

"I can," he said, "and I will if you don't stop that."

She smiled, wicked. "Good."

Permission was all he needed. She writhed like a fury under him while he touched, tasted, owned every part of her. The tumescence that had surprised her jutted between her breasts, her thighs, and finally deep inside her while she moaned into his mouth. He rolled his face away, nestled his mouth against her throat—

Only then did he realize what he'd done. What he'd started he couldn't finish, not without the shedding of blood. Lorelei wouldn't have known this when she encouraged him. Welcomed him. Invited him in without complete knowledge of what her invitation meant.

Fangs pricked his lip. He forced himself to stillness and backed away from her, out of her. Unlike the blood-lust, this was something he could control through force of will. Her hands clutched at his shoulders.

"No. Don't leave me."

Laying a hand against the side of her face, he made her look at him.

"I have to," he said, and her eyes widened as she saw his fangs.

The fear—if it had been fear at all—lasted only a moment. Her hand caught his and brought it back to her, pressing his fingers against the damp warmth he'd just forced his body to leave.

"Can you?"

He studied her face, gauged his body's reaction. His own arousal was what drove him to blood, not hers. Smiling a small, fang-pricked smile at her brazen but rather obvious solution, he pressed his fingers deep into her heat.

She was hot around him, then tight and shuddering as her whole body shook beneath him and he kissed her deep with his fangs pricking her lip. She moaned against him, then went limp and melted again into him, her body seeking his. A surge of body-lust took him, changing too quickly to blood-lust. He sat up, pushing away from her to light another cigarette. For a moment he was afraid to look at her, but when he did, she answered his regard with more amusement than annoyance.

"Having a cigarette after sex takes on a whole new meaning with you."

He smiled as the smoke settled into him, easing the need. His arousal had quieted in spite of the lack of fulfillment and he was content now to lie next to her in the growing dark, feeling her warmth and the way her heartbeat seemed to make the air tremble. As he settled back against the pillows, she found a place for her head against his shoulder.

"Where were you born?"

The question surprised him. He smoked a minute or two before he answered. She said nothing, barely moved, seeming content to wait.

"An island in the Pacific. I tried to go back a few years ago to find it, but I couldn't. I'm not even sure it's there anymore. It's been nearly eight hundred years—the sea could have taken it."

"What was it called?"

"We just called it Home."

Full dark had fallen, a vague shadow of moonlight barely weaving its way past the curtain. They should go, Julian thought, but he lay still, enjoying the weight of her head against his shoulder, the smell of his odd cigarettes and the vague musk left over from Lorelei's climax. She moved again, turning a little toward him and laying her hand against his chest.

"Tell me," she said.

So he wove pictures in the dark, of the bright, warm sun, palm trees, the brown, naked children and the women with their naked, loose, brown breasts. They ate coconuts and roasted lizards on spits over fire pits. They danced sometimes, and sang, and when they danced, the pounding of drums seemed to fill the whole world.

"Paradise," Lorelei breathed, and Julian nodded. It had been—except for the Blood Gods.

He'd been sixteen when the Gods had chosen him. For six years, he'd trained in the Temple, not understanding what waited, knowing only that he'd been Chosen, and it was an honor.

Then, when he *had* understood, it had been too late.

"The Blood Gods were vampires." Lorelei's voice breathed wonderment.

"All the gods who have ever asked for human blood have been." He'd come to the end of his cigarette. He flicked off the ashes and forced himself to sit up. Before he broke the spell, he touched Lorelei's hair, let its silk sift between his fingers.

"We have to go," he said then, shattering the spell they'd woven with sex and with his story.

"Then let's go," said Lorelei, and hopped out of bed.

FIVE

They headed east. Lorelei wasn't surprised. Somehow it didn't surprise her, either, when the streets became darker and more unfamiliar than any New York City street she'd ever seen.

They'd gone past the bad neighborhoods, deeper than drug lords' territory. They'd gone far enough, in fact, that they should have been in the East River. Here, the hookers were thin and pale with fang marks and slashes from razor blades on their arms and throats. Other back alleys carried the smell of urine and garbage—here, the backdrop was the coppery smell of fresh blood.

Lorelei knew she should have turned around blocks ago, when the worst thing lurking behind a Dumpster was a crack dealer or a strung-out junkie. But that inexplicable trust in Julian kept her trailing after him. The same trust that had drawn her into his bed.

Maybe trust was the wrong word, though. Attraction wasn't the right word, either. She felt like she'd known him much longer than a day and a half. Sometimes she felt like she belonged to him. Or at least with him.

They turned another corner. The darkness here was cloying, damp. Lorelei suddenly realized they were descending—that they had been for some time.

"Where are we, anyway?"

His eyes flashed toward her in the semi-darkness, his mouth curved into a half-smile. "Deep within the vampire city. More under the human city than of it. Can't you feel the terror? The pervasive sense of doom and death?"

She made a face. "Save the poetry, Julie."

His eyes narrowed. "Don't call me Julie."

The expression should have frightened her, but he didn't quell the humor in it well enough. She smiled weakly back, disturbed by the sense of comfortable intimacy their exchanged had produced.

He stopped at a crossroads. For a moment, Lorelei thought he might have forgotten his path, then he bent his head and she saw the flare of orange as he lit a cigarette.

"Are you okay?" she asked. If the blood lust had returned, he might need to eat, and as far as she knew, he hadn't packed any raw meat for the trip. And the last thing she needed was for him to drop dead, leaving her stranded in the middle of vampire country.

He took a long drag, released a spice-fragrant exhale. "Precautionary, mostly." He picked a road. "This way." But when he finished that cigarette, he lit another.

They'd entered what appeared to be a deeper part of town, following long stretches of dark, deserted alley. The silence weighed as heavily as the darkness, within it the soft drip of water from the ceiling, up above where the sky should have been.

"This is one of the deepest levels," Julian said. He cocked his head. "We're close, now. I can feel him—"

A dark body vaulted from the darkness, slammed into Julian and brought him to the ground. A knife came down in a silver flash, severing Julian's throat—

The wound closed immediately, so fast the blade was nearly trapped in the healing flesh. Julian grabbed the other vampire's head, one hand on each side. His fingers tightened with a sharp, sickening crack, then his fangs flashed, and he buried his face in the vampire's throat.

Lorelei stood by, breath heaving, horrified, fascinated. The damp dark clawed against her skin, the silence broken now by the wet sound of Julian's feeding. Why did this not repulse her? she wondered. Instead, she had a sudden image of him bent over her, fangs sunk in her own throat. An ultimate intimacy as her life flooded into his body. The step he'd refused to take last night. At the time, she'd been touched, grateful. Now she felt cheated.

Suddenly Julian staggered, breaking the spell. Lorelei rushed to him as he rolled away from his victim, curled into a tight ball of pain on the wet ground.

"Julian!" Lorelei couldn't coax her voice above a whisper.

"Are you all right?"

"No," he managed. "No, God, it hurts—"

***

He'd never experienced such pain. It clawed through him as the vampire's blood coursed through his body, turning every vein, every capillary to searing pain. What was it doing to him? His body stiffened uncontrollably, then went so flaccid he couldn't move. There was no control, no sense of his own body. Only the pain. Even Lorelei's voice hurt when it reached his ears.

Then he heard more than just her voice. He heard her heartbeat, the beats of her arteries, her capillaries, the movement of the valves in her veins, the traveling of her blood. He'd never been so aware of a mortal's blood without hungering—hearing it, feeling it, without *needing* it.

She was there, right next to him, half on top of him, her breath and her voice against his ear. His hands closed on her arms, holding her tight against him. Her breath flooded over his face. Alive. Hot. He wanted her—but he didn't want her blood.

Then he saw the fear in her eyes.

"I won't," he said. "Just hold still and let me listen to you."

Her tension fell away as he held her, and his pain melted as the blood he'd fed on mixed with the blood already filling his veins. Her heartbeat shook his chest, and slowly his own heartbeat shifted until they sounded in perfect unison. Not just the beat of their two hearts, but the beat of every blood vessel, moving in exact synchrony.

He held her there for a long time, until the pain faded, then gently he let her go. She slid away from him, sat on the ground next to him, her blue eyes wide and questioning.

"Are you all right?" she said.

"For the moment," he answered, marveling that she could be concerned for him. He sat up, then stood. "We have to go on."

***

They went deeper, as the ceiling grew higher and the floor descended, until they walked in a cave with vaulted ceilings so high they couldn't be seen in the murky darkness.

Lorelei clung to Julian, afraid of what might lurk in the

shadows. Finally she took his hand, clinging to it. A pulse beat hard through his fingers, the hand warmer than it had been only a few hours ago when they'd made love.

"How much farther?" she asked. Her voice slithered cold up the high, high walls and came back to her a million times, amplified, softened, transformed—ch ... ch ... far ... far ... ther ... ther ... The sound touched her skin, and she cringed.

"Not far," said Julian, and his soft voice fell dead into dead air and stopped.

Afraid to speak again, Lorelei just followed.

After a time, she realized a light had grown far ahead of them. Greenish-white, like cave-light. The very color of it nauseated her. Julian's hand tightened on hers, as if he sensed her discomfort.

"He'll be there," he said softly in his voice that didn't echo, "in the light."

"That's what I'm afraid of."

He smiled a little. The white, sharp tips of his fangs protruded from behind his upper lip. He didn't tell her not to be afraid.

They went on.

***

The light grew. Soon the world was full of it. Lorelei couldn't tell where it came from. It seemed to spill down the walls, onto the floor. The air had become cool, still, and utterly odorless.

She'd stopped holding Julian's hand and now clung to his arm. Fear crawled through her, but he seemed centered, composed. Sometimes his arm came around her, to circle her and hold her for a moment or a minute. His calm radiated into her, and she held onto it as well as she could. The green light fell and fell, and she blinked against it.

How had she come to this place? How had she come to be walking through the unknown bowels of the earth, through caves and tunnels no human could possibly know of, her only guide and protection a vampire? It was too much. So much that she could only keep going, keep following him.

Suddenly they were no longer alone. A pale escort flitted through the falling light, hovering just out of sight. Lorelei sensed his presence, could almost see him if she looked away. Presently, he was joined by another and another, until they were trailed by a half-dozen or more vague figures.

"Children," Julian murmured.

Lorelei wasn't certain what he meant. Then, turning her head, she caught sight of the face of one of their entourage. A child's face with a demon's eyes—a boy or girl of no more than ten, the face pale, small kitten fangs flashing against the lower lip.

"Many of them can't hunt on their own," Julian explained, his voice still a pale murmur, "so the Senior keeps them here."

"At least he takes care of his own." But as she said it, she saw the demon eyes and wondered what price these children paid to be "taken care of."

Julian must have seen the realization on her face, for he said no more about it.

An archway appeared ahead of them. She couldn't estimate its age, but it was easily as old as anything she'd ever seen. Runes in the stone resonated with unbelievable age. Strangely, Lorelei felt like she should be able to read them—as if they stirred some primal memory within her.

"This would be the place," said Julian softly.

"That's what I was afraid of."

He gave her a rueful smile, then passed under the arch.

Lorelei didn't know what she'd expected, but it certainly wasn't this. Beauty, pure, crystalline, filled the room, stalactites and stalagmites that seemed to be made of glass, like the inside of a geode. The strange green light seemed purified here as it was taken in and reflected back a hundred thousand times, from facet to facet and back again. She could barely breathe for the beauty of it. How could something like this exist, and no human being ever know of it?

"This way," Julian said. He seemed to know his way through the maze of corridors, and she followed him. Behind them, the strange, demon-eyed children disappeared into the reflections of light, making their own way.

Julian led her to a narrow passage among the crystals. The passage made a gradual descent and ended at a plain wooden door. So plain, so ordinary in the midst of all the sparkling beauty, and behind it, a plain oak desk in a room cluttered with the kind of paper detritus one might find in a mundane corporate office.

The man behind the desk, though, was far from ordinary. He looked up as they came in, folded his hands on the desk and eyed Julian with a kind of resigned acceptance.

"Julian," he said. His voice made Lorelei's spine pulse. Shatter glass, Lorelei thought. Move mountains.

"Master," said Julian, without a hint of sarcasm, but also without a hint of obedience. They stood looking at each other for a time, then Julian said, "You put out a Call for me. Why?"

The Senior gave a dismissive wave of his hand. His skin was so pale as to be nearly translucent. His eyes spoke of an age Lorelei could only begin to comprehend.

"The Call has been lifted," he said.

Julian lifted an eyebrow. "Why?"

"Because it's too late."

"Too late for what?"

"Too late to stop it."

Julian only stood for a moment. His face remained utterly still, and Lorelei could extract nothing from his expression. Finally, he spoke again. "But it's not yet finished."

"No. No, it is not." He shook his head slightly then. It seemed Lorelei could see his bones through the skin of his face. A strange weight lay in his eyes, something like amazement. It was beyond Lorelei's understanding that a creature of his limitless age could find something to amaze him.

"I have walked through the great forests following the ancient ox," he said finally, "and when I found it, I fed on its blood. I saw the Sphinx built and lapped blood from a Mayan altar. I drank blood on the fields of Normandy and saw a man walk on the moon. But never, never have I seen a vampire become what you have become."

"What have I become?"

"You will know, when it's finished."

"And how do I finish it?"

"You must take my blood."

Julian blinked. Lorelei felt almost as if she were no longer in the room. Certainly the others took no notice of her. She watched as Julian took a single step forward, then stopped, shaking his head.

"You cannot mean just to—let me."

"I can. I can do nothing else."

And, Julian realized, neither could he. The compulsion was greater than anything he'd ever experienced—greater than a need for sex, greater than a need for human blood. Every cell of the Old One's blood sang to him, every cell of his own blood sang back.

He went. Nothing could have stopped him, not willpower, not his cigarettes, not even, he thought, a stake through his heart. He looked into the Old One's eyes and saw an age beyond imagining.

"When were you Made?" he asked, with breathless unbelief at what he saw.

"I was the first," said the Old One, and closed his eyes.

Tears pricked Julian's eyes. He bent forward, kissed the Senior's forehead, then bent to drink.

The Old One stiffened against him as his fangs sank in, until the blood filled his mouth in a hot pulse.

It didn't end there. As the blood rushed into his mouth, the Senior's mind reached out for his, filled it. Julian stiffened, interpreting it as an attack, then realized it was something else. Something that had never happened before. He took more than blood from the other vampire—the first vampire. He took everything.

He saw a memory of a night sky, a sky so old the stars sat in different places. He saw the deep green of infinite forest, as far as even vampiric eyes could see. Heard the thunderous footsteps of the aurochs, the ancient ox. Tasted its hot blood as if on his own tongue.

There was more. Images from a time so ancient Julian couldn't understand it even as the memories flooded him. Images from yesterday, when the Old One had downloaded his e-mail.

Then the pictures faded. The pulse of blood slowed, finally stopped. Julian swallowed, the last of the hot blood going down his throat. Then he slipped his fangs free, and the Old One crumpled at his feet.

And the pain began.

Needles in his blood, fire, ice—he couldn't explain it, couldn't escape it. All his blood aflame, from the big veins in his throat and chest to the capillaries in his eyeballs. He felt as if he were being turned inside out.

Perhaps he was. Everything inside him was changing. The power of the Old One's blood burned away everything he had ever been, leaving behind ... what?

He couldn't think or feel past the pain to discover the answer. Not yet. He could only sink to the floor, and quietly die.

SIX

Lorelei panicked. Under the circumstances, it seemed the most sensible thing to do. Trapped in the bowels of the earth, no idea how to get back where she came from, surrounded by vampires—and Julian, her only hope of knowledge or rescue, had apparently just died.

So she sat frozen in panic, looking at the two vampire bodies tangled on the floor next to her. The Senior's body seemed strangely smaller in death, whiter, and then she realized it was actually shrinking, the skin shrinking as flesh disappeared under it, until the skin enclosed the bones like plastic wrap, and then disappeared, leaving behind a skeleton which changed from brown to bleached white in a handful of seconds.

Next to the bones, Julian lay still.

Lorelei covered her mouth with her hands and breathed, long, slow breaths meant to ease the frantic pounding of her heart and tame the crazed fear fighting at the back of her throat.

"What's happened here?"

The fear came back and grabbed her as the vampire entered the room. As vampires went, he looked fairly harmless—tall and slim, wearing a suit that was too big for him and carrying a briefcase. A vampire accountant, she thought, as she searched around her for a weapon. The only thing close at hand was the pile of bones. She grabbed a femur and brandished it. The bone felt light and brittle in her hands. If she hit the vampire with it, it would either shatter into uselessness or into something with a sharp edge.

The accountant vampire stared at her, his face paling. "Where's the Senior?"

"*This* is the Senior!" Lorelei stabbed at him with the big leg bone. "Don't come any closer."

The accountant dropped his briefcase. "The Senior's dead?"

"Yes." Lorelei relaxed her posture a little. This guy looked about as befuddled as she was.

"What happened?"

"I'm not sure. Julian—"

The vampire paled further, which Lorelei hadn't thought possible. "Julian? There was a Call for him—"

"Yes, there was." She looked at Julian's body, limp on the floor among the white, white bones. "I think he might be dead, too."

The vampire's face gentled at her uncertain tone. "I'm William," he said. "Put down the bone and let's check."

Lorelei hesitated, then laid the femur down with its fellows. It was creepy, anyway, waving a dead bone at a vampire in a baggy business suit. She watched as William knelt next to Julian, gently lifted his head. His lips thinned as he lifted Julian's eyelids.

"He's not dead," he said finally. He looked up, puzzled. "He's...warm."

"He's not supposed to be?"

William reached out and took Lorelei's hand in his. His fingers were cold, almost icy. Lorelei winced, involuntarily and William let her go.

"A vampire is only warm immediately after a kill."

"Then he *should* be warm. He just made a kill."

William nodded, then suddenly stared at her with wide eyes. "He killed—he *fed on*—the Senior?"

Lorelei nodded.

William shook his head. "What *is* he?"

"I think," Lorelei said slowly, "he may be the new Senior."

"You're right," said William, suddenly decisive. "Help me take him into the inner rooms."

Julian's dead weight suddenly seemed less of a burden when he stirred, nearly causing Lorelei to drop him as they carried him through a nearly invisible door in the back of the room. Beyond was another room with a blanket spread on the floor. They laid Julian there, where he again stirred, his eyes opening, then closing again. He curled on his side, into a fetal position, and shook.

"It's as if he's transforming," William muttered. He watched a moment, then suddenly his gaze jerked to Lorelei. "Who are you? His familiar?"

"I don't know." She replied honestly out of reflex, then wondered if she'd just endangered herself. If William had been the old Senior's "familiar"—whatever exactly that meant—Lorelei's status as the new Senior's familiar might give her some clout. Or make him want to murder her. She held her breath and waited for William's response. She was so far out of her depth here.

"If you are, it's within your right to kill me."

Lorelei laughed in a strange, hysterical relief. "Thanks, I'll pass. I think I'm going to need your help."

***

Later, she dozed, sitting vigil next to Julian. The floor of the strange, low-ceilinged room was covered with furs, a few so old they'd crumbled when she accidentally touched them. The one she sat on now was a soft sheepskin, new enough that it carried only a slightly musty odor.

Julian had lain curled up and shaking for a long time, then had suddenly jerked to lay flat on his back, stiff, as if rigor mortis had taken him. Perhaps it had—many things about what seemed to be happening to him made Lorelei think of a death.

She was barely awake when William returned. He sat down next to her. He'd taken off his suit jacket, rolled up his shirtsleeves, loosened his tie. "How is he?"

"How the hell should I know?"

William smiled. Lorelei saw the tips of his fangs. The sight hardly unnerved her anymore.

"I've never seen anything like this before," he said.

"What do you mean?"

"A vampire feeding on another vampire—the Senior vampire, no less. Julian should be dead."

"Dead?"

"It's forbidden for a vampire to feed on another vampire. Not just on principle—it's a horrible death. I saw it once. Not so horrible for the one being fed upon, but for the one feeding..."

Lorelei looked at Julian, frowning. What had she stumbled into? "The Senior told him to do it. It was as if they were both under compulsion."

"I've never seen anything like this, ever."

"I don't think any of you have."

She drew her knees to her chin and looked at Julian. He seemed different. Had he actually changed, or was it only a reflection of her new knowledge? She felt numb. She'd barely been able to accept the fact he was a vampire—now she had to accept he was changing from a vampire into something else, and no one seemed to know what that was.

"Keep everyone out of this room," she said, not pausing to wonder if she was in any position to give orders. "I want him undisturbed until we have some idea what's happening."

William nodded. "That seems wise. I'll do what I can."

***

Blood. Cascades of it, rivers. Without blood, the sun will not return. Without blood, the world will end.

He was the Senior before he had become the Senior, when he had only been the first Bloodborn vampire. The mortals around him had made him a god and fed him.

But as much as he'd been fed, as carefully as his frightened subjects had tended to him, the hunger had never abated. Always there was room for more blood—more blood—more blood—

Not any *blood. Not now. Now only the blood that will make the transformation complete.*

What blood? What transformation?

You will know.

And the blood was everywhere, as if he swam in it, the heat, the thick wetness, the smell, and with it came the hunger—

***

Lorelei woke with a start. Something had changed. Julian still lay next to her, but not so still as he had been. His eyes moved now, deep in dreams. His parted lips exposed the tips of his fangs, and his harsh breathing seemed at times to form words.

That, however, wasn't the change Lorelei had sensed. Someone else had come into the room.

Lorelei sat up. She sensed the stranger's presence, but couldn't see him.

"Hello?" she ventured, scanning the room. There were shadows in the corners, but the room was too small to hide anything much bigger than a cat. "Who's there?"

He stepped forward. He was considerably bigger than a cat, an imposing presence with broad shoulders and his face obscured by the folds of a hood. Lorelei's breath came fast, her heart pounding.

"Where did you come from? Who are you?"

What little of his face she could see hinted at a smile. "You know me."

The deep voice slid down her spine, cold. For a moment, she thought it held a compulsion, then realized it held only revelation. She *did* know him. She'd seen him in her dreams.

"You," she said. Though she'd begun to suspect the memories were more than a child's recollection of a fantasy, she'd hardly thought to meet their central character here. Though she should have. Enough other weird stuff had happened in Julian's presence.

"Who are you?" she repeated.

"He needs you," he said. "He'll know when he wakes up, but he won't want to do what needs to be done. You'll have to make him understand."

"How can I make him understand when I don't understand?" Lorelei's tone was indignant—then, suddenly, she did understand. Horror filled her, and she stared at the cowled stranger. She wanted to jump at him, to claw the cowl from his face, then maybe his eyes. "What did you do to me?"

"It was necessary. Your family carried the proper genetic marker. Very few have it anymore now that the time has come. I only supplied a catalyst."

Lorelei shook her head slowly, afraid to look at Julian, afraid to look anywhere but at the vampire. If she even looked at herself, if she saw her own hands or her own body, she would have to acknowledge this as real.

"Catalyst?"

"Julian has gone through a transformation, but it's incomplete. He must take the final step. If he doesn't . . ." He trailed off, then said slowly, as if dredging the words up one by one from a long-buried memory, "'Without the Changed One all the light in the world will die.'"

Something resonated in Lorelei, as well. Not a memory, or at least not a memory in her mind. Something in her blood, perhaps, the legacy of the genetic marker. "This goes beyond him. Beyond just saving his life."

"Yes. If the dreams we had, if the words we put in the Book, are true, it affects all of humanity." He studied her for a long moment. "Can you finish it?"

She pressed her lips together and nodded. She had no choice. But . . . "Can you tell me what he'll be?"

"I could if I knew," he said, and disappeared.

SEVEN

Julian woke in a bed. The Senior's room, his bed, Julian was certain. The smells told him. There were too many of them assaulting his senses. It seemed he could feel every molecule of the air against his skin.

Another smell drifted by, and he opened his eyes. "Lorelei?"

"I'm here."

He turned his head, saw her, and the hunger drove up his throat, relentless. He closed his eyes.

She sat on the bed beside him and took his hand. "Julian, are you all right?"

"You... you're still here," he managed. He kept his eyes closed. If he opened them, he would kill her.

"Where would I go?" she asked with a wry smile. "There's freaking vampires all over the damn place."

Julian laughed. He loved her, he realized then. Not for her blood or her body, but just for her. Her laugh. Her hand holding his. He opened his eyes. He could hear her blood. Something in it called to him, like the Senior's blood had called. Julian swallowed hard. Carefully, he smiled.

"What happened?" she asked gently.

He shook his head. "I don't know. I honestly don't know."

"You look different. You look pink."

"I've just been born," he said, and realized it was true.

He sat up carefully, in case the pain came back, but it seemed to be gone. "You should go back, Lorelei. It's too dangerous here. I can send someone with you to be sure you're safe."

She shook her head. "No. I'll stay here with you."

Astounded, he asked, "Why?"

She bent forward and kissed him gently on the mouth, without fear. When she drew back, she was smiling. "Because you need me."

God, no. He grabbed her, too quickly, too harshly, closing her face between his hands so he could look into her eyes. And he saw there what he had been most afraid to see. Understanding. Acceptance. She knew what he felt, understood the howling hunger that took him over, demanding not just blood, but *her* blood.

Worse, he had a feeling she knew more than he did.

He released her, too abruptly. "No," he said. He forced himself to his feet and stumbled past her, out of the room, into the light beyond.

Outside, William had taken up a post at the Senior's desk. He sat in front of the Senior's computer, studying an accounting program. Julian couldn't remember ever seeing William doing anything else.

"William—" he began, and then he saw the skull. It sat on the desk in front of William, holding down a stack of papers. Julian walked to the front of the desk. Hanging from the upper edge, dangling down across the front, were bones. Arm bones, the small leg bones. Fingerbones on a string.

"What the hell is this?" he said, barely able to make words.

William looked up. "I'm just calculating expenses—"

"No, you bloodsucking accountant *freak*. The bones, dammit, the fucking bones!"

William glanced at the skull, then shrugged nonchalantly. "It's the Senior. There were some threats made against this office, a few who seemed inclined not only to challenge your ascendancy, but to kill you before you were able to assume your new position. I placed the bones as a warning."

"Get them down."

"Sir, I believe you underestimate the hostility currently directed at you. I think you also overestimate your ability to handle the threat."

"I don't care. Get them down."

William nodded. "All right."

"Get them down, and then get the hell away from my desk."

"Sir."

Julian wanted to spit at the little sycophant. He'd never liked William, had always had an intense urge to slap him around whenever he saw him. Being a minion was one thing—being a minion with absolutely no trace of backbone was another. And he didn't seem at all distressed by the loss of his former master. William quickly gathered the bones and left the room. Julian sat down behind the desk.

He felt strange suddenly, a wave of vertigo flooding his system. He put his head in his hands, then down on the table.

"You know you have to do it."

He didn't look up at the sound of Lorelei's voice. He couldn't. He wasn't sure he'd ever be able to pick his head up off this desk. "I don't have to do anything."

"You can't resist this any more than you could the Senior."

"I can resist. I've resisted human blood for two centuries. I can resist yours."

But he was certain he couldn't. She was right—the pull was too strong. Exactly like the pull he'd felt from the Senior, except even stronger. He needed something, something he could only find in her blood.

"It's the only way to complete the transformation," Lorelei went on. The voice came now from the other side of the desk—she must have sat in the chair across from him.

"Perhaps any human blood would do."

"No. Only mine. There's a genetic marker of some kind."

Julian looked right at her, surprised by her words and then by the fact he could lift his own head. "Who the hell fed you that bullshit?"

She pressed her lips together in irritation, then said, "A vampire came in while you were gone. I don't know where he came from—"

He blinked slowly. "Tall? Broad-shouldered, in a cloak and cowl like frigging Obi-Wan Kenobi?"

"More like Qui-Gon Jinn, but yes."

"Did he tell you who he was?"

"No. Do you know him?"

With a sigh, Julian put his head in his hands again. "We've met. I don't know who he is. I'm not even sure he's a vampire."

"I've met him, too. Before today. A long time ago, when I was a little girl."

Again, Julian was surprised enough to lift his head. "Tell me."

She told him, while he stared in increasing amazement. Then, as she finished, he shook his head vehemently. "No," he said. "I won't kill you. I'd rather die than take human blood. I don't care about the transformation, or whatever the hell's going on—"

"It's important, Julian—"

"Nothing's that important—"

"I don't think you understand—"

"I don't think *you* understand." She opened her mouth to break him off again, and he came to his feet, reaching across the desk to grab her by the shoulders, shake her, make her look into his face, into his eyes so she could see he meant what he said. "I won't kill you, Lorelei."

She studied his face. He meant it, she could see that. He would pass over the transformation and everything it might mean just to keep from shedding her blood.

That was wrong. Deep down in her heart, perhaps as deep as her DNA, as the genetic code that had been planted in her blood, she knew this transformation had to happen. Julian's change meant more than just the change of a single vampire. It meant a change of the world as every vampire on Earth had come to know it.

She looked into his eyes, saw his sincerity. Saw something she suddenly recognized as love. Her own eyes prickled with tears.

She looked into his eyes, and lied. "It won't kill me. He told me that."

Julian's hands softened on her shoulders. He looked away then, so she couldn't see what struggles rose in his eyes. He sat back down, heavily, as if he was too weak to stand any longer.

"How could he know that?"

She shrugged. Fear burned at the back of her throat, but she swallowed it. "How could he know any of this?"

Julian closed his eyes. "I'm so tired."

"You're dying. If you don't take the final step, it'll all be over."

He looked up at her again, desperation heavy in his eyes.

"I don't want to do this. I don't want to *be* this."

"You have no choice."

Slowly, he rose from the desk. He turned and went back through the door, into the Senior's room. Lorelei sat for a moment, gathering courage, then followed.

In the other room, he'd sat down on the furs where he'd slept. She sat next to him and laid her hand on his arm.

"Did he tell you anything else?" Julian asked in a dead voice.

She shook her head. "No." She lifted her hand to his face. "You have to do this now, or it'll be too late."

"Lorelei—"

Her hand cupped his cheek, turning his face gently to hers. "It's all right," she said. "Everything will be all right. But do one thing for me."

"Anything."

"Make love to me."

He bent his forehead to touch hers, looked into her eyes and then closed his. He knew, she thought. He knew she'd lied to him. But he said nothing more, only bending forward again, turning his head until his lips touched hers.

As he pulled her down to lie next to him, he felt completely human. Soft and familiar as she slipped her hands beneath his shirt to feel the hair that curled against his chest, but hard where he needed to be as he rolled her under him.

She thought about the dream again, the dream that was no dream, the images coming to her as his lips touched the curve of her throat. The other vampire, the one who'd marked her, had done it with such delicacy. Julian's lips tasted her throat with a similar care, but he didn't bite. Not yet. Instead, his mouth moved on while his hands drew her shirt up. He mouthed her breasts, fangs pricking her gently. She didn't think he'd even broken the skin until she looked down and saw the small, perfect droplets of blood.

"I'm sorry," he whispered against her skin.

"Don't be," she said, and pressed his head back against her.

His skin grew warmer as he bared more of it, until he lay

human-warm and naked on top of her. He took his time, rushing nothing, learning her as he hadn't been able to do in their first, hurried encounter in her apartment. His hands explored, long-fingered and clever, finding pleasure places on her skin where she'd never known they'd existed. Eight hundred years of experience, she thought, ought to be good for something.

He held her trembling at a peak higher than any she'd ever experienced, then pressed inside her, deep and hard. He was still inside her when the trembling changed to pulsing fire, and as she shattered apart around him, he sank his fangs deep into her throat.

Her orgasm turned orange, then red. Blood pulsed out of her throat as her body pulsed, and he went rigid against her, only his mouth moving as he drew life from her. There was no pain. Lorelei felt only the joining, the fusion of his body to hers where he still pierced her, the fusion of her blood to his as it passed out of her. She became a heartbeat, every pounding pulsation a climax.

"I love you, Julian," she said, not sure she spoke, not sure she could speak.

She pounded and pounded, and the last furious climax took her into darkness.

***

The blood slowed. Julian swallowed, made himself let go. He could still hear her heartbeat, faint but rallying, could still feel her body pulsing around his sex. As his fangs withdrew, he finally softened and withdrew there as well. He'd lost track of his own orgasms, which had pounded in time with each of hers, with each rush of her blood into him.

Gently, he eased her to the floor. Her throat was smeared with blood, but the flow had stopped. He laid a finger on the groove on the other side of her neck and again felt a soft pulse. She was still alive.

He sat away from her and shook.

Unlike the former stages of transformation, this one brought no pain. It was as if his blood had turned to light, flooding his body, cleansing it. All trace of hunger disappeared behind the brilliance. An understanding began, as if his body told him what it had become, but only a little at a time. Each cell had to awaken and tell its story. Only after they'd all spoken would he know the full truth.

He knew a little, though. Enough to bring Lorelei back.

He lifted her into his lap, cradling her. She sagged limply within the support of his arms. Still alive, but fading. He'd left her very little blood, not enough to carry all the oxygen her body needed. Her lips were turning blue already.

He bit deep into his own wrist, let his mouth fill with blood. Then he bent to her, kissed her, pressed her mouth open and let his blood fill it. Slowly, letting her swallow instead of choke, until she moved a little in his embrace, then opened her eyes and looked up at him.

"What happened?" she asked.

"It's over," he told her.

"I'm still alive."

"You sound surprised."

"I am, a little." She shifted away from him, glancing at her nakedness and the smears of blood on her breasts and belly. "I need a bath."

"I'll be sure you get one."

She looked at him then, studying him, first gravely, then with a smile. "You don't look any different."

"I feel different," he admitted, "but I'm not sure what's changed."

She smiled and crawled back into his lap, curling up like a little naked cat. "You'll find out," she said, "and I'll be here to find out with you."

He wrapped his arms around her and held her close, tears springing to his eyes. He hadn't cried in three hundred years.

"Thank you," he said. "Thank you for loving me."

"I had no choice. Now, love me back."

"I do. I always will."

"Good. Now watch over me. I need to sleep."

He smiled, caressed her black, black hair, and watched over her while she slept.

NICHOLAS

Surely a bridegroom of blood art thou to me.
      —*Exodus 4:25b*

In the earliest days, the First Born Ones walked among men, and taught them the ways of the Blood Gods. But others of the First Born Ones denounced the Blood Gods and spoke of the Changing.
      —*The Book of Changing Blood*

A Knight came to us in the dark days. His touch healed the plague. He visited only within our walls, and when we asked in whose name he healed, he said, "In the name of the Eaters of Light, of which I am the only one."
      —*Fragment from a record kept in an English monastery. Received via e-mail by Julian Cavanaugh, sent by the Western European Vampire Alliance*

BEFORE

Vivian's party was, as usual, all the rage. The house crawled with vampires. Mortals, too, dragged themselves in off the street to indulge in the spirit of the evening, or were brought in as invited guests.

This was Nicholas Carrington's third year, and the first time he'd brought a guest. A mortal guest. He was beginning to think it had been a mistake.

He'd been seeing Dina Winters for a few weeks now. She appealed to him. It was possible he'd even begun to care for her. But here, in the middle of the Halloween bash, with real vampires, wannabe vampires and pseudo-vampires everywhere, all he could see, hear, or think about was her blood.

Three years ago he'd come to this party a mortal and left something else entirely. Vivian had brought him, Vivian had changed him. At the time it had seemed the right thing to do, and he still wasn't sure he'd make a different decision, faced with the same situation. Perhaps he could offer Dina the option. But if he did, it would mean telling her what he was. He wasn't sure she was ready for that. He knew he wasn't.

"Nicky, where's the bathroom? I'm supposed to meet Lor in five minutes."

"We're getting there."

"How can it take so long? I swear this is the weirdest house I've ever seen."

"Yes, it is. Here."

He stopped at a door. Perhaps it hadn't been there before, perhaps it had. He wasn't sure himself. It took vampires far older than he to understand the mechanics of this place. Vivian even got lost from time to time, or so she said, and it was her house.

Dina opened the unlocked door and went in, pulling Nicholas after her. He resisted. "No, I'll wait here."

The smile she tilted at him spoke of sex. "Come with me."

He swallowed. Desire for her blood combined with the desire for her body until he wasn't sure he had a single brain cell left firing. "You said your friend's meeting you in five minutes."

She licked her lower lip. "Five minutes can be an eternity if you play it right." Pulling his hand, she drew him into the small, tiled room after her. He was too startled to protest. Up until now, she'd been almost standoffish about sex. Certainly nothing like this. Vivian's incense did weird things to mortals.

She closed the door. Before he could protest, she was half-climbing his body, her mouth questing after his, her hands grasping his shoulders, her knee crooked over the curve of his buttock. His vision went red, and he bent to kiss her. Her mouth tasted wet and salty, and he could feel her blood moving through her lips, her tongue.

"Nicky," she sighed.

He shoved her away. She looked up into his eyes, her expression startled, then staring, fear rising.

"Nicky, no!"

He barely heard the words. It had gone too far. He never should have brought her here, certainly never should have let her drag him into this small room. But it was too late now.

He bent her back while she screamed words he didn't hear. His teeth tore into her throat, and she died.

NOW

ONE

Nicholas woke with a start. Memories fell into place slowly—Julian, the kind of voice compulsion only a vampire of advanced age could accomplish.

Dina.

He smelled blood. Not quite fresh—perhaps an hour old. He rolled over and saw her. He'd killed Dina just before her friend Lorelei had barged in, just before Julian had stopped him in the middle of his bloody feed.

He looked at her, at her shoulder-length blonde hair, clotted with blood. The bloody wound in her throat still oozed. Blood had congealed in her clothes, down the front of her blouse. It had run down her arm and her cupped, outflung hand was full of it. It was hard to think of her as Dina anymore. She was just a corpse, another in a series of corpses he'd left behind. But most of the others had deserved it.

Nicholas took a long, deep breath, inhaling the odor of her blood, the odor of her death...

She wasn't dead.

"Very sloppy, Nicholas." The woman's voice came from the doorway at his back, her tone harsh and clipped. "Very sloppy. But I've come to expect that from you."

He rolled his head to look at Vivian. He felt dizzy, sick.

"She was dead," he said firmly. "I felt it happen."

"You were wrong. Now finish it before she wakes up."

"I can't." He said it bluntly, waited for her challenge. Surely she knew what she'd created, three years ago today.

Vivian arched a dark eyebrow. "Then I will."

"No!" He sat up too fast and grabbed at the floor, the wall, as the world spun around him. Julian had put a strong compulsion on him—the aftereffects would linger.

"No?" she repeated, her tone tinged with angry disbelief.

"What do you presume, *Nicholas.*" She spat his name, and her fangs—white and sharp—peeked between her lips. He closed his eyes. Damn Julian—he could hardly move.

"It happens," he said, his voice thick as blood in his throat. "Every once in a while."

He opened his eyes and sat up to see Vivian staring at him. "*What* happens?"

"They don't die."

Silence pounded through the room. Vivian stared at him while he blinked stupidly, trying to clear the last of the compulsion from his head. Then a sound, soft and strange in the blood-soaked room.

Dina. Breathing.

Vivian stared at her, a strange bemusement on her face.

"Get your head together and pick her up," she said. "Come with me."

***

Nicholas watched while Vivian tended Dina's strangely alive body, washed the blood from her, removed her bloody clothes. The thick, blonde hair, clogged with blood, proved to be a wig. Beneath it her own hair, also blonde, was cropped short. Her panties and bra were strangely pristine, untouched by the red that fouled her shirt. Vivian left those alone. Nicholas was glad. He didn't think he could bear to see her naked, not now, not after what he'd done to her.

Why had he been so stupid as to bring her here? He'd put himself into a situation ready for disaster. Why? Because he liked her. Because he'd wanted to be near her. He'd thought he could control himself—he'd spent the last three years learning the aggressive methods only Vivian's children could master. But the need for blood had come on him so suddenly, so intensely, there'd been nothing he could do about it.

No, not just the need for blood. The need for *her* blood.

"Have you seen anything like this before?" he finally asked, as Vivian buttoned a long white nightgown and covered Dina with a sheet. Dina had barely stirred throughout the proceedings, but her breath came soft and even, filling the room with its small sound.

Vivian adjusted the sheet, as if tucking a child into bed. "Tell me what happens."

He shook his head slowly. "They don't die. Not right away. Something gets into the blood, what little is left, and it reproduces for a while. Then it stops."

"How long?"

"A week, sometimes two."

"And then they die."

He nodded. "Eventually." His voice sounded dead even to his own ears. "I tried to finish the first one when I realized what had happened. It was—" He shuddered, closed his eyes, unwilling to remember. "The pain was horrible. I think I might have died for a time. No one ever told me it could happen that way."

Vivian smoothed a hand over Dina's short blonde hair. "No one knew."

Too numb to be surprised, Nicholas looked at Dina's quiet face. She would awaken soon, he knew, and begin the strange journey toward the death to which he'd condemned her.

He didn't think he could bear it.

***

Dina drifted awake, the world returning to her in a numb haze. She was in a bed under white sheets. *Hospital*, she thought automatically. She'd spent enough time in them lately. But there were no IVs, no nurse call buttons, only a bed with white sheets and a rose-colored coverlet, a cozy room with rosebuds twining up the wallpaper.

She tried to sit up, but dizziness took over, sending her back to the mattress. She ached everywhere. She'd grown used to discomfort and pain lately, but this was different, as if every cell in her body had been affected. Like the flu, but deeper, more pervasive. And her neck hurt, just below her jaw.

What had happened? She couldn't remember anything after coming to the Halloween party with—

"Nick."

"Dina."

The voice surprised her. She'd had no sense of anyone else in the room, but she turned her head and there he was, on a chair by the door, slumped forward, elbows on his knees, fingers laced loosely together. Dark brown hair tumbled onto his forehead above wide-set, almost feminine green eyes. His nose was blunt, a bit too short for his face. He looked tired.

"Where am I?"

Suddenly she realized she was in a nightgown. Someone had changed her clothes. Her heart galloped hard and high in her chest for a moment. What if someone had seen— Then she felt the elastic band of her bra. It was still there, everything still in place. Her panties were still on her as well. The wig was gone. He would wonder why she'd worn it, since as far as he knew her hair had always been shoulder-length. She had no idea what she might tell him.

"How do you feel?" Nicholas asked. He stood and approached the bed, a guardedness appearing in his eyes.

"Awful," she said. "What happened? I don't remember anything after we came in the front door. Are we still in your friend's house? Where the party was?"

He looked away, and when he looked back his face had changed. Eased a little. He smiled. "Yes. You weren't feeling well last night, so Vivian offered to put us up for the night."

"Why don't I remember anything?"

"I don't know." His fingers traced her face gently, from temple to chin. "Can I do anything to help?"

"I could use something to eat." It had to have been hours since she'd last eaten, but she didn't really feel hungry.

He nodded. "I'll get you something." He stepped a little away from the bed. "Sleep," he said, and his voice sounded odd. Furry. "Sleep until nightfall comes again."

He stepped through the door, leaving her alone. She could try to sleep, she supposed, though it seemed she'd already slept for quite a while. Still, as the door closed silently behind him, her eyes drifted shut.

TWO

With only an hour of full night remaining, Nicholas concentrated on the office work Vivian had left for him. He'd done some of it while he'd been back and forth checking on Dina, but it was far from done. What he'd finished had been slipshod, done with great lack of concentration. He was certain he'd misfiled a good many of the papers he'd need to compile her fourth quarter report. And today there was e-mail to sort, as well.

Tonight more than most other nights he resented being Vivian's lackey. It could have been worse, he knew—some vampires used their "children" for more than just office work. But typing and filing and accounting were so beneath him. Some nights he wished she *would* ask him for sexual favors. God knew he was better at sex than accounting. He'd been a musician, not a CPA.

He skimmed through the long list of e-mails, deleting the trash and filing the rest. Vivian's e-mail seemed to get more eclectic and more far-flung every day. Today there'd been messages from Sri Lanka, the Bahamas, and a few countries he'd never heard of. He hadn't even known there were vampires in the Bahamas. Considering the place's reputation for sun, it seemed ironic.

"Almost done with that, I hope." Vivian's silent approach hadn't surprised him. He'd felt her coming as she reached the door. He belonged to her, after all. She had made him.

"Not really," he said, not bothering to disguise his irritation. "I've been distracted."

"That's not my fault, and it's no excuse for not finishing my work." She said it mildly as she sat in an office chair next to him and peered over his shoulder at the computer terminal. "Your stupid mistakes don't excuse you from your duties."

"She's not a mistake, she's a human being," he snapped, then quickly gathered himself.

Vivian eyed him with an archly raised eyebrow. "You should

have thought about that last night, before you killed her. Or didn't kill her, as the case may be." She paused. He refused to look at her, but felt her regard. "How is she?"

"All right at the moment. I put a sleep compulsion on her."

"Which only works on a human being." He refused to rise to her bait. Ignoring her, he concentrated furiously on his work.

After a moment, she continued, "Will the sleep help?"

"A little, and only for a while. Deep sleep seems to help the blood reproduce more quickly. She'll wake up feeling a little stronger, but I don't know how long it'll last."

"You seem to know a lot about this. How many times has it happened?"

He shook his head, lips tightening. He didn't want to answer her question, but he had to. She hadn't put a compulsion on him, but it was more than rude for him to disregard her questions. In fact, it was grounds for her to dispose of him. She owned him. He couldn't remember ever having resented it more than he did at this moment, except perhaps during the first few days after she'd made him. Not that long ago, yet an eternity. "I'm not exactly sure. Six, maybe."

"Do you know why?"

"I have no idea." He leaned his head back, pushing his hands through his hair. He hadn't tried to put the pieces of the puzzle together, hadn't really wanted to. Perhaps he was afraid of what he might find.

Vivian was still looking at him. She had stilled in her chair, sitting so quietly her presence barely affected even the air in the room. "Why did you do it? You seemed to be getting on fairly well from what I saw. I thought you liked her."

"I was hungry," he snapped, then crossed his arms hard over his chest, staring blankly at the keyboard on the desk in front of him. "I don't know. Once the idea occurred to me, I couldn't make it go away. Finally I couldn't stop it. I just . . . took her."

"Compulsion? How could that be? You did well with my training. I thought you'd reached a point where you could always choose your victims."

"It felt like compulsion."

"Was it that way with the others?"

He nodded. Behind his glum silence, he was remembering. Leading Dina to the restroom, through the hallways of Vivian's house, which could confuse the best of mortals and a good many vampires. He'd shown her the way, and suddenly it was as if the whole world existed inside her heartbeat. He'd heard the rushing of her blood, as if he could hear even the valves in her veins tapping open and closed, the soft squish of cells in single file rows moving through the tiniest capillaries. And he'd had no choice but to take her. He barely remembered doing it—just remembered her screams and the thick, sweet taste of her blood rushing into his throat.

He came back to himself, to the sullen self-anger that had overtaken him. Vivian was still looking at him. Her scrutiny disconcerted him. Sometimes it seemed she could look too far inside.

"Do you know what causes the compulsion?"

"No," he answered simply. He didn't want to elaborate, didn't have to unless asked specifically.

She nodded and pressed him no farther. "You've done enough for tonight," she said. "Go back to your room. It's nearly dawn."

He negotiated the strange short-but-not-short hallway that led from Vivian's office to the room where Dina slept. The house existed half on the human plane, half on the plane only vampires could navigate. It made for confusing and uncomfortable passage, particularly for the humans who occasionally entered.

She lay sleeping quietly, her face too pale, the wound on her throat too dark, with bruising spreading down from it. The punctures looked brutal, too much for her delicacy. Shamed he had caused it, Nicholas pulled his eyes away. She was all right for now, as all right as she could be. He left. In his own room, he stripped to his shorts and stretched out on his bed. Not his bed, though, not really, not his room. Vivian's. He remained hers until he could prove he deserved not to be. The bondage irked him more and more as time passed. It had been three years since she'd made him. He deserved a chance to be something other than her thrall.

The approach of dawn pulled at him, drawing him into weariness deeper than sleep, something closer to coma, or death. As the sun rose, he sank into darkness.

***

Dina woke some time later, not sure how long she'd been asleep, and for a moment not sure where she was. Then she turned her head and saw the ivory wallpaper with its twining rosebuds and remembered. Nick's friend's house.

She felt better. The pervasive pain that had greeted her on her last waking had faded, along with the dragging weakness. Carefully, she sat up. Her neck still ached, but her leg— She hadn't noticed that before. How could she have missed it? That pain was gone. A fluke, she thought, a cruel trick of her body.

She eased her legs over the side of the bed, inched forward until her feet touched the floor. Vague dizziness made her head spin, combining with the pain in her neck. She closed her eyes until the vertigo receded, then gingerly stood.

Her legs held. She still felt weak, but not as sick as she had yesterday, or even as sick as she had felt intermittently over the past five years. With growing confidence in her ability to move without falling over, she walked toward the corner, to the chest of drawers there and the mirror above it.

Her face was pale, smudged gray under the eyes. And on her throat, just below the line of her jaw, she saw the source of the dragging ache.

A dark bruise lay below her jaw, nearly black, then purple, then dribbling red and greenish yellow down to her collarbone before disappearing behind the lace-edged neck of her white nightgown. At the darkest part of the bruise were two dark circular marks, covered with rough, black scabs.

Gingerly, she touched the marks. A stabbing pain shot deep into her throat, seeming to arrow straight to her heart. Gasping, she jerked her hand away. A strange wound, she thought. If she didn't know better, she'd think she'd been bitten by a vampire—

Get your hands off me, you bastard.

The thought flashed through her on a wave of fear, and she

took an involuntary step back from the mirror. But the phantom voice faded quickly, with no apparent substance behind it. Where had it come from? Was it a memory, a dream, or something else? She couldn't remember what had happened once she and Nick had crossed the threshold of the strange, big house. She'd been dressed like a vampire, though. Maybe somebody had gotten carried away.

A small sound behind her sent her spinning toward the door. Vertigo hit again, and she grabbed at the edge of the chest of drawers to steady herself. Nick came in, closing the door gently behind him.

"How are you?"

She stared at him as the fear washed through her again. Then she swallowed hard. It was only Nick. She liked Nick. "Better," she said. "What time is it?"

"Just past dusk." He stepped toward her, took her arm. "Can I help?"

She shook her head. "I'm not ready to go back to bed yet." Instead she eased her way to the chair next to the bed and sat, accepting his assistance.

He sat on the bed and studied her. "You look better. Not so pale."

She wondered how pale she'd been before, if she wasn't as pale now. And it suddenly occurred to her that she'd slept again for an undetermined amount of time, and she still wasn't hungry.

"Can I get you anything?" he asked.

She wasn't hungry. She was thirsty, a little, but not so much that it was unbearable. She could only think of one thing she wanted.

"I want to go home."

His lips parted, and for a moment she was sure he was going to refuse her. Then he nodded once, sharply. "I think that can be arranged."

***

"I don't think it's a good idea."

Dina, sitting at the kitchen table, could barely hear the hissed whispers from the next room. She cocked her head, trying to make the words come to her more clearly.

"We can't keep her here forever." This was Nick. His voice carried a little better. When Vivian spoke, it was all Dina could do to tease words from the whispering.

". . . can. We should. She can't remember . . . What happens . . . truth?"

Nick glanced in her direction and Dina looked quickly away, concentrating on the glass they'd given her and what remained of the drink inside it.

"She should be home," Nick finally said, sounding defeated.

Vivian also looked in Dina's direction. "Maybe," she said, and something else, then, "Sorry."

Nick shoved a hand through his dark hair and came back into the kitchen, Vivian right behind him. They both sat at the table. Vivian looked at Dina's half-empty glass.

"How is it?"

Dina turned the glass, making its contents swirl. The drink was colorless and nearly tasteless, but too thick for water. "It's okay, I guess. I think it's upsetting my stomach."

"You shouldn't drink anymore, then," Nick said.

"What is it, anyway?"

Nick glanced at Vivian, who smiled and said, "It's a protein drink."

Dina frowned and pushed the glass aside. She felt strange, as if her body didn't really want her to eat or drink anything at all, particularly not a mysteriously transparent protein drink. "When can we go?"

"In a few minutes," Nick said. His answer surprised her. Dina had expected him to tell her they couldn't leave at all.

"Take your cell phone," Vivian said. "I might need to get in touch with you."

"Why?" Nick didn't sound happy with the request.

Vivian frowned and shook her head. "Something's brewing. I'm not sure what, but if something does happen, I'll want you here right away."

"Brewing? What's brewing?" The words came sharp, too much like a demand.

Vivian lifted an eyebrow and gave him a dark look. "I don't

know, and I don't appreciate your tone. Just be ready. In case." She hesitated. "The Senior put a Call out for Julian for a reason. I don't know what it is, but I have a feeling it's important."

The conversation made no sense to Dina. The only thing she understood was that Vivian had some sort of superiority over Nick, and that she intimidated Dina. There was something about the woman, with her glossy black hair and perfect eyebrows, and the way her regard could shrivel. Dina also understood that both Nick and Vivian knew something she didn't. Something important.

She decided to let it go for now. "I don't have anything to wear. I really don't want to go home in this nightgown."

"I'll get you some clothes," said Vivian, and departed, her footsteps barely audible.

"She makes me nervous," she confided to Nick.

"She makes everybody nervous." He smiled, reached out to touch Dina's cheek. "You're feeling better?"

"Yes." She looked at the mysterious drink, then at Nick. Once she'd thought his wide face open, easy to read. Now it was different. Now it seemed to hide things. "What happened to me?"

"You were attacked by someone at the party." His voice was gentle. "They got a little carried away with the vampire theme. You lost some blood."

"Why didn't you take me to the hospital?"

"It didn't seem serious enough." There. He was definitely hiding something. She could tell from some subtle change in his face, or maybe his eyes. Something that had been open before had closed.

"I find that hard to believe, given the way I felt when I woke up."

"Maybe it was more serious than we thought."

"Maybe I should go to the hospital now." She made a challenge out of it, though she wasn't sure why. She had the feeling neither Nick nor Vivian wanted her examined by professionals.

But his response was placid. "Do you feel like you need to?"

"No," she conceded. "I feel like I need to go home."

"Then let's get ready."

Vivian had put jeans and a soft cotton shirt on the bed in the room where Dina had slept. Nick waited outside while she dressed. She still didn't understand why he had to follow her everywhere. She didn't let him follow her into the room, though.

The jeans were a little big, the shirt purple and just the right size. She liked purple, especially this dark, rich, plum version. Carefully, she adjusted her bra, checking it in the mirror, then buttoned up the shirt. Some of the color had returned to her face, but the deep bruising looked worse, more invasive. The pain had faded, though. And the rest of her body, though still weak, felt better than it had in a long time. She should have been happy, she supposed, but instead it struck her as creepy. Something very strange had happened for her to feel as good as she did.

She should ask Nick. Or maybe not. Maybe she didn't want to know.

THREE

It wasn't the first time Nicholas had been in Dina's apartment. They'd only dated a few times before the debacle of the Halloween party, but he'd been here once or twice to pick her up, had sat on her couch and admired the watercolors hung over the faux fireplace, the display of jewelry on the coffee table. She'd designed the pieces herself, and sold others like them in Lorelei's boutique.

He sat there now, watching the lamplight glint off a pair of dangly gold and turquoise earrings, while Dina rummaged in the kitchen.

"I should be hungry," she said. "I haven't eaten in ages. But nothing looks good."

"That protein drink can be filling." It had actually been plasma, but he didn't think she needed to know that right now. He hadn't been sure it would help, but he'd figured it was worth a shot.

She took a bottle of designer water from the fridge and opened it, sipped carefully. He straightened, alarmed. She smiled and drank a little more.

"There. That tastes fantastic."

That surprised him. Vampires couldn't drink water—it made them violently ill. But Dina wasn't a vampire. He wasn't sure what she was.

Walking dead, some nasty part of his mind said. He blocked it off viciously.

"I should call Lorelei," Dina said, then looked at the clock. "Damn, it's past midnight."

"She'll be sleeping," said Nicholas. Lorelei had seen what had happened Halloween night. He didn't want Dina reminded of that right now.

"Maybe not. Plus she'll be wondering what happened to me." Dina picked up the phone. Nicholas watched, tense, as she dialed the number. But after a few moments, she hung up. "No answer. I'll try later."

Hiding relief, he leaned back against the soft cushions of the couch. He felt sick. He hadn't fed last night, and his blood cried for replenishment. He'd have to slip out and find someone he could leech for a pint or three.

She sat next to him on the couch and sipped her water. "Can I get you something?"

"No, thanks. I'm going to have to leave soon, anyway."

"That's too bad. I'd hoped we could talk."

"About what?"

"You still haven't told me what happened at the party."

"Yes, I did."

"Not in any detail. I want to know who did this and why." She brushed her fingers over her battered throat, wincing.

"Apparently Vivian didn't screen the guests as well as she normally does. We don't usually have this kind of incident." *Usually the victims just die.*

"I guess weird parties attract weird people. Do you know who it was?"

"Somebody who wandered in off the street. He ran off." The lies came easily. He'd become used to lying over the last three years. He supposed it got even easier after a century or so. He couldn't imagine keeping this up for hundreds of years, like Vivian. He stood, looking down into Dina's surprised expression. "I need to go. I can come back in a couple of hours if you want me to."

"Would you please?"

He nodded and left before he could change his mind.

Alone in her small apartment, Dina closed her eyes and fought a sudden wave of despair. She thought she'd gotten used to the awful, lurking knowledge that had haunted her for the past five years, but every once in a while it staged a sneak attack. The strange events of the last couple of days had undoubtedly precipitated this one.

She curled her feet under her and sipped her glass of water. She should be hungry, but the thought of food turned her stomach. With the aching sense of loss chewing at her soul, she turned on the TV in an attempt to chase it away.

***

On the streets of New York City, if you took the time to look, you could always find someone who deserved to die. Nicholas followed the smell of fear. There was a great deal of it in the air, but he could sift through the threads and search out one of them even through the miasma of the city. This thread belonged to a child, and smelled like impending death.

It was easy enough for Nicholas to slip into the building, and he made it just in time, just before the blow that would have sent the boy into unconsciousness.

"Run," he said to the child, putting compulsion in it. "Tell someone what happened."

The boy ran, blood running from his nose, his eye swelling shut. Nicholas' vampiric ears heard the small footsteps patter down the hallway, heard the boy knock on a neighbor's door. All while the father stared in horror and disbelief at the sudden intruder.

"You won't do this again," said Nicholas.

He attacked like a cobra, a lightning-quick strike that sank his fangs deep. He could make it easy—all vampires could—through use of compulsion, if he wanted to. He didn't want to. He let this victim feel all the pain, all the terror, let him feel the darkness encroach as his heart slowed. Nicholas felt the approach of death, stopped just before it was too late.

"You might live," he said, feeling hot blood drip down his chin. "Or you might not. But this was your choice."

He left the man gibbering on the floor, undoubtedly wondering if the blood would ever stop flowing from the wound in his throat, or if the pool beneath him would simply grow and grow until there was nothing left in his body for his heart to pump. Nicholas knew the blood would stop. Agents in vampiric saliva worked to heal the wounds if the victim was left alive, to ensure another meal. Part of Vivian's training had involved learning to feed without killing. But he felt no obligation to inform his victim of this fact. Better to let him look death in the face for a while.

The fresh blood rushed through his system, making him dizzy. He'd gone without for too long. Stupid of him. But there'd been Dina to think of. He'd gotten by on the plasma drink yesterday, but it was never enough, like a human eating sugar when the body craved protein.

He went back to her apartment building and sat on the front stoop, waiting for his body to adjust. Sitting there listening to the too-fast rush of his own blood, waiting for it to slow to a normal rate, he thought. About Dina.

Feeding tonight had been good, but even hungry as he'd been, he'd been able to choose his victim, to control his feeding so he could stop short of killing. Why hadn't he been able to do that with Dina? The compulsion had been so intense, so uncontrollable—

He hadn't experienced anything like it since his first few days of vampirism, before Vivian had taught him control.

He understood that most vampires couldn't achieve that control. Even Vivian wasn't sure why she and her "children" could while others couldn't. But to have the control and lose it—and then to face the aftermath, the return of the victim—why did this happen to him? There had to be an explanation.

Dina had a right to know, he thought suddenly. She had at best two weeks to live before the blood in her body died, and she died with it. She also had a right to know why. He owed her the truth. And if she hated him, if she demanded some sort of retribution, well, he owed her that, too.

He slipped silently in through her apartment window, to wash his face in her sink. Surprised she hadn't heard the water running, he went back out and came into the building the right way, stopping to knock on her door.

She opened the door, looking bleary. The TV droned in the background, voices overlaying a strained laugh track.

"I didn't think you'd come back," she said. She stood to one side, letting him come in.

"I said I would, didn't I?"

She nodded.

"Are you all right?" he asked. She looked like she'd been sleeping, but surely not. She'd spent all day asleep, the victim of his compulsion and the transformation of her remaining blood.

"TV makes me brain dead."

It was more than that, though. Her eyes looked haunted.

Did she know?

He sat on the soft couch and looked up at her. After a small hesitation, she sat next to him and turned down the volume on the TV.

"I wish I could talk to Lorelei," she said. "She's got to be wondering where I am."

"She's not home. You can't do anything about that."

"I don't understand why she wouldn't be at home in the middle of the night."

"Maybe she went home with someone."

"Maybe she was attacked, too."

He looked away. Lorelei *had* been attacked. He'd done it himself, and probably would have finished her if Julian hadn't intervened. Or maybe not. The compulsion had been fading when he'd gone for her. He could have stopped himself. With her, he could have stopped himself.

"You can try her again in the morning," he suggested, knowing full well Dina wouldn't be conscious after sunrise. "I'm sure she's fine."

She nodded, but didn't look convinced. She fiddled with the remote control, changing channels and toying with the volume.

"Dina . . ." She looked toward him, brows lifted in a question. "Dina, I have to tell you something."

"What?" She sounded drained, wearier than she had when she'd first awakened from death. "What is it?"

"Dina . . ." He swallowed, still tasting blood in the back of his throat. "Dina, you're dying."

She looked at him placidly, a small smile curving her lips and a horrible weight of sadness in her eyes. "Yes," she said. "How did you know?"

FOUR

He stared. He'd intended to say more, but her words had changed everything.

"Dina, I'm so sorry."

Her eyes had changed between her words and his. The open, vulnerable sadness had been replaced by a shuttered look. She was protecting herself. From what?

"It's okay," she said, her voice brittle. "I understand how hard it is to be around me. It's been fun. Have a nice life."

"I don't—" He stopped. He wasn't sure what to say, didn't know where she thought the conversation was going. Gently, he lifted her hand in his. "That's not what I meant."

"It doesn't matter. I don't know how you found out, but now that you know, you might as well leave. I don't need to be abandoned again. At this point I'm not sure I even like you, so just go."

"Someone else left you."

Her eyes changed again, the shutters trying to open. The pain behind them was almost more than he could bear. Dina swallowed hard and nodded.

"Then he was a prick."

She let out a strange laugh, almost a sob. "Yes, he was."

"So am I. But I'm not going to leave."

She turned her face away, too late to hide the tears from him. "You should, Nick. You really should."

***

"They said at first it should be treatable. I had the chemo, I had a mastectomy, radiation—but it came back. More chemo, another mastectomy. And then they found more in my leg, in the bone."

She stopped. She'd stopped several times during her near-monologue, and Nicholas had waited, silent, until she was ready to go on. Outside, morning approached, and he could feel the weariness encroaching. Dina rubbed her eyes. "I'm so tired." Shaking her head, she continued. "I'm supposed to see the doctor again for some kind of a prognosis. There's not much chance it'll be good. The party was sort of a last hurrah."

"When?"

"Tuesday."

Nicholas nodded. Today was Friday. Dina might not live until Tuesday. "Who knew about this?"

She shook her head. "Me. My doctor."

"Your parents? Lorelei?"

"I didn't tell Lorelei. My mom died ten years ago from cancer. I never knew my dad. My boyfriend only stuck around for the first round of surgery. He couldn't take anymore after that."

Nicholas nodded. He didn't know what to say. The sun approached, and Dina yawned.

"Go lie down if you're tired," he said. "I don't mind."

"In a minute." She leaned her head back on the couch. "Thanks for listening."

He touched her hair, lifting a short blonde strand away from her forehead. "No problem."

Weariness encroached on him, as well. Only a few hours until sunrise. He needed to go back to Vivian's, or see if Dina's bedroom was suntight. "Dina—"

The doorbell rang. She pushed wearily from the couch to answer it.

It was Vivian. "I need to talk to Nicholas."

Frowning, he came to the door. "I thought you were going to call if you needed me."

She grabbed his elbow, dragged him into the hallway. "This is bigger than I expected. You need to come with me now."

"It's three hours 'til daylight."

"I know. But we need to go Below. The Senior's dead."

Nicholas gaped. "*What?*"

"The *Senior* is *dead*. Julian killed him. Now Julian's the Senior."

He could barely get his head around this. The Senior had put out a Call for Julian, and now the Senior was dead at Julian's hands. "Is he cleaning house?"

"We don't know yet. It doesn't look that way so far. But he wants us all Below."

"And we're just supposed to go so he can kill us all?"

She studied his face, her mouth tight. "You don't know Julian, do you?"

"No, not really."

"He hasn't killed a human in centuries, much less another vampire. If he brought down the Senior, there was a reason."

"If the Senior had a Call out for him, I'm guessing there was a reason for that, too."

"The last Senior spared nearly everyone who pledged loyalty within the first twenty-four hours of his ascension. Are you coming or not?"

"All right, I'm coming. But Dina's coming, too."

"She'll slow us down."

"If she stays here, she'll die. She won't know to keep the curtains closed."

"Then she'll die today instead of later."

He met Vivian's gaze, realizing defiance could get him killed. "She's coming with us."

The tips of her fangs showed against her lower lip, then subsided. "Fine. Get her. We need to go *now*."

He nodded and ducked back into Dina's apartment. The trick, he realized, would be convincing Dina she had to go.

"I don't understand," she protested when he told her. "I'd rather stay here and rest."

"It might not be safe here."

She eyed him with obvious skepticism. "Why would my own apartment not be safe?"

"The man who attacked you at the party. He might come back." The words came out before he could consider them. When she found out what had really happened— "Dina, there are things you don't know. Please come with me. I don't want anything to happen to you."

As he said it, he realized he meant it, far more deeply than he'd ever dreamed he could. The thought of her inevitable death made him hurt in a way he'd never experienced before. It was almost as if his soul ached. If vampires had souls.

Her skepticism faded, replaced by an expression he couldn't read. "I don't know if I can trust you, Nicky."

He felt his mouth twist as he smiled. "You can't. Now come on."

She gave him an odd, narrow look. But she followed him.

***

Nicholas had made a few trips to the Underground with Vivian, helping her run errands for the Senior. The former leader of the Underground had trusted her with his mortal servants, as well as with a half-dozen of the vampire community's legitimate business pursuits, like a highly successful Goth club in Alphabet City and a profitable online venture specializing in vampire memorabilia. It seemed no matter what the era, there were always mortals who hungered for things vampiric. Nicholas had been one of them, before Vivian had taken him Over. He'd worn black capes and fangs on stage when he'd played shithole nightclubs in Jersey. Then his life had changed, and he'd found Vivian.

She led them through a narrow corridor into the wide, crystalline chamber where the Senior's office had been. Dina clung to Nicholas' hand, staring wide-eyed at the glittering walls. She looked scared.

"Are you all right?" he asked her.

She abandoned her fear a moment to give him a sour glare. "I would be if somebody told me what the hell is going on."

"There's been a hostile takeover," Vivian answered. "My boss was overthrown. We're here to meet the new guy."

Dina sensed the hesitation in Vivian's tone. "Are you afraid he might fire you?"

"I'm more afraid he might kill me."

Dina blinked. "What are you? Drug lords or something?"

"Or something," said Nicholas, his voice quiet. He smiled and squeezed Dina's hand reassuringly, but she didn't find herself reassured.

Across the wide room, a door opened. A man came through it, took a few steps toward them, then stopped to light a cigarette. The small flame flared, strangely bright in the wide room, and a thread of smoke curled. He inhaled deeply, exhaled smoke, and waited.

Dina studied him as they approached. He didn't seem

particularly threatening. Six feet tall with black hair that curled a bit against his collar. His face, particularly his eyes, had a vaguely Asian cast. He wore a cream-colored Aran sweater, fashionably faded jeans, and Reeboks. Scary.

But Nick's hand tightened on hers as they approached. Their small party stopped a few feet away, close enough to smell the smoke from his cigarette. It didn't smell like tobacco. It was spicy, strange. He flicked ashes to the floor and gave them an apologetic look.

"Sorry about the smoke," he said in a voice that sounded strangely like water. "I don't need them any more, but two hundred years of an oral fixation is hard to break." He drew another drag, then turned back to the door. "Come with me, please."

They followed, Dina more confused than ever. But when they stepped into the office, all her questions vanished at the sight of a familiar face.

"Lorelei!" Dina ran to her, grabbing her friend in an over-enthusiastic embrace, nearly knocking her down. "I was so worried about you!"

"Dina?" Lorelei's voice sounded weak. Enthusiasm fading into concern, Dina stepped back. Her friend's face had gone gray, her dark blue eyes suddenly huge in her round face. "My God, Dina."

"Lorelei, what's wrong?"

"I saw you—" She broke off, her gaze moving over Dina's shoulder to Nicholas. She grabbed Dina's hand, jerking her closer. "You need to come with me *now*."

Dina glanced back at Nicholas. "Nicky—"

But he looked strangely bleak. "Just go. You would have found out sooner or later."

Nicholas watched the women leave, feeling suddenly sick. He'd wanted to tell Dina the truth himself, not have Lorelei relate the gruesome scene that had transpired on Halloween night. Julian laughed a little, but not without sympathy. "It'll be hard to put a good spin on that."

Nicholas looked up at the new Senior, swallowing his anger. "You don't understand."

"No, I don't. But I was there, and I saw you kill her. I also saw you nearly kill Lorelei. As the new Senior, I could have you sent into the sun right now, just for the hell of it. Feeding is one thing, but that was obscene." The sympathy had faded from his voice, replaced by thin harshness. Something had changed. His face was different, his voice, the color of his skin—

"What are you?" said Nicholas. Next to him, Vivian stiffened.

Julian smiled and drew a drag from his cigarette. "I'm the new Senior. Other than that, your guess is as good as mine."

"Forget the girls," Vivian broke in. "What's going to happen to us?"

"You and Nicholas, I assume, will fall asleep in a couple of hours."

The silence hung a moment, just long enough for Nicholas to wonder if he or Vivian would ever awaken from that sleep.

"And you won't?" Vivian's voice harshly broke the silence.

"No."

If he was trying to intimidate them, he was succeeding. Nicholas had thought of Julian as a weak sell-out, hiding from the rest of his kind, refusing, by all accounts, to take any human blood. But now....

Now he oozed power. More than the previous Senior had, and the previous Senior had been centuries older. Something had happened between Halloween and today. Something more than a changeover of power.

Vivian moved a little closer to Nicholas. The action surprised him. She'd never come to him for comfort, no matter how subtle. "What do you want from us?"

Julian snubbed out his cigarette and smiled. "From you, Vivian, I want a full report on all the businesses you handle. Not just the numbers—I can get that from William. I want to hear about business plans, policies, projections for the future. As for you, Nicholas—" His gaze turned, and Nicholas actually felt his stomach quivering as it touched him. "I want to know what happened with Dina. You need to tell me everything."

FIVE

"Lorelei, you have completely and totally gone off the deep end."

Lorelei just shook her head, looking sad, angry, and frustratingly sane. Surely, Dina thought—hoped—her friend had lost her mind. If there were any truth to this story...

"You don't remember anything, then?" She sounded tired.

"No. I remember meeting Nick at the party, then I remember waking up in bed, and Nick came to help me."

"He didn't hurt you?"

"No. Why would he hurt me?"

"Because he *killed* you, Dina. I watched him do it, and then he tried to kill me."

It didn't sound any more convincing than the last time she'd said it. Dina just stared at her. Lorelei looked tired, but Dina *was* tired. Exhausted. She'd have to lie down in a few minutes, or fall down right here on the floor.

"How could he have killed me? I'm alive, right now, talking to you."

Lorelei's hand whipped toward her, and Dina flinched as her friend grasped her throat, pressing against the bruises. She'd almost forgotten about them, but they hurt now as Lorelei dug in her fingers.

"Are you sure?" She let go, just as Dina was about to ball up a fist to defend herself from the sudden, illogical attack. "He's turned you."

"Turned me into what?"

"Into one of them."

"A vampire." She let sarcasm drip. She reached out herself, touching marks on Lorelei's throat, but lacking the courage to return the pain Lorelei had inflicted. "What about you? What have they made you into?"

Lorelei's mouth tightened, her brows compressing in irritation. "That's different," she said sullenly, then added after a moment, "I don't know. But Julian's good. Nicholas—"

"He hasn't hurt me. Not since I woke up in that bed. He's been good to me."

"Maybe he just feels guilty."

Dina rubbed her eyes. They kept sliding closed, heavy and gritty with her need to sleep. "You have no reason to lie to me, Lorelei. But I need to talk to him about this. And this vampire stuff—it's just crazy."

"Then tell me why you suddenly can't keep your eyes open just because the sun's coming up."

"I'm not drinking anybody's blood."

"Not yet."

"I really need to go to sleep."

"I know." Lorelei took her hand and led her to a door at the back of the small room. "I'll take you where you can rest."

***

Nicholas had half-expected Julian to issue an instant execution order. It would have been fully within his rights as Senior, and would have set an example for others who might take innocent and unwilling victims. There'd been a rash of that lately, in spite of the official codes of conduct. The previous Senior had turned a blind eye, recognizing the impossibility of enforcement. Julian seemed inclined toward a different approach.

Apparently the fact Dina hadn't actually died tempered the situation a bit, though, for Julian listened, frowning, to Nicholas' story, smoking meditatively as he considered the details. Vivian had left some time ago, escorted by William to a place where she could sleep.

"This has happened before?" he asked when Nicholas came to an awkward finish.

"Yes. A few times. They always die."

"You have no idea why?"

"None."

"But when it happens, the killing is always prompted by intense compulsion?"

"Yes."

Julian snubbed out his latest cigarette. He smoked like a chimney, judging by the overflowing ashtray. Nicholas wondered exactly what he smoked. There wasn't much tobacco in the mix, and it didn't smell at all like pot. Given those facts, Nicholas wondered what he got out of it.

"I'm going to place you under house arrest until we get this figured out. You'll be sleeping soon, so I'll escort you to a room. In the meantime, I'll have Dina's blood tested and see if we can find anything."

Nicholas stared. "Have her blood tested?"

"To look for abnormalities." Julian stood and stretched, then gestured for Nicholas to precede him out of the room. "You don't have much time. We should go."

"Who's going to do the testing?"

"I'll be awake for a while, along with the human servants. Lorelei can help."

"You didn't Turn her?"

"I'm not sure what I did to her."

"And you?" Nicholas couldn't help the question, impertinent as it was.

Julian only smiled. "We're not sure about that, either."

The room seemed ordinary enough, but Nicholas knew that if he tried to leave it he'd be intercepted and probably killed when Julian left him. So he made no effort to plan an escape. He just stripped to his underwear and crawled under the bedclothes. When dusk came, perhaps there'd be answers.

***

Dina drifted out of that strange, intensely deep sleep to see Lorelei leaning over her, a frown between her delicate, black brows.

"How do you feel?"

Dina considered. "I've been worse."

"Did you feel better yesterday?"

She frowned, wondering at the strange questions. "Maybe. I'm not sure. Why?"

"Because I'm trying to figure out exactly what that bastard Nicholas did to you."

"Lor—"

"No. I don't want to hear any more of your rationalization." She straightened. "Come on. We need to talk to Julian."

She went without protest. Obviously Lorelei felt strongly about the situation, though Dina still found it difficult to believe that Lorelei honestly thought Nicholas was a vampire. And Julian, too, apparently, as well as Vivian. Maybe Lorelei had tried some mind-altering drugs at the Halloween party, and they'd done permanent damage to her brain.

Her lack of protest, though, had less to do with respect for her friend than with the fact she was too tired to worry about any of it right now. She felt like she'd only had an hour or so of sleep. She also felt like she had the flu. Her body ached, bone-deep, everywhere. Her surroundings looked strange, like everything was the wrong color. Her chest hurt, as if her heart struggled to beat.

It wasn't as bad as the aftermath of chemo, though. She decided to tough it out.

Julian sat behind a desk in what looked like a mundane office, working at a computer. Surely vampires weren't computer literate. Didn't they spend all their time reminiscing about the 18th century or something? The strangeness of her thoughts didn't register immediately. Lorelei told her to sit in a chair across from the desk, and Julian looked at her.

He was old. She could tell that from looking into his eyes, and the realization shook her. He didn't look more than thirty, but his eyes—those eyes had been around for a long, long time.

She swallowed. "Are you—are you really a vampire?"

He smiled a little. "I used to be. Now—well, we're looking into a variety of possibilities."

"That's not what we're here for," Lorelei broke in. Rudely, Dina thought. But Julian looked at her with a deeper, wider smile. The age in his eyes turned to warmth, and Dina shivered again. This man—or whatever he was—loved her friend. How? They couldn't have met before the party.

"I know, love." He spoke gently, and Dina wished the voice had been directed at her. It thrummed with beauty.

"We're going to press charges."

Dina blinked at Lorelei's pronouncement. "Charges? What charges?"

"Against Nicholas," Julian said. "As Senior, I've determined his attack on an unwilling victim to be prosecutable. I could order him killed, but I'd rather go through the formal Tribunal."

"Would they order him killed?" The very idea appalled her. Did they consider her an unwilling victim? Of what? She had no idea what might have been done to her at the party, or who'd done it. Plus there was the added wrinkle that he hadn't killed anyone.

Julian returned his attention to her, his deep, deep eyes once again mild. "If the charges are proven, the penalty is death."

"How can you prosecute him if the victim has no recollection of what happened and there are no other witnesses?"

"There are witnesses," said Julian. "Lorelei saw him take you, and so did I."

"But I'm not dead."

He traded a strange glance with Lorelei.

"He should die for this," she said.

"It's not time yet." Julian stood, walking around the desk to kneel next to Dina's chair. "We have to have a talk. A very long talk. Nicholas and Vivian need to hear this as well. Only then can we decide what should be done."

***

"A blood test?" Dina looked impulsively at the bend of her right elbow. Sure enough, there was a small mark, its edges tinged with blue. "This is ridiculous. I'm getting a little tired of waking up with mysterious wounds."

Julian smiled. "I don't blame you."

They still sat in his office, but Nicholas and Vivian had joined them, in chairs next to each other opposite Dina and Lorelei. Julian perched on the desk amidst a clutter of papers. Behind the desk was the last member of the group, a mild-looking man with glasses and a receding hairline. Julian had introduced him as Dr. Greene. The sheer ordinariness of her surroundings struck her as surreal.

"Why did you do this?" Vivian asked. Her voice was quiet, as if she knew something the rest of them didn't.

"Nicholas told me about the occasional strange results of his feeding. I want to find out what causes it. Then, perhaps, we can find a way to cure it."

"What causes it?" Nicholas asked.

Julian looked back at Dr. Greene, who rose and came to stand in front of the desk, carrying a manila folder. He consulted the pages.

"Dina's blood is dying," he said. He barely glanced at her, then shifted and let his gaze meet hers. "I'm sorry to put it so bluntly, but that's the truth."

"Why?" she managed. Everything felt so unreal, his words had little impact.

"As near as I can tell, the exposure to Nicholas' vampiric blood caused your blood to replicate rapidly until all the lost blood was replaced. However, it began to die again almost immediately. Within the next few days, there'll no longer be enough living cells to sustain life."

"Replicate rapidly," Vivian repeated. "Like cancer."

"Very much like cancerous cells," Dr. Greene confirmed. "Except in this case the result is beneficial rather than detrimental."

Dina folded her hands hard in her lap. Cancerous cells. "Could my own cancer have caused that reaction?" She asked the question almost without thinking, then kept her gaze fixed on Julian, ignoring the shocked, gaping look on Lorelei's face.

He nodded slowly. "How much cancer?"

"Extensive."

"There's more to it than that," said Vivian.

"Yes?" Julian's attention moved almost languidly to Vivian.

Vivian shifted under the scrutiny of the others in the room. "We all have to find our way through the conundrums of our way of life. My way was to focus on mercy killings. Over the past century, I'd estimate ninety-five percent of my victims were afflicted with incurable cancer."

"So the blood that's sustained you, the blood you used to make Nicholas, was formed and reformed over at least a hundred years from blood drawn from cancer victims." Julian looked again at Dina, but spoke to Nicholas. "Were you aware she had cancer?"

"No." His voice was soft and thick. Dina had never heard

him sound like that. Looking at him, she expected to see tears, but found only a strange, drawn look of desperation.

"Were you originally one of Vivian's mercy killings?"

"Yes. But at the last minute, she offered to bring me over."

Dina stared at him. He'd been a cancer patient, too? She wanted to ask him about it, but Julian's questions moved the discussion on.

"Vivian, have you brought over any of your other mercy killings?"

"Not for a long time, though I offered it to most of them. The majority were elderly and didn't find the possibility attractive."

Julian leaned back in his perch on top of the desk, considering. "Dr. Greene, do you think Nicholas' compulsion could be a result of this pattern? That he was drawn to take Dina's blood because of her condition?"

Dr. Greene considered. "It's possible. In which case, perhaps the compulsion exists because he holds some latent ability to heal, and that's why those victims always come back."

"But—" Nicholas broke in, then hesitated. "Afterwards, if I take them again—it's hideous."

"There's an element missing." Julian jumped decisively down from the desk. "Dr. Greene, I want you to run another series of experiments. I'll tell you what I want, but we need to do this quickly and thoroughly. Dina's life depends on it. Dina, Nicholas and Vivian, I need a blood sample from all of you."

***

"You heard what he said. He as much as admitted it."

Dina clasped her arms around her knees. She was so tired...

"I can't believe this. It's crazy." Vampires, real vampires, drinking blood and turning people—turning *her*—into walking zombies. It wasn't real life. It was some nutty horror movie.

"What did they do to you, Lor, to make you believe it?"

"Not 'they.' Julian just dragged me along for the ride." She shook her head. "I saw his throat slit open to the bone, and he got up and walked away. I saw—" She stopped. "I had no choice but to believe, Dina. Neither will you by the time this is over."

"So I'll either believe or die?"

Lorelei studied her, her dark blue eyes suddenly wide and moist. "Why didn't you tell me?"

Dina shook her head. "It's not like we were soul-deep friends or anything. We were business associates more than anything else. I'm sure we both have a lot of secrets."

"But if you were that sick—"

"I wasn't 'that sick,' Lor. I was dying. I still am. As soon as someone decides this craziness is over, I'll go back to the doctor, and they'll probably cut more pieces off me and radiate me some more and pump more chemicals into me, until I get sick of it or until there's nothing left." Her voice broke, and she stopped, biting hard on her lower lip, wrapping her arms around herself, feeling the artificial softness under her arms where the softness had once been natural. "Or maybe I won't go back to the doctor at all. Maybe I'll just let it run its course. Let Vivian kill me. Do you think *she* could get it right?"

Her laughter was strained and false, but Lorelei answered it with a sympathetic smile. "You won't be going anywhere for a day or two," she said. "Let's make the best of it." She stood. "Let's go see William. Julian can't stand him, but I think he's a hoot."

***

Outside, night was wearing down. Nicholas knew because his new room—his house arrest room—had a window.

It was a small window, high on the wall across from the bed. Closed, locked, and covered with a tinfoil screen, it let very little of the outside world in. But it was enough.

A human wouldn't have noticed the changes in the quality of the dark that leaked around the edges of the screen. It still looked like nighttime—dark, deep and velvety, tinged with star- and moonshine. But to Nicholas it was edged with a threat of gray that hadn't been there an hour before. Dawn approached on slow, soft feet.

It presented no threat to him. Even if it were full daylight outside, not enough light could come through the screen to hurt him. But the implication of the window didn't escape him. If there was a covered window, it could be made into an uncovered window. And then he would die.

Outside, footsteps echoed. Nicholas looked up, as he had every other time he'd heard footsteps in the hallway. For the past several hours, they'd tapped past from time to time, always moving on. This time they stopped. Someone knocked.

"Nicholas." Julian's voice. There was no anger in it.

Nicholas looked up at the window. "Come in."

Julian did, his booted feet nearly silent on the wooden floor. "Dr. Greene has completed the tests." He stopped a few feet away and clasped his hands behind his back. Nicholas suddenly felt like a three-year-old. In vampire terms, that was exactly what he was. A three-year-old vampire being addressed and possibly chastised or sentenced by an eight-hundred-year-old Senior.

"What were the results?" He could barely bring himself to ask the question, afraid the slightest offense might cause Julian to take away the tinfoil screen.

But Julian showed no anger, his voice pleasant as he said, "We can save her. You and I, together."

He swallowed. "What's the catch?"

"You might have to die."

***

He had little choice but to see Dina. Julian saw to that. And Lorelei, blue-eyed and meddling and surrounded with an aura unlike anything he'd ever encountered, went with him.

"She'll need me there," she informed him in a brittle voice. "When she starts to believe, she'll need me. And I don't trust you, you blood-sucking bastard."

He tried not to take offense, but couldn't help wondering how Julian put up with her. She certainly had no qualms about speaking her mind.

He hadn't seen Dina since the night before, when they'd dragged him off under "house arrest." Seeing her now as she sat on the bed in her small, windowless room, was like being slapped across the face. So small and gray, her face drawn and the bruises on her throat nearly black. He'd seen that before, a few days before death.

Under Lorelei's narrow, disapproving gaze, he sat next to her. "How are you?" he asked gently.

"I'm tired." She rubbed her face. A blue bruise rose beneath her fingers, faded slowly. "They tell me I'm dying. I mean, faster than I was dying before."

"I'm sorry."

"Sorry they told me that awful lie?" The words should have held eager hope, but were instead laced with sarcastic desperation.

"No. Sorry I did it."

"Then you admit it?"

He shrugged, resigned. "I have to. I can't lie anymore." He passed a glance to Lorelei. "Particularly not here where they'll kill me for it."

Dina only laughed. "Whatever."

"You're not angry?"

"I would be. I'd be killing you with my bare hands if any shred of me actually believed this bullshit." She flopped back on the bed, eyes closed. The bones of her face strained against her gray, tired skin. "If I'm dying, it's because my body finally decided to give up. It's been fighting cancer for five years, and if that's the decision it's made, I can't blame it. But you a vampire who's turned me into a zombie? Bull and shit."

"Dina—" Lorelei started.

She sat up rapidly, and her face went bone-white for a frightening moment. She didn't seem to notice. "Lor, I don't know what that freak Julian told you, or what he did to you to make you believe it, but if you could get your sense back, you'd know it's just a bunch of psychos who make up stories to justify a really sick obsession."

Nicholas looked at Dina—really *looked*—in a way he hadn't looked at a woman in a long time. What had attracted him to her in the first place? Had it been the blood compulsion that had grown and grown until he could no longer ignore it? Or was it something else?

She looked so small and frail right now, the color gone from her face, her eyes wide and stark, bruises rising and fading on her skin as she moved. And it made his heart ache.

If he made her remember, made her believe, she'd hate him. If he let her believe he was innocent, just playing along with the others' games, she'd die, perhaps as early as tomorrow.

His heart hurt.

He took her chin gently in one hand, watching the bluing of her skin beneath even that soft touch, and turned her face toward him. He could see the tracery of veins beneath her skin. This close, he could smell the death of her blood, sweet and cloying.

"Dina, I want you to understand something. I care about you. I don't want you to die."

She shook her head, a soft smile curving her mouth. "You can't stop it."

"But I can."

She opened her mouth to speak, but he said, "No," vibrating the word with compulsion. It wasn't great compulsion—young as he was, he couldn't muster much—but it closed her mouth, because she was a human and weak, with her blood dying within her. He bent toward her, his breath caressing the line of her jaw, then his mouth touched the bruises on her throat. He sensed Lorelei's movement, her tension and her small jump forward, but he only kissed Dina's throat, his lips soft and his teeth retracted.

Then, with all the compulsion in his power, he whispered, "Remember."

She stiffened next to him, convulsed as her eyes went blank. Her mind retreated into memory. He felt it when she went. Went with her. Lived the moment of betrayal as she'd experienced it, when the man she'd thought she trusted had slammed her into the wall and killed her. Lived his own memory at the same time, tasting her blood in his mouth, feeling it leaving her body in torrents, feeling her horror as she realized her heart was slowing, would stop, would end.

She jerked away from him, her eyes back to the present.

"No."

So white. She was so white, even the shadows under her eyes turning white as she stared at him, the truth returning to her.

"No."

She scrambled away, and suddenly Lorelei was there, her arms around Dina, her body between her and Nicholas.

"Get out," Lorelei said. "Get out now."

He backed away, reluctant.

"*Get out now!*"

Lorelei's eyes flashed blue. As if a hand had pushed him backward out the door, Nicholas went.

***

Dina sagged against Lorelei, the tears finally going dry. It seemed she'd been crying for hours. Maybe she had. Her body ached, and she'd never felt so tired, not even after her cancer treatments. Everything about her body felt wrong, from the way her skin no longer seemed to fit to the way the prosthetics in her bra no longer wanted to stay in place. In a sudden fit of anger, she reached into her shirt and yanked out the bra and substitute breasts, throwing them across the room.

A moment later, she realized what she'd done and looked at Lorelei. Her friend stared at the bra, the prosthetics falling out of it, swallowed, then looked back at Dina.

"You have to decide what to do," Lorelei said gently.

"I can't believe this is real."

Lorelei smiled wryly. "I know how you feel. It was the same way with Julian."

"But Julian didn't try to kill you."

"Even so, he came awfully close to it."

Dina shook her head. "I don't understand any of this."

"You're not alone. Strange things are afoot here, believe me." She took a long breath, drawing Dina close again, cradling her. "I don't want to sit here and watch you die."

"I could have done it alone, if it weren't for Nicholas."

"Hey." Lorelei's voice chastised softly. "I'd be back home and my life would still be normal if it weren't for Nicholas. He started all of this when he did what he did to you. He nearly killed me, too, you know."

Her voice had hardened at the last, and the brittle iciness in her eyes surprised Dina.

"I don't want to hate him," Dina said. "I don't think... I don't think he'd hurt me now."

"I want to rip his heart out with my bare hands," Lorelei said, the iciness gone now, the words spoken like average conversation. "But if he can save your life, I say we let him."

"And if it kills me?"

"Then you're no worse off than you were before. And based on my experience, dying at his hands would be much more pleasant than dying the way you are now. Or dying of cancer, for that matter." She smiled a little. "They make it like sex."

Dina closed her eyes. So tired. She wondered if she could open her eyes again, then did, and looked at her hands. "This came from Julian, this idea about healing me. Do you trust him?"

"Yes."

She nodded. "I guess that's all I need, then."

***

Dr. Greene touched a button, displaying the last slide in his presentation.

"After exposure to blood samples from both of you, Dina's damaged blood reaches this stage after approximately thirty minutes."

Nicholas looked at the slide, frowning. Nearly half the broken, damaged cells from the previous slides had transformed into plump, red, healthy cells.

"How precise are the ratios you've quoted, Doctor?"

The doctor looked at him, but briefly, his attention quickly returning to the slide. "They're precise."

Leaning back in his chair, Nicholas crossed his arms over his chest and looked at the ceiling, letting his breath out slowly. "So she only needs a one-to-four ratio of Julian's blood, but nearly a one-to-one ratio of mine."

"That's right."

Julian grinned, his expression not at all friendly. "She'll have to damn near bleed you dry, Nicky, if she wants to live."

Dr. Greene cleared his throat. "Since you're a man, though, you have a slightly larger blood volume—"

"Bullshit," said Nicholas mildly. "There won't be enough left to keep me going, and I'll be too weak to feed." He leaned forward again. "Can we set up a transfusion process so my blood will be replaced as soon as it leaves?"

Dr. Greene exchanged a glance with Julian. "No. The transfused blood will mix with yours. If this is to save Dina's life, your blood has to be in a completely pure state."

He nodded. Immortality, he'd thought. But it would only last three years. What a pisser. He might have done better with the cancer.

"We'll do whatever we can," Dr. Greene went on, "to save your life as soon as Dina's recovery is assured."

"It doesn't matter." He pushed out of the chair, went to stand by the wall. He wished there were a window. Not so he could die, but just so he could see out, look at the world one more time before he left it. "I did this to her. I have to fix it." He turned back to the others. "When do we start?"

"As soon as possible," said the doctor.

"Dina needs to decide," Julian added. "Lorelei's with her. As soon as we hear from her, we can begin."

"I want to talk to her," said Nicholas. He looked at Julian. "Get her to talk to me."

Julian smiled, some of the ice gone from his eyes. "I'll do what I can."

***

She wasn't hard to convince. Nicholas stood outside the door and heard Julian say, "He wants to talk to you." Dina answered, "Then let him in."

Nicholas entered the room carefully, wary eyes on Lorelei, who seemed omnipresent lately. "Alone," he said to her.

"No," said Lorelei.

He started to contradict her, but Dina interrupted. "It's all right, Lor. Leave us alone so we can talk."

He knew Lorelei wanted to protest, but she didn't. Instead she went to the door while he sat on the bed next to Dina.

"Dina—" he began, reaching for her hand.

"No." She drew her hand away from his questing fingers. "I want you to talk to me first. I want to hear your side of the story."

"Which story?"

"The whole thing. All of it. From the beginning."

It seemed fair. He looked at her white hands where they lay folded in her lap, like small birds dying.

"When you're thirty, you don't think much about cancer," he began, then slid Dina an apologetic look. "But you know that, don't you?"

She nodded, too tired to take offense. Closing her eyes, she sank into the pillow, letting his words swirl around her, trying to accept their picture of who he was.

"It was this never-ending gastrointestinal thing, then God-awful back pain. I finally gave in and went to the doctor . . ."

Tests had revealed a pancreatic tumor. It had lurked there long enough to begin to press against the nerves of his back and invade his liver. It was inoperable, and the outlook was poor.

He would beat this, he'd decided. But months later, after chemo and radiation, after macrobiotic diets, homeopathy and acupuncture, the outlook had been even poorer. He was dying. He knew it, refused to accept it, couldn't face it.

There'd been a night nurse at the hospital, a beautiful woman with dark hair and violet eyes. Nicholas had flirted with her when he'd had the strength, convinced himself he'd get better if for no other reason than to give her the good tumble he thought she deserved.

One Halloween night, weeks after he'd checked himself out of the hospital, sick of tubes and fluids and toxic chemicals that weren't helping him, she appeared at his apartment door and invited him to a party. She took him to her house, a strange place in a weird part of town where even stranger guests had gathered. There she took him to her bedroom.

"I have a gift for you," she said. "You don't have to take it if you don't want it."

He hadn't believed her at first. That she could offer him a peaceful death in her arms seemed likely—but eternal life? But she kept talking, talked all night. As the sky began to change from black to deep indigo, Nicholas had finally agreed.

"Do it," he said, only half-believing. Whatever happened, it would be better to die in her arms than in the stench of the hospital. He had no family—his parents and sister had been gone for years, victims of a drunk driver, and he'd never had much contact with any other relatives. It was one of the first questions the bewitching nurse had asked him, testing him, he thought, to see who might miss him. His bandmates were all he'd had left, and they'd blissfully moved on with another lead guitarist when he'd ended up in the hospital. He had no one.

So, with only hours left before sunrise, Vivian had taken and remade him. He'd left his apartment that night for the last time. To the outside world, he had to be dead now, until anyone who would have known him was gone.

In New York City, becoming someone else was an easy thing. So he'd done it, under Vivian's guidance. As time passed, on some days, he wished he'd just let the cancer devour him.

He'd worked out his own bargain with the world, with his need to feed. He watched people along society's fringes, and if they killed or abused the innocent, if they branded themselves animals in his eyes, he fed from them.

Then had come the first incident, when an innocent had drawn him so strongly he couldn't resist the call of blood. She'd come back from what he'd been certain was death. He'd tried to kill her again and nearly died himself in the process. By the time he recovered, she'd died again.

It made sense to him now, the call of cancerous cells to his own vampiric blood, made of Vivian's centuries of feeding on cancer victims. But the call hadn't been there when he'd first met Dina.

"I'd just finished treatment," she told him as he paused in his story. "Most of my cancer cells were dead."

He nodded, the picture becoming clearer if not easier for either of them to take. "It wasn't until the cancer began to regenerate that I felt the compulsion. It came so gradually I didn't notice it, until that night at the party, where there was blood everywhere. I looked at you and I didn't see you anymore, didn't hear you. All I knew was your blood, that it called me and I needed it."

Dina blinked tear-filled eyes. "There was something between us, before…before all this."

"Yes. Yes, I think there was."

"Can there be something again? If I live through this?"

"That's up to you." It occurred to him that he was more likely to die now than she was, but he said nothing. He was certain Julian had withheld that information, and he thought he knew why. If Dina knew her cure could kill him, would she refuse to let him heal her? He had a feeling she might. He couldn't allow that. It wouldn't be the right decision for anyone.

"I remember what you did to me now, because you made me remember it. But I remember something else, too. When I looked into your eyes that night, right before—it wasn't you."

He nodded. "It was the blood, the compulsion. If I'd been in control, it never would have happened."

She moved closer, touching his chest with her white hands. "Nicky, I forgive you."

He laid a hand over hers. "Thank you." Her skin was cold, and he sensed the slow, sluggish struggle of her blood. "Will you let me try to fix this?"

"Yes."

Looking into the softness of her eyes, he knew she didn't understand the risk he took. He didn't care. "Then I'll do it," he said.

He wanted to touch her then, to kiss her, caress her, let his body show her what he'd begun to feel for her. But even his fingers, gentle on her hands, left them shaded with bruising blue. He didn't want to hurt her—he'd hurt her enough already. Gently, he kissed her lips, withdrew before anything else could grow from the touch.

"I'll get Julian."

SIX

Dina had expected a hospital room, or at least something similar. Instead Julian took them to a prettily appointed bedroom where a rose-pink quilt tumbled over a high bed.

"No needles?" she said. Nicholas sat on the bed, strangely quiet.

"No," said Julian. "This is best done the natural way."

"You mean...with teeth?" A tendril of fear curled low in her stomach.

"Yes." This from Dr. Greene. "Scientifically, I'd have to say we could administer the blood through an IV tube. But when it comes to this kind of thing, I'd feel safer for you if we follow Julian's instincts." He smiled at her surprised expression. "I may be a hematologist, but these folks know more about blood than any expert I've ever met."

So the doctor's recommendation was to trust the vampires. An odd turn of events, to say the least. She looked at the bed and Nicholas, who now half-lay across it, leaning against the rose-colored pillows, legs crossed at the ankles. A seductive pose, to put it mildly.

They make it like sex. Lorelei's words suddenly came back to Dina. "Well," she said, still afraid, "I guess it can't be any worse than chemo."

She lay on the bed and suddenly found herself aware of the presence of the others in the room—Lorelei, Dr. Greene, Julian, Vivian. Then, as Nicholas' arms went around her, drawing her down next to him, her world shrunk to the green-brown of his eyes.

His hands moved gently, easing her down on the bed, encouraging her to stretch out next to him on the soft quilt. He drew her close while his eyes held hers, his hands tracing her body. She forgot to flinch when fingers brushed her flat chest and the scars where breasts had once been. He smoothed his hand over her, over her shirt, tracing her contours, rubbing the scars through the cloth. He said nothing, while his eyes took her in.

Her world had become green and gold, full of his eyes and nothing else. No one else existed. His eyes were full of silence and light. He lifted his wrist to his own mouth, then to hers.

Until the taste of blood touched her tongue, she didn't realize what he'd done. But when he offered her his wrist, her mouth latched to it greedily, drawing blood from the veins he'd opened with his own teeth. Thick, sweet, coppery, the blood flowed down her throat, warming her.

Her own heartbeat became a sudden presence in the room, pounding like a deep-toned drum. She felt her pulse shake down to her fingertips, felt the movement of precious cells through each capillary. It was strange—not quite painful, but so deep within her it could not be escaped. She seemed surrounded by the woolly thickness of the trance Nicholas' eyes had put on her, though his eyes now were closed, his mouth slack and his head rolling back on the pillow.

She was hurting him. The realization came to her suddenly, as coherence lanced through the trance. She pulled back from his wrist, seeing suddenly the flow of blood that seemed too slow.

"No," she said through the blood in her mouth.

"Don't stop." Julian's voice, vibrating through the air. She had no choice but to put her mouth back to the flowing blood and drink.

For a long time, then, there was nothing but that, the hot blood flowing down her throat, making her heart beat, making all the veins in her body pulse, flowing through her arteries, bringing her skin back to life.

"Take him." Julian's voice again, and Nicholas' wrist was pulled away from her mouth to be quickly replaced with another, again flowing with blood. "Drink this."

She drank, and Julian's voice went on above her. He shifted her, easing her off Nicholas while hands took him from the bed. He hung limp in Vivian's arms as she lifted him and took him from the room, followed by Dr. Greene. They both moved quickly. He was too still. She tried to ask about him, but Julian pressed her face back against the bleeding wrist, which Dina only then realized was his. Julian's blood tasted different, cooler, thicker, smokier. She took a long, hot drink—

"Julian..." This was Lorelei, her voice soft and concerned.

"Yes," he said. "Stop. It's enough."

Dina drew away. And the pain began.

***

She woke some time later, after the worst of the pain had burned itself out, and sleep had dragged her into forgetfulness for an eternity of hours. She lay alone now in the rose-pink bed. She felt alive.

Pain still haunted her arms and legs and a spot just below the beating of her heart. But it was a shadow of what had burned through her before. From what little she remembered of her death, this had been worse. But now it was over.

Birth must hurt like that, she thought. Not giving birth, but experiencing it. Because she felt as if she'd been born, as if everything within her had been remade and restored.

"Nick," she said suddenly, and sat up.

Her head swam, but only a little, and she heard her heartbeat in her ears. At the same time, she realized she hadn't heard that sound in several days.

"He's not here."

She looked toward the voice. Lorelei sat in a chair by the door. Dark circles arced under her gray-tired eyes. "How do you feel?" she asked.

"Better, I think," Dina answered. "No, I'm sure I feel better."

Lorelei smiled. "That's good. I'm sure it wasn't very pleasant for a while there."

"No, it wasn't." She paused, letting herself feel. "I feel different."

"How?"

"I don't know. But I haven't felt this way in a long time." Suddenly it occurred to her. "Since before the cancer." She bit her lip as a thought rose, a wonderful thought too much to consider in case it might be wrong.

Lorelei spoke it anyway. "They probably cured you."

She closed her eyes, opened them again. "That's not possible."

"Of course it is. Every blood cell in your body has died and been replaced by new blood."

"Vampire blood."

"That's right."

"I'm one of them now?"

She shook her head. "I don't know. Dr. Greene showed me the slides. Nick's blood is definitely vampiric, but Julian's is something else. When the two were mixed, the result appeared to be normal, healthy cells, but it's possible that appearance is misleading."

"Then what's happened to me?"

"Don't ask anybody that question. They'll just tell you you'll have to wait and see."

Her tone drew Dina's attention. "You, too?"

Lorelei nodded. "Julian took a good deal of my blood and replaced it with some of his. Dr. Greene's taken several samples from me since and still hasn't figured out what happened. Julian's blood shouldn't have reproduced enough to save me from the blood loss, but it did, or mine reproduced faster—he's not sure. I'm not a vampire, though. I don't get dragged down into the Sleep, and I can still face sunlight. As far as I can tell, nothing's changed."

"You have, though. You've changed."

"A little, I suppose. Being around vampires will do that to you."

"That's not all, though. There has to be a reason why you're still here. You love him, don't you?"

Nodding, Lorelei said, "Yes."

Dina wasn't convinced. It was hard to be convinced of anything in this place. "Are you sure? You can't have known him that long. Are you sure it's not just some mind trick of his?"

Lorelei laughed. "Relatively. Doesn't matter much either way. He's awfully good in bed."

Dina returned the laugh. Maybe Lorelei hadn't changed so much, after all. She crossed her arms over her chest, hugging herself, then looked down involuntarily.

"Did you want these back?"

She looked back at Lorelei, who was holding up her bra and prosthetics. They looked strange in Lorelei's hand, alien. "No. Not right now."

She laid them on the table next to the bed. "Doesn't seem fair, does it? They can bring you back to life, they can grant you immortality if you want it, but they can't make anything grow back."

"Then what the hell good are they?" She said it mildly, but an unreasoning anger rose behind the words. Anger, fear, and the same despairing loss she'd felt after each mastectomy. Tears rose. She swallowed hard to keep them back. She could have broken down here with Lorelei, but she had to ask another question first. She looked away, gathering herself. "Where's Nick? Is he all right?"

Lorelei didn't answer right away. She turned back to find her friend looking studiously away, at a corner of the windowless room.

"Lor, what is it?" Her fear shifted, strengthened. "Is he all right?"

"Julian's with him," Lorelei said slowly, still not looking at her. "Julian and Dr. Greene. And Vivian, I think. They're trying."

Her eyes met Dina's then, and Dina stared as realization flooded her. "He knew, didn't he? He knew this could kill him."

She nodded. "It was more than that, though. He knew it would probably kill him. There was more than a passing chance."

"Why didn't he tell me?"

"Because he didn't want you to give up your life for his."

"Why should he give up his life for me?"

"Because he killed you."

There didn't seem to be an answer for that. Dina looked at her hands, where the pink had returned, and she could no longer see the blue-black, dying veins through parchment skin. "I want to see him."

"Then let's go."

***

Looking at him, it was hard to believe he wasn't dead. His skin as pasty-white as Dina's had been, no breathing stirring his body, he lay on a hospital bed in a specially appointed room deep within the Underground. Dina had followed Lorelei for what seemed at least a mile before they'd reached the locked and barred door that led to a hallway smelling of antiseptic. An IV stand stood next to the bed, feeding blood into a vein in his arm. Dr. Greene stood next to it, marking information down on a chart. He looked up as the women came in.

"Hello," he said, smiling only a little. He glanced at Nicholas' still body and started to say something else, then shrugged and went back to his chart.

"How is he?" Dina ventured.

Julian rose from a chair in the corner. Dina started. She hadn't seen him sitting there. "It's not good." He looked wan. Blood stained a bandage on his wrist where Dina had drunk.

Dr. Greene looked up from the chart. "He's gone into a deep coma, not unlike the daytime Sleep. It's keeping him from dying, but it's also keeping his body from processing the new infusions. As long as blood moves into his system, he'll stay alive, but the blood keeps dying. In this coma, his body can't dispose of the dead cells. Eventually they'll build up to a point where they'll kill him."

"There's nothing you can do?" It seemed wrong that she, who'd been so close to death, should be alive now, while he, who'd faced immortality, should die this way. For her.

"I'm doing everything I can. I have tests running in the lab, and if something works, we'll put it to work right away. But until I get a clearer idea of how to proceed, I can't do anything more than what I'm doing now. And what I'm doing now will eventually kill him."

A silence fell, like a single teardrop, filling the room. Dina stared at Nicholas' silent face and swallowed hard. "If there's anything I can do..."

Dr. Greene smiled gently. "I could take a blood sample from you. I'm not sure what the process has done, but there's a slight chance we might find something. I already tried Lorelei, and that got us nowhere."

"Anything."

"Sit down, then."

He took the sample, and she watched as the thick, garnet fluid filled the tube, turning it from glass to a great, ruby jewel. A beautiful color, she thought. A life color. He withdrew the needle and folded her elbow back on a wad of cotton.

"I'll take a look." He lifted the test tube to the light, turning it as he peered through its garnet contents. "I'll head to the lab right now, in fact, if you'd like to stay here for a bit."

"Yes, I'll stay," said Dina. She rubbed her arm. It ached where he'd drawn the blood, up the length of the vein, seemingly all the way to her heart. Or perhaps her heart hurt for another reason.

"Julian, I'll need you," the doctor said.

Julian nodded and rose to follow Dr. Greene out the door. He paused as if to speak to Dina, then just shook his head and left. Lorelei followed him.

Dina scrunched down, drawing her knees up to rest her heels on the edge of the chair. She leaned her head on her knees and looked at Nicholas.

So still. He couldn't answer any of her questions, not even the ones she most wanted answered. For a time she watched him, until his image blurred in the gathering of tears in her eyes. She left the chair and slipped into the narrow bed, fitting herself against him under the blanket.

So cold. She pressed tight against him, trying to will her warmth past his skin, into his body where maybe it could awaken his sluggish blood.

Suddenly it all seemed hopeless. He'd saved her life—but for what? Could she go back to her old life now, knowing what she knew? Would they even let her? But could she stay here without Nick? She pressed her face between his shoulderblades, against his cold skin.

"Don't die on me, Nick. It's not right."

"It's also not necessary."

Dina jerked in surprise, shrinking behind the width of Nick's shoulders. Carefully, she craned her neck up, peeking over him.

She hadn't heard anyone enter the room, but there was someone there, standing on the other side of the bed near the door. He was tall and wore a long, dark brown robe. The robe's cowl obscured his face.

"How'd you get in here?" she whispered. She slid out of the bed, as if standing to face him gave her some power.

He smiled. "Through the door."

Smartass, she thought, then looked at him. Maybe not. Maybe he'd meant *through* the door.

He was tall, monkish within the shadows of the hood. Then he pushed the cowl back and revealed his face. She looked at his eyes, and suddenly couldn't breathe.

He seemed like just a man at first, pushing hard at forty, with a scar across his nose and a haphazard brown beard softening the roughly hewn lines of his face. But his eyes— They were blue and infinite, and if Dina hadn't believed in the immortality of these people before, she did now, seeing those eyes.

She breathed hard a few times, filling lungs seemingly pressed empty. He only watched her, so still she wondered for a moment if he was there at all, even though she could see him clearly.

"It's not necessary?" she repeated, surprised she could remember the words, uttered an eternity ago.

"No. Julian can save him." He took a step toward the bed, a scarred finger brushing Nick's dark hair. "I would, but there's not quite enough left. My way would kill him."

Few of the words made sense. She jumped on the few that did. "Julian can save him?"

"Yes."

"Does Julian know this?"

"No."

Dina blinked. "Were you going to tell him, or should we just let Nick die?"

He smiled at the harshness of her tone. "I'll tell him." He closed his eyes, then looked at her again. "He's on his way."

"Okay, you're freakier than he is."

He grinned, and she decided she liked his smile. Except if she looked at his eyes while he smiled, it was too much. They seemed overfull, as if some of his infinite years had been irrevocably lost to him.

"I should hope so. I've worked hard to achieve that goal."

"How old *are* you?"

He shrugged. "I'm not really sure anymore."

She might have questioned him further, but Julian arrived then, slamming through the door to the small hospital room, Vivian, Lorelei and Dr. Greene right behind him. At the sight of Dina's companion, he came to an abrupt stop. A moment of chaos behind him somehow resolved itself without injury.

"You again," Julian said. "What the hell do you want?"

"I've come to help." His gaze locked with Julian's.

"I want answers first," Julian demanded. He seemed unfazed by the eyes, but then he carried centuries in his own. Not like the other man, though, not so full of years his eyes could barely hold them.

"You'll have answers," the man said. His voice was soft but strong, like a fall of rain that after a thousand years causes a cliff to fall into the sea. Its accent was odd and unfamiliar. "It's time for the answers to begin."

"You disappeared before, when you healed me. Where did you go?"

"Away. It wasn't time."

"Can you say something that makes sense, please?"

The man smiled. "You can save him. I can show you how."

It made sense, but Dina could tell the statement had caught Julian as much by surprise as it had her. He swallowed, then recovering quickly, said, "How?"

"Come with me. I'll show you."

Julian studied him a moment. Dina's breath quickened, and she wanted to scream at him to just take care of Nick, for God's sake. But Julian said slowly, "I want a name. You haven't given me a name."

"What good would it do you? I've had thousands of them."

"Pick one."

"Adam. Belial. Corbin once, I think. Lucien most recently. Take your pick."

They stared at each other a moment, Julian and the many-named stranger, and Dina wondered how Julian could meet those endless eyes without losing himself. Then, suddenly, he nodded.

"All right then, Lucien most recently. Show me."

Lucien knelt next to Nick's bed and took Julian's hand. "Touch him. Take his hand and see what you feel."

Julian glanced at Lucien, then lifted Nick's limp, white hand. He closed his eyes.

There was a long moment of silence in the room, so deep it made Dina's head swim. Julian bent over Nicholas, eyes closed. Nothing happened. Silence rained down on the room, filling every corner.

Suddenly Nicholas took a deep, shuddering breath and opened his eyes. His white skin flushed pink, and he moaned with his breathing, which seemed to have taken him over until he could do nothing else. Julian, still holding his hand, cupped his face with the other, until his breathing eased. Then he cradled Nicholas' head against his chest while he plucked the IV tube from his arm.

"No more of this," he said. "He won't need it."

"What did you do?" asked the doctor.

Julian combed long fingers through Nicholas' dark hair, while Nicholas closed his eyes and breathed. The sound brought tears to Dina's eyes as his breathing settled into a soft, normal rhythm.

"I don't know." He turned to Lucien and Dina saw his face, full-on. Something had changed. His eyes had become heavier, as if his soul had aged a century in those few seconds. "Can you tell me?"

"I can. But it will take time."

Julian nodded, his gaze going back to Nicholas. "Later, then." He stood, staggered. Lucien caught him. "I need to sleep."

"You do."

They left, the two of them and Lorelei with Dr. Greene. Vivian stood staring, then looked at Dina.

"I think the world just came to an end."

Before Dina could ask what she meant, Vivian had followed the others out the door. Dina settled back in her chair and put her chin on her knees to wait for Nicholas.

SEVEN

How many times, Nicholas wondered, drifting out of black haze, *must a person die before he gets it right?* At least twice, the answer must be, because he'd botched it this time as well as the last.

Either that, or hell was a clean white hospital room in the Vampire Underworld, with Dr. Greene standing next to him muttering at a chart.

He remembered little after he'd opened his own wrist, offering it to Dina. His whole world had become a shuddering heartbeat after that, a life-rhythm slowing around him until it disappeared. Then nothing, until his body had filled suddenly with warmth. He hadn't awakened, not really, but he'd dreamed. Odors, mostly, a strange smell like a vampire's smell, but older, stranger. And warmth, someone holding him perhaps.

He must have made a sound because the doctor turned to look at him. "You're awake."

Nicholas nodded. "Yes."

"How do you feel?"

"I'm not sure."

The doctor nodded. "You're still down two pints of blood, but you'll be fine."

"I need to feed." But the hunger wasn't there.

"No. Your blood's reproducing itself."

Nicholas stared. His blood hadn't reproduced itself in three years. "I don't understand."

The doctor smiled wryly. "Nobody does." He opened the door. "You have a visitor waiting. Shall I let her in?"

"Vivian?"

"No. Dina."

He swallowed, dumbfounded again. Slowly, he nodded.

She walked into the room, and he felt dizzy looking at her. Smiling, she sat, not on the available chair, but on the edge of the bed right next to him, where her warmth reached him through the blankets.

"How are you?" she asked.

"Better than I'd expected. I expected to be dead."

Her hand reached up and came to his forehead, brushing his hair back gently. He closed his eyes a moment, lost in the beauty of the simple caress.

"It wasn't supposed to be like this," he murmured.

"How was it supposed to be?"

"I was supposed to die, and then you'd remember me forever as the one who gave up his life to save yours." His head spun. He didn't feel quite right, as if he were dreaming, or heavily medicated. "It would have been nice, I think, to have been remembered that way."

"I would have missed you."

"Why?"

"You still saved my life, whether you died to do it or not."

"But it wouldn't have been necessary if I hadn't killed you first."

She yanked gently at his forelock, then let her hand fall back to her lap. Wooziness filled him again. It wasn't a sick feeling, more like an overload of his system. He wondered if it had to do with the blood, living blood pumping through his veins for the first time in three years.

"I was dying when you met me," she was saying. He focused, listened hard to hear her over his own pulses. "I had a few months to live, maybe a year if I was lucky. Now—" She took a long breath. The look on her face told him she still couldn't quite believe what she was about to say. "Now Dr. Greene tells me the cancer's gone."

"Wow." He couldn't think of anything else to say.

She smiled. "'Wow' is right." Again her hands came up, this time closing around one of his, her fingers kneading his palms, the back of his hand. "I think it's why you had the compulsion. Somehow, your body—no, your *hunger*—knew you could cure me. It just didn't know how."

"But the others. There were others before you, who died after I fed on them. I couldn't have cured them, not if Julian's blood was a necessary component."

"You carried the first catalyst, and that's what drove you."

Her hand tightened on his, hard, and he heard tears in her voice. "I'm *alive*, Nick. And so are you. We should make something good out of that."

"So, would I have to die, then, for you to love me?"

She smiled. "I don't think that will be necessary."

He tried to sit up, thinking he might lean forward and kiss her, but his head spun, and he clutched at her hand.

"Take it easy," she said, standing to help him lie back down. She settled him against the pillows, then climbed back into the bed. Smiling, he put his arms around her.

"You make me dizzy."

"I don't think it's me."

"No." Moving carefully, he managed to meet her lips with his. "Not just you, anyway. My heart's beating, my blood's moving—I don't think I was this alive when I was alive."

"What did he do to you?"

"I don't know. But whatever Julian is now—" He broke off.

"What?"

"It's amazing. It scares me."

"Vivian said she thought the world had just ended."

"She might be right." Julian, Lucien—they were both something so new, yet Lucien's version was apparently unimaginably old. It made no sense. It would change everything.

He drew Dina closer. The strange dizziness had faded, his system adjusting to the living, growing blood, and all he could think about was her warmth, her *life*, so close to him. He pressed his lips against her throat, feeling the blood move and desiring it not at all.

"Are you hungry?" she whispered.

"Just for you."

She let herself melt against him while his hands explored. It didn't even occur to her to flinch or draw away as his fingers slid under the tails of her shirt, up her stomach, as his hands moved against the long, sickle-shaped scars on her chest. He touched them, drew his fingers over and down them, tracing the long, angry lines, and suddenly they weren't angry. They were part of her. They had, at one time, saved her life.

But he paused then, suddenly, and said in her ear, "Is it all right? Does it bother you?"

"Of course it does," she answered, surprised at the half-laugh in her voice. "I'm a freak."

He laughed, more surely. "*You're* a freak?"

"Okay, you win." How could she have imagined merely a week ago that she could be lying in bed with a man while he shimmied off her shirt, laughing about her scars? It was a sweet and lovely thing, and she was glad she'd lived to experience it.

Whatever had made Nick dizzy and unsure before, it seemed not to bother him now as he slid her out of her jeans. With her face against his warm shoulder, she wriggled against him as his wide, bare body slid against her and pressed her down. Feeling his arousal against her, she tipped up her hips to meet him, and he came hard inside her. A sharp rhythm brought him pounding deep, and his hand between them cupped her into a hard, wet fire. It rose, spiraled, and her heart seemed to lift within her to meet his until they beat together, as if they shared a body, shared blood, shared the deep, flooding power of orgasm. Her world turned to brilliant, opalescent fire.

They came down together, and his lips moved against her ear. "God," he breathed.

"No," she said. "Just Dina."

He laughed, nuzzling her. "I can smell your blood, but I don't want it. I can hear it, but I'm not hungry." A hot, deeply felt sigh ruffled her hair. "It's amazing."

"How long do you think it'll last?"

"Long enough to make love to you again?"

She smiled. "That would be good."

He kissed her, long and deep. There were questions, she knew. Many questions, particularly for Lucien. Nick, she was sure, wanted the answers as much as she did.

But they could wait.

LUCIEN

By night on my bed I sought him whom my soul loveth: I sought him, but I found him not.
    —*Song of Songs, 3:1*

    Ea said, "I did not tell the gods' secret—rather it came to the wise man in his dreams."
    So Enlil went into the boat and took me by the hand. "From this moment," he said, "you shall live at the mouth of the rivers, and never die."
    —*The First Book of Gilgamesh, as recorded by Aanu, c. 5,000 BCE*

The First Born have taken demons' names, but in time they may choose new names. In that time a light in the world will transform the world, and those accursed at the beginning may yet be blessed in the end.
    —*The Book of Changing Blood*

PRELUDE

In the few days since Halloween, everything Vivian knew had changed. It seemed weeks—months, even—had passed since the death of the Senior and Julian's rise to power. Even knowing the Senior had allowed himself to be killed, she couldn't help thinking of it as a sort of military coup. It still surprised her to see Julian walk out of the Senior's office in sweater and jeans, his young, not-quite Asian face and slim body incongruous with her perception of what the Senior should be. She couldn't shake the image of the bulkier former Senior vampire, his darker skin and wider jaw.

It occurred to her she'd never known his real name. Perhaps it was better that way. She could remember him always as the Senior, and leave Julian to be Julian.

She didn't trust Julian. Not yet. She didn't know him well enough to trust him. And although the fact he hadn't killed her when he'd come into power spoke well of him, his presence made her nervous. Maybe because no one knew yet exactly what he'd become.

She'd seen something of his transformation, though, when he'd brought Nicholas back from the brink of death. Lucien, the mysterious, tall, inconceivably ancient vampire in the cowl who kept turning up at odd intervals, had shown him how to do it. Julian had accepted his revelations, sparse as they'd been, without hesitation. Perhaps Vivian should follow his lead and let herself relax in the face of the new leadership.

Nicholas certainly seemed unconcerned, but then he'd just come back from the dead for the second time in his life and probably couldn't help being happy about it. As they sat in the Senior's—Julian's—office, he seemed content to absorb whatever came his way. Vivian sat next to him and noticed that his constant, vague presence within her mind had changed. She'd Made him three years ago, and the relationship created a superficial mental bond. She couldn't read his mind exactly, but she always knew where he was and had a general idea of how he felt. The connection was different now, as if a thin, not-quite-opaque curtain had fallen between them.

They were all there now, all the major players—Julian and Lorelei, Vivian, Nicholas, and Lucien—all summoned by Julian for reasons still unknown. Lucien was for once without the overly dramatic brown robe and cowl, clad instead in ordinary jeans and a plain green sweatshirt. Vivian wasn't sure why the monkish attire had bothered her so much. It seemed affected, she thought. Too much. Plus it reminded her of things she'd tried for centuries to forget.

If she were honest with herself, though, she'd admit that Julian and Lucien both gave her the willies. Particularly Lucien. Looking at him made her feel like someone had just walked over her nonexistent grave.

Julian took a cigarette out of his pocket and held it up, looking at it as if he were trying to decide whether or not to light it. Next to him, Lorelei regarded the cigarette balefully. He didn't look at her, but seemed acutely aware of her disapproval.

"So how are you feeling, Nicholas?" he asked.

Nicholas shrugged. He certainly looked better than he had three days ago, when he'd given nearly all his blood to Dina to save her life. He looked different, in fact. Vivian wasn't sure why—then it clicked. He looked less vampiric. He looked alive.

"Good," he said. "Very good, in fact."

"And Dina?"

Nicholas' soft smile warmed Vivian's heart. Her boy was in love. It looked good on him. "She's fine. Doesn't like going to mysterious meetings that last all night, though."

Julian smiled. "Not a problem. I'm sure she could use the rest." He put the unlit cigarette back in his pocket and turned toward Lucien, who sat behind Julian's desk. Vivian had wondered why Julian had let Lucien take the position of power, but now she realized it didn't matter. No matter who sat where, Julian had complete control of the room. "Now. Lucien. You need to answer a few questions."

Lucien shrugged. His deeply serene stillness affected even the deep, oddly accented timbre of his voice. "Ask them."

"First of all, who exactly are you?"

"That's a long story."

"Then you might want to start talking."

"How long do we have?"

Julian looked at his watch. "The sun just went down, and it's November. You've got quite a while."

Lucien settled back in his chair. "Good. Then I can start at the beginning."

THE BEGINNING

The Mountains of the Mother's Spine
10,000 BCE

The four virgin girls stood in a small huddle, shrouded in dark linen. They shifted uneasily, and from time to time one would move as if to talk to one of the others, but then would turn back and speak not at all.

In front of them the Mother's Womb opened like a dark maw in the mountain, belching incense. Mylie, at the front of the line, could smell it, spicy, thick. It made her head spin. From beyond the door came the sounds of chanting. The shamans called the gods. Behind her one of the other girls choked back a moan of fear.

Mylie closed her eyes. She would be first. She had no idea what would happen to her within the Womb's walls. The shamans had told them they would join with the gods. She assumed it meant she would die. They would be sacrificed, all of them, their blood spilled to appease the angry god who, over the past two years, had nearly decimated their village by withholding rain.

The smell of incense grew stronger. A shaman appeared in the doorway, necklaces of teeth and bone rattling around his throat. He took Mylie's arm and drew her into the cave.

Her feet failed her, digging into the dirt as her breath came suddenly fast and her heart beat hard in her throat. The shaman gave her a hard look and jerked at her arm. She stumbled across the threshold of the cave's entrance. As she breathed the thick incense inside, her courage returned.

Her heart still beat hard, her breath still came fast and shallow, but she followed the shaman with a semblance of calm. He let go of her arm, but his demeanor registered no approval. He merely stared straight ahead into the incense-fogged interior of the cave.

In the pit at the center of the cave a fire burned. There was no other light, no windows or torches, and the red-orange light of the fire writhed on the painted mud walls. The shamans—six women, two men—stood in a circle around the fire. They sang in a language Mylie had never heard before. The sound of it made her skin prickle with fear.

The shaman grasped her arm again, steering her forward. She saw then the crude stone altar set in the center of the flames, the fire lapping all around it.

"No," she said, the word torn from her in spite of her effort to remain silent. Her feet stopped moving again, digging into the ground. But here there was no loose dirt to dig into, only hard-packed earth. The shaman jerked at her arm, yanking her toward the fire.

Another shaman came forward from the circle and took her other arm. The two men pulled the robe from her, leaving her naked. She shivered even in the heat, afraid. The men took her arms again and forced her up to the edge of the flames. Desperate, she looked toward the women shamans, who still stood singing. They would not return her gaze.

She was inside the circle of chanting now, close enough to the fire to feel the heat writhing up her legs. It hurt already. She thought she would die there of fear. She wished she would. It would be better, faster, than the flames.

Then, all around her, the chanting changed. It seemed to fill the air, not just with sound but with touch, pressure, heat and colors. The sweet, dark smell of the incense filled her head. She felt herself lifted but didn't know what lifted her. Her body moved over the lapping flame, until she lay upon the altar.

She felt no heat, only a pressure against her body as she lay on her back. What had seemed reality a moment ago now seemed a dream, vivid and clear, but not quite real.

The pressure grew, molding her body, heavy against her belly and thighs. Still the fear seemed distant, another woman's fear, as the smoke above her coalesced. A figure grew there, a man but not a man, dark, with eyes that seemed to open into another world.

Transfixed by the eyes, she moved with the corporeal smoke. It covered her and suddenly entered her. Heat filled her in a flash, as if the fire around her had come into her body, and she screamed. But then the fire had become another sort of fire, and she writhed with it as heat filled her, as the smoke filled her, as whatever had entered the smoke came deep and hard within her.

Then the fire became only fire again. Hot and deadly, it lapped at her feet, and she screamed with the pain. But the chanting took her again, and somehow her body moved away from the flames. A moment later she stood on the packed dirt floor a few feet from the fire and the altar. Shamans stood to either side of her, holding her up as she shook and sobbed. But it seemed another woman shook and sobbed while she watched from deep within herself, marveling at what had happened.

She had mated with a god.

The shamans, touching her more gently now, put her robes back over her. She quieted as they led her through a dark passageway of the cave, toward a circle of light that led outside. Everything seemed different to her now, the colors on the walls brighter, the ground softer beneath her bare feet. The opening the shamans took her to was surrounded by a bright red border. They stepped through.

The cave's back way opened on an open area, a place where flowers could have grown if there had been rain, but there had not been rain for a long time. A natural curve of stone surrounded the small courtyard, broken by four round openings. Four small, natural caves.

"You will have a room here," said the shaman. "Each of you your own. Your families will come at times to visit you. We will see to your food and drink and your comfort in all things. You carry the god's seed within you. You will be blessed, and you will bring us salvation."

She stared. "What do you mean? How long will we be kept here?"

He led her forward into the courtyard, toward the first opening on the left-hand side, toward the small cave where she would live.

"Until the child comes."

***

Six Months Later

The children had all come early, within minutes of each other. Four children, healthy and bawling. Two mothers dead. The other two nearly so.

Mylie had lived, but barely, and she felt life ebbing from her as the shamans took her child. She saw little of him, except that he was big—bigger than any newborn she'd seen before. She'd spent the night surrounded by the screams of the other women, the wailing of the babies, the smell of blood. The shamans seemed unconcerned with the fate of the women, only with the children.

Mylie barely remembered the past stretch of hours. Only the sounds, her own pain, the child tearing out of her body. Now they wouldn't let her see or touch it.

One of the shamans passed her bed, bent to adjust her blankets. She turned her head to look at him, and he started.

"You live."

"Yes. For now."

He grunted. "Mere mortal women could not expect to safely deliver the children of gods."

"No one could have thought of that before?"

The shaman looked at her darkly. "We were dying. All of us. It seemed worth the sacrifice."

Mylie had birthed a god—his disapproval frightened her not at all. "I want to see my child."

"That is not possible. The children have been taken into the temple. They will be raised there."

"I have milk. I could feed him."

The shaman snorted. "A god-child feasting on the milk of a human breast? An appalling thought." He lifted her blankets, glanced at the ruin the child had left behind. "You will die before dawn. There's nothing I can do."

He left her then, apparently unaffected by her glare.

A few cots down, the other still-living mother moaned. She and Mylie had been the largest of the chosen girls, which was probably the reason they'd survived the births. But the priest was right. Mylie didn't have much time left.

***

Outside, night had fallen. The last of the roaming shamans

departed, taking the dead with them. Only Mylie and the other girl remained, and the other girl had fallen silent. Dark shadows swam around the room, around their fur pallets, swarming up the paintings on the walls. The god lurked within them, perhaps. Did he mourn the deaths of the girls who had birthed his children? Mylie found it hard to imagine.

The shamans were gone, and the room lay in a dead quiet. Mylie lifted her head. Across the cave a door opened into another chamber, where there was light. The shamans had taken the babies through that door, into whatever chamber lay beyond it. She could walk that far, she thought, perhaps steal a glance at her child before the last of her life leaked away.

Pain flared, then faded as she moved. Perhaps it meant death was near. It didn't matter. Gathering what little strength remained, she edged off the pallet. She wavered to her feet, took one step, two. Step after step came together in a blur as the world faded around her. When it returned, she was standing in the open doorway.

A pale light filled the small room, touching four small, sleeping faces. They lay next to each other in a small clump. She stood just inside the doorway, watching the wavering light of the sacred oil lamps play over the babies. Which was hers?

She took a few more steps, until she stood next to the sleeping babies. Then, strength departing, she sank to the dirt floor.

Darkness took her for a moment, a soft, welcoming wave. This was death, she knew, waiting for her. It didn't seem so bad. Soft, gentle. A warm place.

But it let her go. She opened her eyes, and she was still in the small room with the babies. One stirred a little in his sleep. They all slept peacefully, the sound of breathing soft in the small room.

But not all. At another, sharper sound, she looked up and saw a small pair of eyes fixed on her. Returning the startlingly clear gaze, she pulled herself along the floor.

This was the one. Her child. He knew—she could see it in his bright, gray-blue eyes. She reached out, and his hand came out from under the soft blankets to meet hers. Small fingers touched hers, the contact no more than a breath.

Suddenly the room seemed lighter, the darkness more distant. The soft touch of death receded. Mylie moved, just a little, and took her son's hand in her own.

And he, only hours old, smiled.

***

She lived, which was unexpected. The shamans murmured to each other about it as the other three girls were buried deep within the cave. She heard murmurs, too, that one of the children had fallen into a deep sleep, and that they were concerned about him, afraid he might die.

He didn't die, though. She'd known he wouldn't, and when he woke a day later she knew it instantly though the shamans still kept her separate from him, where she rested and continued to heal.

She sat up in her small bed, amazed at the lack of pain, and looked toward the door leading toward the children's beds. As she looked, a small voice sounded in her head, wordless but somehow communicative. *Be well,* it seemed to say. *Sleep and heal.*

She smiled to herself and lay back down, and slept.

***

When she woke that evening the pain was gone, and so were the shamans. Darkness filled the room, ebbing and flowing with the light of a small torch near the door where the shamans came and went. She sat up, then stood, and walked to the room where her baby slept.

A thrill of fear passed through her as she opened the door. Last time, she'd known she would die if she was caught, but then she'd had nothing to lose. Now she had life again and the possibility of losing it if the shamans found her treading on what they had declared to be sacred ground. But the sacred child had lived within her sacred womb, so why should she not be able to approach him?

Again her gaze went directly to him, the small bundle with piercing blue-gray eyes that looked at her from a round infant's face. More than an infant's soul moved behind those eyes, though. He smiled when he saw her, and his hands struggled beneath the layers of swaddling.

She came to him and knelt on the ground. For a moment she only looked at him, then gently she picked him up and cuddled him against her. Her heart pounded in her throat as she unwrapped the layers of blankets to free the tiny hands. They reached toward her, seeking her face. She let them touch her, held a finger out for them to grasp. Then, with a quick look over her shoulder at the silent, closed door, she drew the child tight against her and gave him her breast.

She already ached with the milk beginning to build up within her, and when the tiny, hungry mouth latched onto her, both breasts poured, soaking her tunic. She bit back a small laugh, afraid someone might hear.

There was no one to hear, though, and for what seemed a very long time she sat there on the dirt floor with her half-divine son, watching him drift into sleep, until his mouth went slack and fell away from her nipple, and the milk dribbled white upon his round cheek. Smiling, she wiped his face dry, laid him back in the bed, and went back to her pallet on the floor.

The next morning, the shamans declared her well enough to leave the sacred cave and return to her father's house. She didn't want to go, and her family was wary of her, as if they feared her. When that night her father neglected to ask for her help with the goats, she knew nothing would ever be the same again.

ONE

"...still there was famine for a long time. After the drought came floods, and men began to kill each other. It hadn't happened before, at least not there."

Vivian shifted in her seat as Lucien paused. He seemed unaware of his audience, staring off into far-distant memory. Across the room, Julian tapped ash from his cigarette into an ashtray. Lorelei gently took the butt from his fingers and snubbed it out. Nicholas, on the loveseat next to Vivian, drew lines on his sneakers with a black pen. No one seemed bored, but it had been a long story.

"We, of course, were blamed for it. Our births were supposed to have appeased the gods, and instead it seemed we had angered them. They tried to sacrifice us to their god, but we wouldn't die. One of us they hacked to pieces and sent floating down the River. Someone found the pieces and stuck them back together, and they lived again."

"Except no penis," put in Vivian, then shut up, shocked at the sound of her own voice.

Lucien turned slowly to her, dragging himself back from the story. "Pardon?"

"The god was hacked to pieces, and they found everything but his penis. It's Egyptian myth. Osiris and Isis. Osiris got chopped up by Seth, Isis put him back together."

Lucien nodded slowly. "Interesting. I can't say I've heard that one." He swiveled his chair around to face them more fully. "But none of this happened in Egypt. Maybe the story got picked up later—"

"Or you're just confused." Again, Vivian surprised herself. She was being remarkably bitchy. Maybe because outside daylight approached, and Lucien was still going on and on and on...

"Viv—" said Julian softly, warning.

But Lucien laughed. "That's entirely possible. Some days I can't remember shit." He pushed himself to his feet. "I forget my manners. Some of you need to sleep."

Nicholas yawned. "That would be me."

"And me," Vivian admitted reluctantly.

"What happened then?" said Julian. "If you and the other three were the first of us, what happened after that?"

"We bred," said Lucien simply. "We passed along a genetic marker than enabled Julian to become what he is. And we created others much as you do, through exchange of blood. The result was sterile creatures who live on blood and hide from daylight."

"The father of the first children—of you and the three others—was he a god or a demon?"

Lucien shrugged. "Both. Neither. Who can say now?"

Julian snorted. "As always, you've been less than enlightening." He took out another cigarette, and Lorelei deftly plucked it from his hand. "We'll talk more."

Lucien gave him an indulgent smile. "Yes. We will."

Vivian stood and stretched. "I'll have to excuse myself, I'm afraid. The sun's coming up."

Lucien rose from his chair in an easy, fluid movement, and lifted Vivian's hand in his. "We shall talk later, as well."

He kissed the back of her hand softly. Vivian stared at the top of his head as he did it, surprised at the tremor of feeling that passed up her arm from the place his lips had touched. And when he looked up, and his gaze met hers, she had the strangest feeling she knew him. Not from a few days ago, when he'd arrived to help Julian save Nicholas's life. From before. Long before.

"Yes," she said, barely aware she spoke. "Yes, I'd like that."

TWO

Lucien watched as everyone but Julian filed out of the office, Nicholas stifling a yawn. It surprised him he'd talked so long. It hadn't seemed like more than a few minutes.

It was a hard story for him to tell, though, and he wasn't even sure all of it was true. Those parts that had happened before his own birth he'd gleaned from stolen conversations with his mother, Mylie, and from various lectures the shamans had given him while he was growing up, usually after they dragged him back to the sacred caves after those stolen conversations. The shamans had probably exaggerated. Mylie had probably downplayed her accounts. She'd been that kind of person.

He missed her even now, sometimes. She'd lived a good life but a lonely one, feared by everyone she knew. But she'd dealt with it well, even found humor in it. And she'd had the last laugh by outliving every one of them. By the primitive reckonings of the time she'd lived nearly 125 years. Whether her long life had been the result of her congress with the god, or Lucien's healing, he had never known.

Julian spoke suddenly, breaking through Lucien's musings. "If you're going to be around for a while this time, I'd appreciate it if you could take a look at this." He'd been tapping at his keyboard and now swiveled his computer monitor so Lucien could see it. It displayed an Internet navigator window, filled with lists of e-mails. "The messages come from everywhere, all over the world."

Lucien bent forward to look. It was a massive leap from the story of his infancy in prehistoric Europe to an Internet navigator, but he'd learned to deal with such things a long time ago. Julian went on. "The Senior before me had been collecting them for centuries. He thought they were parts of the Book of Changing Blood. I believe Vivian and Nicholas catalogued most of them."

Lucien nodded. It seemed strange, looking at not-quite

familiar words he hadn't seen in at least a millennium. "Yes," he said.

Julian seemed to expect a longer answer. "Okay...I have two questions for you, then. Is there such a thing as the Book of Changing Blood? And are these parts of it?"

"Yes," said Lucien. His smile went unanswered. He cleared his throat. "These categories—I assume the Senior assigned them?" The messages were sorted into folders by region—Asia, Polynesia, Western Europe, Eastern Europe and a dozen others representing Africa and North and South America, then were subdivided from there into "Book," "Not Book," "Maybe Book," and an intriguing folder entitled "Bullshit."

"I think so. You'd have to check that with Vivian."

"How old was he? The Senior?"

Julian shrugged. "I don't know. He remembered aurochs."

Lucien lifted an eyebrow in surprise. "He must have been one of the first, then. Surprising. I actually didn't think any of the Bloodmade Children were that old."

"I saw the memories when he died. I still have some of them. They're fuzzy, though. Like dreams."

Julian's eyes had gone distant. Lucien waited for him to come back. A few seconds' delay, a few hours—it mattered little to him. He could barely tell the difference between a week and a decade anymore. After twelve thousand years it hardly mattered.

"There are patterns," Julian said after a time. "Particularly if you read all the messages within a group. You start to see certain things emphasized, certain phrases appearing over and over. Would you recognize them, if they were part of the Book?"

Lucien snorted. "I wrote the Book. Well, not by myself. Aanu and I found each other coming out of the ground I don't know how many years after the Black Sea—I think it was the Black Sea—flooded. We'd dreamed the same dreams, under the mud." He paused, remembering the flood and the years he'd spent dead, then slowly reviving, in the deep layers of mud. Nobody had bothered to tell him to build an ark. Too bad—it would have come in handy. "We put the Book together by transcribing the dreams, hoping it would guide the Children.

Later, in Egypt, the Dark Children destroyed it. We were supposed to be demons, always and forever. Any suggestion we might be able to change was blasphemy to them."

Julian's eyes went distant again as he digested this. "Do you think there's a hope of piecing it back together?"

Lucien had opened one of the messages and was scanning the contents. Many phrases here did, indeed, seem familiar. The Book, yes, but corrupted from the original. "There's a hope. If I could remember it all, I'd write it down for you from memory. Unfortunately, my brain doesn't work that way. I'll need as many pieces as I can collect."

"I think you'll find a good starting point here."

"It appears that way." He leaned back in his chair, studying Julian's quiet face. His woman, Lorelei, had gone to bed a few hours ago, leaving Julian to smoke in peace. Lucien didn't mind. He enjoyed the sweet smell of the cigarettes. "However, more important than the words of the Book are the changes you've undergone. You'll discover more about the Book from inside yourself than you'll ever understand simply by reassembling and reading it."

"The Book could tell me about myself. How can I tell myself about the Book?"

"You *are* the Book." Lucien laughed at the obvious irritation on Julian's face. "Reassembly of the Book has been a quest of the Children for a long time. There is certainly some value in it."

"Then you'll help me?"

"As much as I can."

"And will it make sense when we're done?"

Lucien snorted. "Don't expect miracles."

THREE

Yawning, Vivian slid into her bed, under the cool cotton blankets. Tucking the quilt around her, she wondered again why she'd treated Lucien so sharply. It wasn't in her nature to lash out at people. She'd been more the Ice Queen type, closing herself off as much as possible. Emotions hurt too much, especially when you had to carry them around for an eternity. When she brought death to those who asked her for it, sometimes she hurt, but not for very long.

In the back of her mind she still felt Nicholas fluttering there, full of his love for Dina. It was all he could think about these days, and it had stepped up a notch since he'd left the meeting. Perhaps they were making love now, or maybe just being in the same room with her did this to him. She envied him.

Or maybe not. After all, he had his Maker eavesdropping on him. Her own Maker had disappeared without a word of explanation, without even telling her what he'd caused her to become, over six hundred years ago.

It didn't seem right that she should infringe on Nicholas like that. If he'd been one of her intractable and annoying earlier Children, she wouldn't have cared one way or the other, but Nick deserved better. He was the only one left, too. The intractable, annoying Children had managed to annoy themselves into an early loss of immortality. She couldn't say she missed them.

Outside, day approached inexorably. She could feel it in her bones, in her slowing blood. As sleep eased over her, she played with the thread connecting her to Nick. And suddenly she knew she could break it.

Smiling, she took up his feelings within her mind, held them one last time, then let them go.

Goodbye, she thought as the darkness took her under. *Goodbye, Nicky.*

***

England, 1390

Death reigned in those days. Reigned in black pustules and coughing, in black smoke pluming over the cities with the burning of pile after pile of bodies. Screams of pain and of mourning filled the air at all hours of the day or night. Hope had come to an end, and God reclaimed the world.

Hope still held part of Vivian's heart, small and trembling, as she walked up the long trail to the distant cloister. Stories had come from that place, about the monks there. They helped the ill rather than turning them away, nursed them as best they could. Some people even claimed to have come back alive and healed from the place. It wasn't unheard of for a man to live through the Plague, and many who had come here had lived. Many more than seemed normal.

Some spoke of the touch of God within those walls. Still others spoke of bargains struck with Satan. Vivian didn't care which was true. She only wanted to live.

By the time she reached the end of the trail, she thought it might be too late. She could barely move, her arms and legs weak and shaking. It took a great effort of will to reach up and grasp the bell pull. But when she collapsed, her weight dragged the rope down with her, sending the bell pealing into the cloister beyond.

Time passed, and she might have slept. She wasn't certain, as her mind drifted in and out of awareness. Finally a tall, robed figure appeared. Perhaps he had opened the tall door first. He must have. As Vivian peered up at him she saw the open doorway behind him.

He knelt next to her, bringing into view a long, sober face partially obscured by a brown cowl. "Child, why do you come here?"

Vivian stared up at him. Was he an angel? Surely not. Surely an angel wouldn't have asked such a stupid question. "I want to live," she said, and tried to reach for him.

The man's expression didn't change. Strong hands touched her, arms reached under her. "We'll see what we can do."

***

Within the cloister walls Vivian found, for the first time in months, air free of the stench of burning bodies. The place smelled of gentler things, of earth and baking bread. The man carried her to a room and gently settled her on a mat on the dirt floor. Her body ached with the need to breathe. She lay still, wondering how close the hand of death lay, if it reached out to touch and claim her even now.

"Rest," said the man. "The Father will come for you soon."

He disappeared out the door before Vivian could ask if he meant a particular monk, or the Lord Himself.

She drifted again, breathing as best she could, her lungs thick with fluid. She'd watched her mother die, her sister—had nursed them as well as she could before the sickness had claimed her, too. Her father had left them all and tried to burn the house down on his way out the door. Vivian had stopped the flames. Perhaps it would have been better to let them burn. Surely death from fire couldn't have been worse than the Death which had come.

She didn't want to sleep, afraid she might never wake up. But sleep claimed her, anyway, and she drifted into a velvety darkness. Pain still lurked at its edges. That must have meant she was still alive. It was hard to tell sometimes.

When she woke again, it was suddenly, her eyes flying open to stare at the rough-hewn beams in the ceiling. *Not dead yet*, she thought, and wondered what it would be like when she did die. Probably much like that velvety sleep, but without the gnawing pain. Perhaps it wouldn't be so bad to let it happen.

No. She wasn't ready. Something inside her screamed that it just wasn't time yet.

But had any of the thousands who'd died been ready? Why should she be allowed to choose the length of her life? More powerful forces than her own mind ruled that realm.

Then she heard a sound. A soft rustle to her right. Carefully, she turned her head.

Another monk had come into the room. Taller and broader than the first, he seemed almost to fill the whole room. A cowl shadowed his face. All she could see was the strong, hard jut of his nose.

"Yes?" she croaked.

He came closer, then knelt next to her, shifting as he moved so the shadow of the cowl always obscured his face. What did he not want her to see?

"Be still," he said. His voice was barely audible, and rough, as if it cost him dearly to speak at all. His hands came out of the folds of his robes and touched her. "How long have you been ill?"

"Not long." Her voice, too, took a great deal of effort. "My family died before me. I tended them as best I could."

He gently lifted her tunic, looking at her bare skin. Before she could give it thought, he had disrobed her completely and was looking beneath her arms at the black, swollen lumps there.

"You are near death," he said quietly.

"I know. I feel it."

He looked into her face, and for a moment she saw the glint of his eyes and a small piece of his face. Scars puckered his skin, as if he'd been terribly burned. So that was what he hid. She wanted to push back his cowl and look. What could be so terrible, as long as it wasn't the face of Death himself?

He skimmed her body lightly with his hands, a physician's touch, warm and careful. Eyes closed, he seemed to be analyzing her condition with his fingers. She dared a glance downward and saw that even his hands were scarred.

Then his touch shifted. He laid his hands on top of her head and held them there a long time, then moved them over her eyes, over her collarbones, over her stomach, then low on her belly, just above her sex. Each time he moved he sat utterly still while a strange warmth grew on her skin. Her mind drifted, moving away from the pain and into a dark, quiet place where the pain was only a memory.

After a long time he leaned back, sagging as if weakened. Then he straightened and looked at her face, again allowing a small strip of light to penetrate the shadows of the cowl. "You will be well in time. It was not too late. Try to sleep." He drew a folded blanket from the foot of her mat and gently covered her with it.

He left her wondering at the strangeness of it all. And she

did sleep, long and deeply, and without dreams.

***

The Present

Vivian woke suddenly, gasping. She rarely dreamed during the Sleep, but when she did it was usually like this—memories so vivid they could have happened yesterday, rather than hundreds of years ago.

She hadn't thought about those days in England for a very long time. The memories weren't pleasant. The story of how she had become a vampire was one she rarely thought about, much less shared. But every once in a while, the remembrance came back to haunt her in her sleep.

She sat up and pushed damp hair out of her eyes. Darkness had just fallen outside, and her borrowed blood still moved sluggishly. She needed to feed.

Vivian had great control over her hunger, as did all her Children. She wasn't sure why, but had always accepted and taken advantage of the ability. Now she put her needs out of her mind as she dressed and headed to the kitchen for one of the specially prepared plasma drinks she always kept on hand. Dr. Greene, a hematologist who lived and worked in the vampire underground, had formulated the mixture for her several years ago. Others of the vampires had found it helpful, as well.

She hadn't quite reached the kitchen when she realized someone else was in her house. Not an uncommon occurrence—her house sat on the unstable junction between mortal reality and the vampire underground, and various vampires wandered into it from time to time. But she was certain she'd been alone last night when she'd succumbed to the Sleep in her own bed. The presence tickled at the back of her mind, like a vague odor, but she couldn't quite pin it down. Not hostile, though. That she was sure of. So she fetched her plasma, then strolled through the house, trying to track the presence down.

She found it—or, actually, him—in her office, sitting at her computer desk. Lucien looked up as she positioned herself in the doorway, leaning against the frame and sipping her breakfast.

"Good morning," he said. "Sort of. Good evening?"

Vivian smiled. "Something like that." She gestured toward the computer. "Finding everything you need?"

"Not really. Where's the 'on' switch?"

Fighting back laughter, Vivian crossed the room and pressed the switch on the surge protector strip with her toe. "Better?"

"Much. Thanks."

The sounds of the booting computer filled the room as Lucien leaned back in his chair. "Julian showed me some of your e-mail earlier today. It's quite interesting."

Vivian sat on the edge of the desk, adjusting her lightweight robe to cover her thighs. Or most of them, at least. Lucien seemed to be enjoying the view. She let one flap slip off her knee.

"I haven't had much time to read any of it, just sort it as it comes in. What I've read is—well, I guess interesting is a good word."

"How long had the Senior been collecting it? The previous Senior, I mean."

"Years. Before I showed up to do the grunt work." She gave a light laugh. "I think he thought he could reconstruct the Book of Changing Blood."

The computer had booted up by now, and Lucien was frowning at the terminal. "He got a good start. I'd say better than half the text is here in one form or another."

Vivian stared. "The text of the Book? I thought the Book of Changing Blood was a myth."

"No. It's real enough."

"Are you sure?"

"I wrote part of it."

She could think of nothing to say to that. He'd lost interest in her knees and was absorbed in the computer screen. Vivian watched his face, gone quiet and contemplative. He had scars, thin lines across his nose and curving under his chin. One made a line from the top of his ear to the bottom, as if the ear had been torn off at some point. How did a vampire get scars? But he'd said he wasn't really a vampire.

The cool, gray-blue eyes scanned from side to side, and again Vivian was struck by the familiarity of his face.

"Have we met before?" she asked suddenly.

He turned his eyes to her slowly. "A few days ago. There was the incident with Nicholas..."

"Smartass. I mean before that."

He smiled a little. "I'm sorry. It's all I remember."

"Then we haven't met before?"

"We might have."

She shook her head. "We must not have."

"Why would you say that?"

"Because you'd remember. I'm unforgettable."

His smile widened. "I'm sure you are. But so am I, so why can't you remember?"

"Touché." She slipped off the desk and walked around to stand behind his chair. "Indus Valley," she said, reading from the screen. The e-mail consisted of a graphics file, showing a wall full of carved hieroglyphics. "Can you read that?"

"Some days. Can't quite manage it today, I'm afraid."

"So today you can't remember if you met me, and you can't remember how to read ancient hieroglyphics from the Indus Valley, either? What day will you be able to remember? This Wednesday, maybe?"

His implacable smile didn't waver. "Thursday, more likely."

"Are there translations attached with the pictures?"

"No. Nobody's cracked this code yet."

"But you can read them?"

"Eventually, I'd remember the language."

"Then why don't you go help out the poor mortals who've been working on translation?"

"Because I remember enough to know there's quite a bit there those poor mortals don't need to know. At least in this excerpt."

He switched to another note, in another obscure language Vivian didn't recognize.

"Here," Lucien said. "This I can read. 'From the Mother's Spine came the First Demons, children of the union of the gods and the chosen virgins. They passed out of the Mountain Lands into the East Lands. . . .' That's the end. The note says somebody burned the rest of this particular scroll."

"You can read that, but you can't remember that other language?"

"I've been alive twelve thousand years. There's a lot of shit stuffed up there."

"So maybe you'll dredge up the answer to my question some other time?"

He turned toward her, looking directly into her eyes. She saw perhaps a thousand years there. How could it be possible to carry more? "It's entirely possible that tomorrow or the day after I'll wake up and suddenly remember exactly when I met the Vampire Vivian. The first moment I saw that sleek black hair, the first time I looked into those violet eyes." He leaned forward and touched her cheek, tracing a rough, scarred finger over her skin. She trembled deep inside, a quick, difficult tremble that eclipsed everything else for a moment. "Did I touch you then?" he said. "Back then when we first met?"

"I don't think so." Her voice betrayed her, shaking. She swallowed to steady it. "That I would have remembered."

FOUR

After she'd left, Lucien sat for a long time staring at the computer screen, reading nothing. Vivian had said she'd gone to find Julian, but Lucien suspected she'd been as moved by their brief encounter as he had.

Perhaps not quite as much, though, and that only because he knew things she didn't. Like exactly the moment they'd first met, and how, and why, and what had happened after. It didn't surprise him she'd forgotten.

After twelve thousand years of existence his memory was spotty, but some memories couldn't be shaken. He remembered his own birth, the encounter with his dying mother, the times he'd died, and the time he'd spent with Vivian, several centuries ago. Everything else came and went.

He nudged his mind back to the present, always a difficult proposition, and focused on the e-mails. The Senior had been collecting this information for a long time. Julian had shown him a drawer in the Senior's office full of papers dating back to the early 18th century—all part of this same continuum of data, all bits and pieces of the Book of Changing Blood.

He'd written part of it, along with Aanu, but could remember none of it. But when he read excerpts, he knew which were legitimate, which were corrupted, and which came from entirely different sources. He didn't think the whole document was there, in spite of the massive quantity of information the Senior had gathered over the years, but a good portion of it was. Perhaps enough to answer Julian's questions.

"'Light will become dark, and dark light. The light will feed upon the light, the dark upon the dark,'" he read. He hadn't written that one. That sounded like Aanu's work. Lucien's sections weren't quite so obscure. "'Those who feed upon the light will war against those who feed upon the dark, and the outcome will determine the course of the universe.'" A bit overstated, that, but Aanu had always been melodramatic.

Melodramatic or not, though, the days spoken of were

coming. Julian's transformation had begun the process, and what had happened with Nicholas and Vivian represented another piece of the puzzle.

Speaking of Julian…

He looked toward the door a full second before Julian entered. "Come in. Have a seat."

Julian did. He took a cigarette from the breast pocket of his shirt and toyed with it, flicking it across and through his fingers in a skilled juggling motion.

"Smoke it if you like," said Lucien.

Julian shook his head. "Lorelei wants me to quit. I don't need them anymore."

"There's no tobacco in them. What's the harm?"

He shrugged. "She says the smell makes her sick. It didn't used to. I guess the shaman herbs made the difference."

Lucien nodded. "You'd do anything for a woman you love."

Julian cocked an eyebrow. "You know that about me, do you?"

"No, I know that about myself." He shifted in his chair, tapped the computer screen. "Has anyone compiled these fragments other than to divide them into categories?"

"There's a document on my computer where someone tried to set a large group of the verses in order. I think the Senior did it, and I don't know how accurate the work is."

Lucien studied Julian a moment, considering his next words carefully. So far Julian didn't seem to harbor a volatile temper, but sometimes it was hard to tell. "I don't presume to tell you what to do. You're the Senior, after all, and I have no intention of usurping power rightfully earned."

"You could. You're older than I, and more powerful."

"Nevertheless. The community has no need for that kind of turmoil right now."

Julian nodded. He balanced the cigarette between his lips, then laid it on the desk. "What is it you don't want to tell me to do?"

"It's my feeling that compilation of this data must be made a priority. I know the answers to many of the questions floating around this place right now, but there are other answers within the Book."

"You wrote part of the Book. Can you help with the compilation?"

"Absolutely. I'd like someone to work with me."

"Who do you want?"

"Vivian."

"Why Vivian?"

"She's worked with this material before, if only in a superficial way. She has a feel for it."

Julian picked up his cigarette again, put it back in his pocket. "Take whoever you need. Whatever you need. If Vivian's not enough, Nicholas should be helpful. He's worked with the material, as well. And I could probably get Lorelei to help you."

Lucien shook his head. "Just Vivian for now. I haven't decided who else to trust. Except you, and I think you have other things to worry about. Or you will."

"In that case, maybe this is a bad time to quit smoking."

***

Vivian rubbed her eyes, then laid her head down on the desk. Scanning through e-mail after e-mail gave her a kind of motion sickness that was about the most miserable thing she'd ever experienced. She glanced over at Lucien, sitting at the other desk, looking through the printed material. She couldn't quite tell from here, but it looked like he might be reading Cuneiform.

"I think I'm going to barf," she muttered.

He looked at her, smiled, and said something. She had no idea what, or what language. Probably whatever language he was reading.

"Excuse me?"

His smile changed to one of pained amusement. He closed his eyes. When he opened them again, he said in English, "Sorry. Do you need to take a break?"

"Do I ever. So do you, if you can't remember what century you're in."

"That's really not very vital information. Time's relative, after all. On a day-to-day basis it's more important to remember who's your friend, who wants to kill you, and where your next meal's coming from."

He left his chair and came to stand behind Vivian's, his hands settling on her shoulders. His big fingers pressed gently into her tight muscles, easing the tension.

"What *do* you eat, anyway?" Vivian ventured, as the warmth from his hands spread down into her shoulders.

"It's hard to explain."

"I'm fairly intelligent. Give it a try."

"Well…" He broke off as his hands pressed harder into her. The increased pressure hurt at first, then her muscles softened like wax beneath his touch. The warmth turned to a deep heat that eased down her shoulder blades and wrapped around her body, soaking through her skin into her heart.

"Do you feel that?" his voice came in a soft murmur just behind her head.

"Yes." She could barely speak through the deep relaxation. "Don't stop."

"That's what I do." His hands shifted down her back, and the stupefying heat shifted with it, spreading further down. It caressed her thighs, penetrated her sex. "I feed on life energy."

Her eyes snapped open, and she jerked half away from him, but his hands kept their hold, easing her back down. "Stop, then," she managed through the lassitude. "Take any more, and you'll kill me."

"Do you feel like you're about to die?"

She considered. "No. Not really."

He chuckled. "I take the energy, then give it back amplified. It passes out of you into me, energizes me, then goes back into you in a transformed state."

If she closed her eyes, she could almost feel the ebb and flow of the energy, transferring from her to him and back again. It wasn't a bad feeling, but the power kept growing. It felt good now, but sooner or later it would have to reach some limit beyond which her body couldn't handle it anymore. Still she held still, wondering what would happen.

"That doesn't make sense."

"Not really. But it's what I do."

She fell silent a moment, just feeling. Her reaction to the

peaking energy was all too familiar. It was going to fire off in the only way it knew how.

"Maybe you should stop," she said. Her voice shook.

He laughed softly and let go of her. Still, her body shuddered. She swallowed hard as, against her will, the tremors started. At least he wasn't touching her now. In fact, she sensed he'd turned away, his attention taken again by the scattered papers as she held very still, trying not to give any outward indication that her body had just exploded into fireworks.

When it had passed, she looked at him with watery eyes. He had, indeed, returned to the papers, seemingly no longer interested in her at all. Anger surged. How dare he take liberties like that? She barely knew him.

"You had no right," she bit out through clenched teeth.

He looked up, his face unreadable. "It was an accident."

She shot to her feet, glaring, fighting to keep her legs steady. They were undeniably noodley. "If you ever do anything like that to me again without my permission, I'll rip your throat out."

"Point taken."

He seemed contrite enough. She hesitated, deflated, but decided she wasn't ready to accept an apology. Gathering strength to keep her legs from collapsing, she stormed out the door.

Lucien watched her go. As she slammed the door behind her, he smacked himself in the forehead with the heel of his hand. What the hell had he been thinking? He'd been careless, let the energy grow too fast. It had seemed like a good way to start breaking down her barriers—when had she closed herself off so thoroughly, and why? But he'd forgotten their ties of blood would cause a quick bloom. Under other circumstances, she could have enjoyed it. They both could have. But this had been too sudden.

"You'd think," he muttered bitterly, "a guy could manage to learn something in twelve thousand years."

***

Vivian's angry retreat took her to the kitchen. She hadn't realized it until that moment, but she was hungry. Scary-hungry. She'd had her usual drink upon awakening, but if a mortal had crossed her path she would have given serious consideration to a feeding frenzy.

Fortunately there were no mortals in her house at the moment, except Dina, and Vivian wasn't entirely sure Dina fit that category anymore, since Nick and Julian had cured her.

The kitchen was deserted. She snagged a bottle of plasma and cast a baleful eye over the jug of unpasteurized milk and the package of raw chicken breasts Julian had contaminated her refrigerator with. He had to keep his food somewhere—there were no refrigerators in the Underground, and Lorelei's apartment was too far for everyday trips. He'd vaguely promised Vivian recompense of some sort. At least he hadn't made a mess. Curious, she opened the meat drawer and found a tray of raw fish and something that looked like part of an octopus.

"Bleah," she said to no one. "And people say *my* feeding habits are disgusting."

She sat down at the kitchen table, her thoughts turning again to Lucien. Had she overreacted? She wasn't sure. It was entirely possible he'd honestly made a mistake, rather than committing a deliberate invasion. As she sipped from her bottle she found her eyes closing, her memory recreating the heated sensations his touch had aroused. As much of a shock as it had been, she wouldn't mind having him do it again.

No, she couldn't call this a violation. She'd been violated before and this was nothing like that. Lucien's intentions had been good.

A shadow passed behind her and she turned, startled. Lucien stood behind her, uneasy. He touched the table, his gaze seeming to measure the distance between them.

"Yes?" Vivian said.

"I'm sorry."

She gave him a moment to twist in the wind, but he didn't seem to be twisting. He stood very still, his blue-gray gaze direct on hers. Suddenly guilty, she gave in. "I overreacted. It's okay."

"May I explain?" His voice was gentle.

Something in her brain perked up. She'd thought his face looked familiar before. Now his voice seemed to be activating the same, unreachable ghosts of memory.

"Of course."

He sat. He looked huge in her plain wooden dining room chairs. "Your energy is different from that of most of the Children."

"Why is that?"

"The one who Made you." He paused. "He was one of the first demons."

She shrugged and looked away. She'd spent several centuries trying to forget about that particular vampire. "How should I know? He never told me who he was, and after he Changed me, the bastard disappeared." Then she realized he hadn't asked her a question. Rather, he'd stated a fact. "You're certain of this?"

"Only a First Child would have responded so quickly."

She looked at the table, old anger struggling to surface. "Well. Another piece of the puzzle that is me."

A soft mass of silence filled the room, then he said softly, "He wouldn't have left you without a reason."

"And how the hell would you know that?"

"I knew them all. We were brothers."

"Nice." She drained her bottle and set it on the counter next to a half-dozen others. Dr. Greene would collect them in the morning, sterilize and refill them. "Well, if you see your brother, let him know I'm looking for him. I'd like to have a chat."

He looked away that time, watching his own big fingers trace the line of the grain in the wooden table. The silence was no longer soft, but carried sharp edges. Again, Vivian wished she hadn't lashed out.

"Lucien—" she started, but a third joined their party then. Nicholas, a bit short of breath, his brow tight with concern.

"Viv, you have a phone call in the den."

She straightened. "Who?"

"Evelyn."

FIVE

Gently, Vivian hung up the phone. She'd expected this news, but it was never easy. Wishing she were alone, she turned to face Nick and Lucien, who in some misguided sense of duty had followed her.

"What is it?" Lucien asked.

"I have to go," she answered. "Evelyn needs me."

"She's dying," Nicholas explained. Vivian tossed him a hard look.

"And you're going to help her?" Lucien's voice was gentle.

"Yes. It's what she wants."

"I could save her."

The words startled her. She hadn't thought of that. Then reality returned. "She's eighty years old."

"Still. You might want to ask her."

"Fine. Come on, then."

***

Vivian checked the time before they left, though her internal clock told her what she needed to know. They had enough time to make the trip and be back before sunrise. Barely. She made her preparations quickly, ignoring Lucien as he shadowed her. She didn't want him along. What she had to do was best done in private. But he was right. Evelyn had to make an informed choice.

Evelyn lived in a bad part of town easily accessible from the Underground. Most bad parts of town were easily accessible from the Underground. It had been designed that way, or perhaps made that way by the combined will of the vampires who currently inhabited it. Bad parts of town had always been easier for their kind to move through and find nourishment from.

Vivian moved through the world differently, though. She met her "victims" at hospitals throughout the City, where she presented herself as a night nurse. She'd never been a nurse in any official capacity, but it was easy to slip under the radar in a place as big and impersonal as a New York City hospital, especially at night, especially when your talents involved a certain amount of subtle mind control.

In the hospitals she looked for people like Evelyn, people like Nicholas had been. Suffering souls facing their last years or months or days of life. Modern medicine could do little for them but let them die, often painfully. Vivian could do little more, but at least she could eliminate the pain when patients were ready to move on. Or, in rare cases—Nicholas had been one such—she could offer immortality.

Evelyn had no interest in immortality, though Vivian had offered as she always did. She would have made a terrible vampire, Vivian was certain. Entering the old woman's small apartment, Lucien a shadow at her heels, she faced once again the dark solitude that reigned there.

Evelyn lay stretched out on the couch, wrapped in a cream-colored afghan she'd crocheted herself a half-century ago. A small black-and-white TV played a few feet away, the bent antenna on top supplying a snowy, distorted signal. An infomercial, ubiquitous at this time of night.

The old woman didn't move as Vivian entered, and for a moment she thought she might be too late. Then Evelyn's chest rose in a soft sigh, and her head turned.

"Hello." Her ghostly blue, watery gaze drifted over Vivian's shoulder. "A guest?"

"A friend," Vivian explained hastily. "I came to carry out your wishes as we discussed, but he wants to make another offer."

Lucien stepped forward. "I could heal you," he said simply.

To Vivian's surprise, Evelyn laughed. "Whatever for? I'm eighty years old. Even if you could heal the cancer, how much time would it buy me? Five or ten years?" She laughed again, the sound surprisingly cheerful in the dismal room. "I've got no one to live for, anyway. It's time to let go."

Lucien knelt next to the couch. Evelyn looked into his face with a soft smile as he laid a big hand on her white forehead.

"I envy you," he said, then kissed her softly on the mouth.

He stepped back, leaving Evelyn with a surprised look on her face. Vivian stepped forward then.

From the shadows near the doorway, Lucien watched. Vivian had knelt next to the couch and held the old woman's hand, caressing it with both of hers. They talked softly for a time, but he couldn't hear what either of them said. The light from the television fell on them like a benediction.

He looked around the dark room. Like the TV, it seemed to be all in black and white. There were a few pictures here and there, old photographs of a handsome man in military garb. On a table near the couch was a triangular wooden box with a glass top. An American flag was folded inside.

A life lived alone, he thought. His awareness swirled around the room, gathering sensations. This man, in the old photographs, was the only man she'd ever loved. They'd been engaged before he'd left for Europe, and he'd died before he could return. There had been no wedding, no children, no future.

She'd had happiness in her life, though. He was certain of that. She was ready to die, but he felt no despair. Only acceptance. She knew she would see him again, her young man who'd been lost to the war.

A long and quiet life, alone but somehow not lonely. He gathered the sense of it from the air, from the memories layered on the trinkets in the house, from the energy the old woman had left behind on everything she owned. He smiled to himself, thinking how much he envied her ability to die.

Vivian had bent over her now, her mouth against the old woman's throat. Evelyn smiled as the soft throb of her life faded, then disappeared.

Vivian straightened, tears glistening on her face. Lucien started to move toward her, then stopped, knowing his interference, however well-meant, wouldn't be accepted at the moment.

Instead he stepped back a little more, until his back touched the door, leaving Vivian as much to herself as he could. After a few minutes she straightened, pressed a hand to her mouth and stood.

"Vivian—" he began, but she lifted her free hand to gesture him to silence. She found a phone on a table and picked it up, dialing 911 to report the discovery of a body in the apartment.

She refused to give her name.

Hanging up, she gestured to Lucien. "Let's go."

He followed her out of the small apartment and back out into the dingy streets. She wasn't well, he realized, sensing it in the downward flow of her energy and seeing it in the paleness of her face.

"Let me help," he said.

"I'm fine."

She led the way back to the warehouse that connected to the Underground, and not until they were safely out of the human realm did she let herself sink to the floor. No humans could follow them here, not even the gang of probable drug dealers who'd been following them, likely with intent to hold them up. And here, when the sun came up, Vivian could sleep safely, even if she had to do it there on the wooden floor.

He wouldn't let it come to that, though. The floor was dirty, and she'd wake up with woodgrain patterns embedded on her face. Kneeling next to her, he brushed hair out of her eyes. Her face was twisted in pain.

"What?"

"It was too much. I had the plasma drink before—I can't hold all the blood."

She convulsed around the pain. Lucien could feel it in his own body, something worse than nausea as her body tried to expel the excess she'd consumed. He lifted her half from the floor, cradling her in his lap.

"Let me."

"No," she said weakly.

"I know what I'm doing this time." He held her closer, and she moved against him in tacit agreement. "Besides, so what if you have another orgasm?"

She almost laughed, then fell limp in his arms as he embraced her shoulders with one arm, the other hand pressing into her stomach. Threading bits of her life energy into his own, he absorbed the pain, then moved enough of his own energy back into her to burn away the extra blood pooled in her stomach. He felt the pain ease, then her pleasure began to build as their energies twined together.

She opened her eyes just as he backed away. "Was it good for you?" he asked.

She did laugh then, a full, round laugh. Then, just as suddenly, she pushed her face into his chest and began to cry.

"Is it always like this?" he asked as her sobs began to subside.

She moved back and rubbed the tears away. "No. But what was I supposed to do? Tell her I'm sorry, but I can't help you right now, I just ate?"

He laughed softly. "I didn't mean that. I meant this." He caught a tear on his finger and looked at it a moment before brushing it off on his shirt.

Her face stilled, eyes darkening with memory. "Usually worse. Usually they're so much sadder."

"She was ready to go."

"Yes. She was at peace. But I saw—" She stopped, her eyes closing hard.

"What?"

"At the last. I saw the light, and her fiancé. He was there for her. They don't always let me hold on that long." New tears welled, and she dashed them away, more harshly this time. "It was her gift to me, I think."

"And you're thinking you may never get to see that light in person, because of what you let yourself become."

She looked away, her eyes distant now. "I'll see it eventually. I'll die someday, even if I have to trot myself out into the sun to do it."

He cupped her face in one hand, turning it back toward him. "Not today."

"No. Not today."

He bent forward, and his mouth found hers, gently at first, then he could no longer hold himself back and pressed hard into her, taking whatever he could. He would have stopped if she'd drawn away, but she didn't. Her arms went around his neck, and she returned his kiss with as much passion as he gave, so much more than he'd expected.

Then, suddenly, her hands were under his shirt and she had taken control, urging him to more than he'd imagined ever taking from her, but she gave it to him and then took from him.

It wasn't a good place, but he had his big coat, and he spread it on the floor as she twisted it off him. For a moment he thought he should stop her, then he saw her eyes. She knew what she was doing.

Vivian knew exactly what she was doing. It was the same thing that drove mortals to sex after a funeral, but more so. Faced with the reality of the final completion her soul might never find, she had to reach out for the greatest completion she could give her body. Lucien had just gotten in the way.

It was more than that, though. She had to admit that to herself as she took the final step and slid him inside her. He was big and ready and, she suddenly realized, as fertile as any mortal. The thought made her ride him harder, fighting tears as she remembered the other, primal thing she'd given up.

And she hadn't even given it up willingly. Not really. The one who'd Turned her hadn't explained anything, and then he'd disappeared, leaving her to find her way all on her own. Leaving her to forget how to feel anything but disgust for herself and for the thing who had made her. It had taken her centuries to discover a way back to some portion of her humanity, and even that had proved a long and painful road.

She was striking him, she suddenly realized, beating his chest with her fists as she crested and shuddered on him. His hands closed around her wrists, stopping her assault, then he closed his eyes, and she felt him come hot inside her. Alive, she reminded herself, everything pouring into her was alive. And everything it met within her was cold and sterile.

She collapsed forward onto his chest, sobbing, and he held her as she wept out her heart, wept out six hundred years of pain, until finally he said softly into her ear, "It's almost daylight, love. We have to go."

But she couldn't stop, and the tears kept coming as he wrapped her in his big coat, picked her up, and carried her down into the Underground.

SIX

When the Sleep took her she went back to the place in her dreams where she'd left off the last time. After the healing. Why did her subconscious keep dragging her back there? This was all right, this part, but there were other places she didn't want to go.

Helpless, she followed the tide.

***

England, 1390

When she woke she felt weak, but much of the pain had gone. Her breath came more easily. When the monks brought her food, she ate it carefully, and when it was gone she felt stronger.

Her healer came to visit her later that afternoon. Seeing her sitting up on her pallet, he smiled, though she could barely see the smile through the shadows of his cowl.

"You're feeling better," he said.

"Yes." Tears suddenly clogged her throat as she realized the magnitude of what he'd done for her. Had he not come to her yesterday, she would be dead now. "Thank you," she managed.

He reached out, his rough-woven sleeve falling away from his big hand, and touched her cheek. The ridges of scars felt harsh against her skin. "It's what I do."

He smiled again and left her.

***

She didn't speak to him again for weeks, though she saw him often as she wandered the walkways and attended the services. He would watch her from across the room, his eyes bright under his hood. His regard made her warm—she didn't know why.

Though she grew stronger every day, she had no desire to leave the cloister to rejoin the dying city below. What was left for her there? Her whole family was dead, most of her friends either dying or dead. In the cloister it was quiet, without the smell of death and the dark, overhanging atmosphere of doom.

She was a woman, though, and so couldn't stay forever. After a month the Senior Abbott took her aside.

"You were welcome to stay here to heal, but I think it's time you must let us go," he said gently. "This place was not meant for women."

"What is there for me?" She asked him the question, since she hadn't come up with her own answer.

"I don't know. Perhaps God can answer."

But her prayers of late had brought her little in the way of inspiration. She felt as if she'd been set adrift. She sat for a moment looking at her hands, uncomfortable, wishing she could simply disappear into the shadows of the cloister and haunt the place, never have to face any other world again.

"I'll go," she finally said. "It's best."

That night she gathered her things, planning to leave in the morning. There wasn't much to gather. Her robes, a triptych and a string of paternoster beads she'd been given for devotions, and the small amulet she'd worn when she came here, a memento of her mother. Her belongings were few enough to tie in a small cloth and hide in her pocket.

She took the beads back out and sat on her pallet fingering them. "*Pater noster*," she began, "*qui es in cailis—*"

Someone knocked on her door. Her praying came to a staggering halt as she looked up, startled by the sound. She'd had so few visitors since she came here that the idea of someone on the other side of the door actually frightened her for a moment.

The knock came again. Unsure, she gripped her beads and rose, opening the door.

The healer stood behind it. He looked down at her through the shadow of his cowl, and she saw sadness in his eyes.

"I heard you're leaving," he said.

"Yes. I've been asked to leave."

He hesitated, and she heard him swallow, the sound oddly loud in the silence of the room. "I wish you could stay."

She stared at him, amazed at the emotion in his voice.

"Why?"

His cowl shifted as he turned his head, enough that she could see his small smile. His gaze had found something on the wall behind her, avoiding her eyes. "I've been out of the company of women for a long time. It was nice to have you here."

Silence held them both for a time, he standing in the open doorway, she just in front of him, gripping the beads, unsure what to do or say. Finally he said, softly, "I know it's not appropriate, but might I come in?"

Immediately, she stepped back. "Please do."

His presence seemed to fill the small room, his height and breadth almost too much for the doorway as he ducked a little to come in. He closed the door behind him, and Vivian's breath jumped thick in her throat.

There was no place to sit, really, but he lowered himself to the floor, folding long legs under him. She sat as well, fluttery with anticipation.

"I came only to say goodbye," he said, then paused. Candlelight flickered on his face, fighting the deep shadows that hid his features. Still she could see little but the glint of his eyes and the hint of tortured scars. His mouth moved slightly, then he went on. "But I would ask something of you, if you would grant it to me."

"What's that?" She wanted to say, *Anything*. Fear stopped that word. But she owed him everything. What could he ask of her that she wouldn't be willing to give?

"Touch me."

She wasn't sure what to say. It seemed a simple thing. Her hand lifted, then a flicker of candlelight caught a ridge of white on his face, and she hesitated. "Why?"

The glint of his eyes held hers. She thought she could make out their color—dark blue, perhaps gray. Sad. He made a vague gesture toward his face. "I've been…this way…for a very long time. People look at me in fear when they see my face, but it's only scars. Nothing they could catch, nothing that could hurt them. I came here partly to get away from what my face inspires in others. Here I can hide, and touch no one. But to go without human contact, particularly the touch of a woman…

It's been more painful than I could have possibly imagined."

She looked at his hands, folded in his lap. The scars there were long, white, angry, winding all around his fingers and across the backs of his hands, disappearing into the sleeves of his robe. "You weren't always a monk."

"I'm not a monk now. I've taken no vows. They let me stay here because of my gift. Those in town who crossed themselves and cringed in fear when I passed now come begging for me to heal them." His voice carried no bitterness. "But that touch is a different thing. If I could be touched out of—" He stopped.

Brave, she gave him his words. "Out of love?"

A wry smile twisted what she could see of his mouth. "Love would be too much to ask. Affection, perhaps. I'd even accept pity."

She shook her head. "You'll get none of that from me. No pity." Love didn't seem like such a difficult thing, she thought in a flash, though she barely knew him. Something about him made her feel gentle inside.

Decision made, she laid the beads aside and came to her knees. Looking up into his face, she could see past the shadows to the ravaged skin he tried to hide. Burns, she thought. Only burns could make that kind of scarring, as if parts of his face had melted, like a candle. Perhaps he had been handsome once. The rise of his cheekbones suggested a good shape to his face, but it was hard to tell.

She hesitated not at all as she lifted her hand, slipping it inside the folds of his hood until her fingers met the roughness of his scarred skin. She traced the slickness and the harshness there, feeling the lines of brutal burning. For a moment she wanted to pull away, automatically repulsed. But another urge came stronger, and she fitted her palm against his face, feeling as much as she could through simple touch.

Thank you. She heard the words—but did he whisper, or somehow speak within her head? She moved closer, looking up into his eyes. His lids drooped half closed, the gray eyes beneath barely focused. As she drew even closer, his eyes drifted shut.

She didn't think about what she did, she only did it. His soft intake of breath as she kissed him nearly jarred her back to herself, but she only pressed closer. His body, scarred as it was, was strong and solid as she pressed against him. His arms came slowly around her, as if he were slow to realize what she did.

She kissed him firmly, her hands on his face, feeling the scars that seemed even to wind inside his mouth. No one could have suffered like this and survived, she was certain.

What happened to you?

With her mouth occupied with his mouth she couldn't speak the words, but the thought floated clear and bright to the front of her awareness. And was answered.

Red fire fell from the sky, poured along the ground. Black ash filled the air as far as the eye could see. Screams rose on all sides as running feet pounded vainly, trying to escape the inevitable flow of death.

She jerked back, startled by the sudden, vivid image. "That…happened? You burned in that?"

He nodded, his gaze sober on her face.

"You—You should have died."

"I did."

She moved back away from him, fear fluttering deep within. It seemed distant, though, as if it belonged to another Vivian, one who had lived a long time ago. She moved away, but her hands found his and held them. "What are you?"

He smiled a little. She could see his face now, all of it, even the deep, red rivers of scars that spilled down from his forehead. "You don't want to know."

"Should I be afraid of you?"

"Never."

He kissed her then, softly, on the forehead. "Thank you. I shall miss you."

His hands slid from hers, and he went back to the door. Fear rose in her, but not fear of him. Fear she might never see him again. "Find me," she said as he opened the door. "Please."

He readjusted his cowl, putting his face again into impenetrable shadow. "I will."

SEVEN

The Present

When she woke, she realized two things. She was in her own bed, and she wasn't alone. She didn't remember making it to her house. She must have succumbed to the Sleep while Lucien was still carrying her, and he must have put her in bed. Tucked her in. Left a nightlight on, just in case.

And he was still here. A rustling sound behind her told her that. She rolled over and found him sitting at her vanity, looking through a folder full of pages covered with what looked like Egyptian hieroglyphics. Not the picture kind from the tomb walls, but the shorthand "cursive" type used by the royal scribes.

"Anything interesting?" she asked. The roughness of her voice surprised her. From crying, no doubt. Weeping herself silly. Well, she'd embarrassed herself in more ways than one with him yesterday.

Strangely, though, she didn't feel embarrassed. She wasn't sure how she felt, in fact. For centuries now she'd so carefully calculated every emotion that she had a hard time figuring out the spontaneous ones when they slipped by. And this one had done more than slip by. It had pounded past every safeguard she had in place. Now she had to deal with it.

He looked up and smiled gently. "Lots interesting. I can remember how to read this today, too. I had to quit on the cuneiform. It dropped out of my head at about noon yesterday."

"Do you sleep at all?"

"Sometimes." He laid the folder aside and stood, moving his chair to sit next to her bed. "Once a week, I guess. Sometimes not that much. I don't really keep track."

"You just sleep when you need it?"

He shrugged. "Or when there's nothing better to do."

She considered. "If you don't sleep, how can you dream?"

"I've had a thousand years' worth of dreams. I think my subconscious told me everything it thought I needed to know."

The openness on his face disconcerted her. She looked at her hands. She'd broken a nail yesterday, probably in the warehouse, scrabbling to get his clothes off. "Should I apologize?"

"Not necessarily."

"I mean—" She stopped and closed her eyes. Not only could she not look at him, it bothered her to be able to see him out of the corner of her eye. "I was angry at you for what you did to me, then I—" There was no point even trying to finish that sentence. She didn't know what to say, how to put words to the emotion that had filled her, and still lingered.

"It was fun."

Surprised, she twisted her head toward him. He was grinning, and she couldn't keep from grinning back. "Okay, whatever."

"I'm open to try it again if you like."

Now she flushed. "Maybe later."

They had work to do, though, and the hours just after midnight found them cloistered in Vivian's office, he on the computer this time, she leafing through the pages, finding bits here and there in medieval French and English that she could read.

They worked in silence for a long time, then Lucien bent his head back, rubbing his eyes.

"See?" Vivian said, smiling.

"I do. Want to trade places?"

"No. I had quite enough eyestrain last time, thank you very much."

"I guess we should take a break, then." He stood and stretched, something popping loudly in his back as he bent backwards.

She watched, enjoying the lithe movement. For a moment she considered getting naked with him for their break. It would certainly be relaxing.

He bent over the desk where she was working, sorting out a few pages she'd found illegible.

"Can you read those?"

"Maybe." He sat down and frowned at them, then turned

them upside down. "There we go."

"I thought we were going to take a break."

He lowered the pages. "Sure. Did you have something in mind?"

She was certain he was having the exact thought she'd had only moments before, but his face betrayed nothing. Trying in vain to fight back a blush, Vivian said, "I'd hoped we could talk."

"Oh. Well, talk, then."

She grinned. "On second thought, rub my back."

He came to his feet and took up the position, kneading her stiff shoulders. The warm energy eased up her spine, then down, until she closed her eyes and hummed with pleasure.

He seemed to have more control this time. She relaxed into the flow of warm energy, feeling the patterns as they grew and moved through her.

"I think I understand how it works," she said after a time. "When you heal, you take a piece of the victim's life force and magnify it, then give it back."

He dug his thumbs deep into her shoulder muscles. "Yes."

"And that's why you couldn't heal Nicholas. Because he was too close to death. If you'd taken what was left of his life force, he would have died before you could heal him."

Lucien leaned back away from her. She turned, studying his inscrutable face. She felt clear-headed again, about as clear-headed as she'd ever felt in her life.

"Actually," he said, "I lied about that. I could have cured him. I've gotten quite good at manipulating miniscule sparks of energy. He had enough left to work with."

"Then why did you say you couldn't?"

"Because I wanted Julian to do it. He had to learn what he could do, and what he can do is vastly different from what I can do."

"How so?"

"He feeds on energy, as well, but he doesn't have to take it away to amplify it. He can work directly within the life force of the other person. It's much less dangerous."

She stared at him. "I don't understand. How did he become

this?"

"He went without blood for nearly two centuries. He consumed the blood of a First Child—your previous Senior, who must have been Made by someone like me, one of the First Demons. Then he took Lorelei's blood, which contained the final catalyst, which I activated in her when she was six years old. It's all in the Book, though it didn't make sense to us at the time. When we wrote down the dreams."

"Does Julian understand this?"

"Yes. I spoke to him, told him how to work with it."

"That's good, because it makes no sense to me."

"It doesn't have to make sense to you. You only need to understand what you have become."

"What have I become?"

"You can make healers. Nicholas was your first as far as we know."

"Because I took the blood of so many cancer victims over two centuries."

"Yes. If you took the blood of, say, AIDS victims for a substantial amount of time, you could probably create a healer for that malady, as well."

"But two centuries…"

"It doesn't take that long. But, as I understand it, you've Made very few children, so you just didn't find out until you Made Nicholas."

"Why me? Can any vampire develop that ability?"

"No. Only someone Made by one of the First Demons."

She turned forward again. "So we're back to him." Her voice prickled with bitterness.

Lucien set his hands against her shoulders again. "Yes. We're back to him."

She closed her eyes, remembering the dreams. They hadn't taken her to that final memory, that place she didn't want to go. But now, with Lucien's hands comforting her, it seemed almost safe. She drifted…

***

They had asked her to leave, and she went, but she had nowhere to go. Her family were all dead, the house where they had lived burned to the ground in an attempt to ward off more infection. But, having been thwarted once, the Death seemed to want no more to do with her.

She went from house to house, nursing the ill where she could, rewarded with food, a blanket, a dipperful of water. At first it hurt her to watch her patients fade and die, but after a time the faces all began to look the same. She always did what she could, and it never changed the outcome.

And every Sunday, as if drawn there, she walked up the long path to the cloister door, stared at its wide, carved wood, fingered the bell pull. Then she turned around and walked back down the hill.

One day, on her way through the town, she had the feeling someone followed her. She stopped and looked, but saw nothing to confirm her fears. But the next Sunday, and the next, the same tickle of apprehension followed her.

The next week she brought a knife, taken from the kitchen of the family she'd just nursed along to inevitable death. It never occurred to her simply to not go. The compulsion was too strong, and she saw no need to fight it.

But on that day she discovered her pursuers were more than her imagination. They came from the bushes bordering the too-secluded path. There were four. The knife did her no good.

They stripped her and went through her pockets, finding the paternoster beads and a few meager trinkets she'd collected over the past months. Death hovered in a black cloud as one of them wrapped her own belt around her throat and squeezed it tight. What strength was left in her for fighting faded rapidly as her body fought to breathe. Death reached out to touch her face—

A roar erupted from the bushes, followed by a form nearly human but perhaps not quite. The pressure on her throat eased suddenly, and she heard screams. She tried to see what was happening but her vision had gone blotchy, red and black with pain and loss of breath. Her body slumped to the dirt, fighting. With breath back in her body she could smell now the coppery thick odor of blood. Pain stabbed through her.

Then arms lifted her, and she looked up into a face wrecked by scars. He cradled her close against his bare skin. He'd shed his robe, presuming, she thought, that the sight of his naked, ravaged body would frighten her attackers more than that of a cowled monk.

"My beautiful lady, what have they done to you?"

She looked up at him, her vision fading, and felt his warm tears touch her face. "I don't know. Do I die?" She remembered hands on her, vague pain, but her awareness had come and gone as the belt tightened around her throat. Whatever they had done, she didn't want to know.

He nodded.

"Can you save me? Like before?" Death stood tall and black right behind him. She had never seen Him so clearly, not even when the Plague had nearly taken her. Fear rose and choked her.

"I can save you, but not like before. There's not enough life left in you—" His voice was thick.

"Please—" It felt like the last word she would ever say.

"I have to tell you what it will be like—"

Death's long-fingered hand reached toward her face. "Just do it—please—"

She felt her breath stop, heard her heart sputter, and then nothing more.

***

Vivian's head jerked hard to one side, and she opened her eyes, realizing how far she'd drifted into memory. She hadn't fallen asleep—she only slept during the day and then it was the familiar vampiric coma. But she'd never lost herself this way before.

"Lucien?" she murmured. His hands steadied her head, their movement still gentle on her, soothing.

"Yes?"

"That was your fault, wasn't it?"

"Yes."

She pulled away from him and turned around, looking into his placid face. "Why? Why do you want me to remember?"

"Because you hate him so much."

"Why shouldn't I hate him? He Made me and then left me."

He studied her in silence for a moment, then lifted his hand to gently brush her cheek. "He had a reason."

"And how the hell would you know?"

"The question is, do *you* want to know?"

The question caught her by surprise. She mulled. Her abandonment had haunted her for a lifetime, had colored everything she'd become in her six centuries of immortality. Finally she nodded.

"If you can tell me, I want to know."

"Then turn around."

She did, and he set his big, scarred hands on either side of her face.

That part of her memory had been silent for her lifetime. Stilled by the death that had nearly taken her then, she had assumed. A memory like that could never be recovered.

But as Lucien cupped her face in his hands, the images came back. They flittered along the edges of her consciousness, begging for her attention.

"Let go," said Lucien gently, and again she was certain she'd heard his voice before. She let her eyes drift closed, let the memories return.

They were strange memories, stored more in her skin than in eyes or mind. The scarred monk had cradled her in his strong arms, held her against his naked chest. She felt soft warmth on her face—his tears. The pain in her broken body had faded, separating from the main stream of her consciousness.

She was two people, two streams of feeling. One writhed along a ribbon of harsh pain, twisting toward death. The other lay curled in a wide, warm lap, reaching toward life.

His heart beat hard beneath his ravaged skin, the sound filling her head until nothing else existed. Her memory supplied all the sensations—the sound, the touch—but no sight, no odor. She floated through it, no longer aware of the present except for the vague pressure of his fingers against her wrists. In the memory they had merged, she consumed by him. He must have taken blood—what remained of logic told her that in a barely audible voice—but she didn't remember pain, only the soul-deep merging as her blood was taken away and given back.

She remembered so much, things she'd had no idea lived within her mind, and she wondered if the memory were truly hers, or half his, left behind with the blood he'd sacrificed to save her life. But he would have been able to see, to smell, and still all she remembered was the embrace of his whole body against hers, the pounding of his blood.

She felt her own life escape, slipping by her like a firefly in a black velvet night. But he grabbed it somehow and brought it back. It seemed he cupped the little light with hands of soft power and nursed it until it glowed bright again, then gently set it back inside her soul.

Then there was blackness again, this time the dark of sleep, and Vivian opened her eyes to look into Lucien's. For the first time she truly saw his face, the barely visible web of scars that still trailed over his features. The deep, clear, gray-blue eyes.

She caught a breath that tried to choke through her throat, and jerked her face out of his grasp.

"My God," she whispered. "It was you."

He sat silently, studying her face. How could he have done this to her? Bad enough he'd abandoned her then, but to insinuate himself into her life this way, without telling her—

But he was talking now, and the soft movement of his voice made her listen.

"It was the only way I knew, then, to save you. Now...it could have been different." He took a long breath, then went on. "They found me there, with you and with the dead men. I was convicted of their murder, of your rape. They took me away in irons and hanged me the next day. I was in the ground nearly a month before I healed enough from the hanging to dig my way out."

She stared at him, barely able to conceive what he'd suffered.

"By that time," he went on, "you were gone. I looked for you nearly fifty years, but never found you."

"Maybe you didn't try very hard." She couldn't forgive him. Not yet. What he'd done had changed her too much.

"I didn't know where to look. But now I've found you, and really it didn't take that long—"

She shot to her feet, clenching her fists to keep from slapping him. "Six hundred years! It took you *six hundred years.*"

He shrugged. "It's not that long. Not for me."

"For me it was a lifetime."

The tears burning on her lashes infuriated her. She spun on her heel and left him alone with the computer and the pile of nearly impenetrable, musty papers.

***

With a few hours left until daylight, Vivian walked. Or, for a time she thought she only walked. Then she realized the truth. She hunted.

She hadn't hunted in centuries. But the memories had brought her back to those early days, when she'd awakened from death consumed with blood lust. For weeks she'd hunted mindlessly, taking whatever blood crossed her path. With the world still surrounded by plague, the deaths disappeared in the mass of other deaths, but later she'd realized what she'd done and the guilt was more than she could bear.

But she hunted now. In the streets of New York City, the smell of blood and death everywhere, in these places where new kinds of plague took their toll.

She found her victim in a homeless man slumped against a Dumpster. He held part of a hamburger and a half-empty bottle of whiskey. Unconscious, he stirred not at all when she bent close to him. The reek of his body barely registered, drowned in the smell of his blood.

But as her fangs sank deep, she recognized the flavor of the blood. Yet another cancer victim, unconscious now not from drinking, but from the advanced state of the disease. The alcohol had blurred the pain, and as she drank deep she sensed the flow of his gratitude. His last breath departed easily. He was ready to go.

When he was gone, and she was satiated, she arranged his body carefully, straightening his ragged clothes and his dirty hair. A peaceful expression had settled on his ravaged features.

Even then, she thought, in those first weeks, had she been

drawn to the dying? She'd been surrounded by victims of plague. It wouldn't have been hard to take victims from those about to succumb.

It pained her that she didn't know, and would never know for sure, because the blindness of that time had blanked out her memory. And if he hadn't left her, if he'd stayed to guide her through those days, things could have been so different…

They'd hanged him. She'd had no way of knowing that. All these years—centuries—she'd hated him, and he had died for what he'd done to protect her.

She left her silent victim and wandered again, no longer hungry, listening to the sounds of the night. Sirens, squealing tires, screams. A baby crying. Laughter. A gunshot somewhere in the distance. She thought of the sounds of medieval England, the smells there which were nearly as dark and textured with rankness as the smells of this place.

Rounding a corner, she put a hand in her coat pocket. Smooth wooden beads rolled against her fingers—the paternoster beads they'd given her in the monastery. The beads she'd never let go of, because they reminded her of him.

She stood silent there for a long time. Someone brushed by her, then looked back over his shoulder, unable to quite make her out as she stood there so silent and so still she barely existed. Her fingers moved along the smooth beads, the Latin of the prayer filling her head. She'd never even bothered to learn it in English.

She had loved him then. Whether she had realized it or not, she had loved him. She remembered the way he had responded to her touch, the way she'd responded when she touched him. She remembered the softness in his eyes within the horrible scars on his face. Perhaps he had loved her, too. In any case, he'd died for her. And, coming back, had changed her.

She looked up at the sky. Not brightening yet, but she could feel the approach of the sun. She turned around and walked back the way she'd come.

***

Lucien lingered in Vivian's house only long enough to be sure the computers were all turned off, the papers put away.

Then he began the strange walk back to the Underground. He took a wrong turn halfway there, but found his way nonetheless. Dawn lurked close when he arrived at the door outside Julian's office. The wide, sparkling chamber was eerily silent. He could feel the vampires that called the place home, their deep sleep a sort of soft, breathing sound in the back of his consciousness.

Julian was awake, though. Julian rarely slept, appearing to need it no more than Lucien did. He knocked on the office door.

Julian answered the summons. A deep line lay between his brows, and he waved absently to Lucien.

"What's wrong?" Lucien asked.

"Nothing." Julian crossed the room to sit on the low couch, sighing as he sank into the cushions. "Lorelei."

"Women," said Lucien.

Julian's mouth tightened. "It's more than that. It's…complicated." He plucked a cigarette from a box on the desk and lit it. "What did you want?"

Lucien took a computer disk from his shirt pocket and passed it to Julian. "The work's not done yet, but this section should interest you."

Taking a long, apparently satisfying drag from the cigarette, Julian went to the computer and put the disk in the drive. Lucien waited until Julian looked up, eyebrows raised.

"That's you," he said quietly.

"'The Eater of Light arises to break the ranks of the Children. Those who choose to walk in darkness will rise up in hatred to end the changing of the blood.' This makes no sense."

Lucien shrugged. "We had dreams, the two of us. We did the best we could. Dreams are a tricky business."

"All that impenetrable symbolism from the collective subconscious."

"You've read some Jung, then."

"Hell, I talked to Jung once. Never did understand what the hell he was getting at." He turned his attention back to the computer. "'If the Eater of Light fails to turn the others to light, those who walk in darkness will prevail, and the earth will suffer.

Not only the Children, but the mortals of the world will walk in rivers of blood.' It's like any other prophetic vision. It makes no sense, and you could interpret it eighteen different ways."

"But you are the Eater of Light."

Julian studied him through narrowed eyes. "How do you figure?"

"I showed you, with Nicholas. You feed on life energy, but at the same time you give it back. I feed on life energy, but my feeding diminishes it. Yours increases it. If you fed on a mortal, gave him what you have…"

"I would change him?"

"Yes. You could always give mortals immortality, with the price of the vampire's way of life. But now the gift you could grant is of a much different sort."

"Then what have I done to Lorelei?"

"She's still in flux from feeding on your blood, but something very strong grows in her."

"It's called her anger." He laughed dryly. "Never mind. That's my personal trial."

"Partly. But before it's over, I think there'll be wider implications."

"Can you say anything straight out, without leaving four thousand questions behind?"

"No."

Julian leaned back in his chair, shoving a hand through his hair. "So, these Children who walk in darkness—who are they?"

"There was another faction, even back then, who rejected the visions. It's the reason the Book was lost in the first place. No change should come—we're meant to be demons, and to follow whatever path leads us deeper into that part of our nature. They refuse to accept that we were left with another choice. Or at least refuse to accept that it's the proper choice."

"And where are they?"

"Everywhere." Lucien shrugged in vague apology for the flip answer. "I'm sure they'll turn up soon, when news starts to travel."

"Great." He snubbed out his cigarette, staring at the remains. "Why me?"

"Because you took the first step. You found a way to become something else."

"I can't be the only one."

"You won't be, in the end."

"And the picture becomes remarkably clear."

"At least you know you have something to look forward to."

Julian shook his head, lighting another cigarette. "I guess a prophecy wouldn't be a prophecy if you could just come out and say it."

"Time is too fluid for that."

Julian gave him an odd look, but Lucien didn't elaborate. He didn't know how. It was one of those things you just couldn't understand until you'd lived twelve thousand years. He stood. "I'll talk to you later. Give my regards to Lorelei."

***

When she went to her office the next evening, Vivian was surprised to see not Lucien but Julian sitting at the desk, looking through the computer files.

"Hello, Viv," he said. "How are you?"

"Where's Lucien?"

"He asked me to take over for him today. He seemed to think you'd be happier that way."

Vivian nodded. Understandable how he'd come to that conclusion. She wasn't sure he was right, though. She felt a need to protest, to justify herself to Julian, but all she said was, "I see."

They were silent for a time, Vivian looking through the loose pages where she'd left off yesterday. Then words came out of her mouth. She listened, wondering what exactly she'd decided to say.

"Did he say anything to you?"

Julian looked up, eyebrows compressed. "About what?"

"About why I might be more comfortable."

"Not really. Why?"

Vivian opened her mouth, closed it again. "Nothing. Never mind."

Julian looked back at the computer, still frowning. After a

moment he clicked the mouse. The printer moaned to life, coughed out a single page. It sounded very close to death, Vivian thought. They should get a new one. Then she wondered what exactly Julian had printed when he snatched the page off the printer and half-ran out of the room.

She sat down at the computer but could find nothing out of the ordinary either in the e-mail he'd been perusing or the word processing program running in the background. Perplexed, she clicked through a few programs, trying to see if he'd hidden anything. She really didn't know enough about computers to figure that out, though.

Then she found another open window, underneath the Internet navigator and the word processing program. Julian had left the computer logged on, and the window listed all the other computers in the Underground that were also logged on. Julian's was one of them. That computer had been logged in for the past three hours.

It wasn't Julian, then. Vivian chewed her lip, then clicked on the icon that identified that system. Hands poised over the keyboard, she wiggled her fingers a moment, then typed, "Lucien, is that you?"

The wait went on forever. Finally his answer came back.

"Vivian?"

"Yes."

"Are you speaking to me again?"

She smiled. Despite herself, a warmth grew in her chest. "If this counts as speaking, then I suppose yes."

"Good."

She drummed her fingers on the keyboard, thinking, then erased the stray letters she'd accidentally typed. "I need you to do one thing for me."

"What?"

"Just give me a reason. It doesn't have to be a big reason. Just any reason, why it took you so long."

The pause dragged out for what seemed like hours. Vivian chewed on a fingernail.

Then his answer appeared. "I guess I just lost track of time."

She laughed, but it sounded more like a sob. Bending her head back, she stared at the ceiling until tears no longer threatened.

"You're an asshole," she typed. "Get over here."

He was there almost before her fingers left the keys. He stood at the door and looked at her, a smile on his mouth, his gray eyes more open to her than she'd ever seen them. There was love there, and hope.

"If you ever lose track of time again," she told him slowly, "you might also lose track of a few limbs." She stood, walking toward him, her whole body hot and tingling. "Better yet, remember that story I told you about Osiris?"

He nodded slowly, a grin making his mouth lopsided. "You mean where they cut him up and his wife found everything but the really important part?"

"If you can't keep anything else in your sorry excuse for a memory, remember that. It could save your...neck."

"Point taken," he said, then lifted her in his arms and made it impossible for either of them to say anything at all.

***

Darkness filled the room like smoke, an unnatural darkness that seemed not to obscure the light, but to eat it. Within it darker forms moved. Mouths opened, the darkness inside them blacker than emptiness. Cold flowed out of their gaping depths.

Lucien woke with a start. The cold still gripped him as Vivian moved closer, wrapping an arm around his waist from behind. Her lips touched his back, between his shoulder blades.

"What is it, love?" she mumbled sleepily.

His hand closed tight over hers. "They're coming."

LORELEI

Better to live on a corner of the roof than share a house with a quarrelsome wife.
 —*Proverbs 21:9*

His name will not be spoken. He devours men and gods. He eats their powers and swallows their souls. He devours hearts and incantations. He drinks blood and knowledge. Those who live within these walls are soulless. He has eaten them.
 —*An inscription in hieroglyphics on the wall of the Lost Pyramid. Sent via e-mail to Julian Cavanaugh by the Egyptian Vampire Enclave*

When blood moves again within the Transformed One, he will bring forth life out of death. His blood will live again, and he will create his own heir.
 —*The Book of Changing Blood*

ONE

Lorelei Fletcher.

Lorelei Fletcher.

She looked at herself in the mirror and barely recognized her own face. It had been this way for too long. She didn't think she could stand it anymore.

It would be easier if she had some way to know exactly what had changed back in November, or if anything had changed at all, when Julian had taken her blood and given it back. He'd changed, that was certain. But she didn't know if she had, and the question ate at her, refusing to let go.

Over the right shoulder of her reflection, she could see Julian curled up in bed, naked, a sheet tangled uselessly around his knees. It was the first time he'd slept in a long time. He didn't seem to need it anymore, or at least not much of it. But last night he'd slipped into the bed with her, curled up against her and cradled her, demanding nothing more. The gesture had touched her, and her eyes still felt tight and puffy from weeping.

Because it hadn't been enough.

She straightened her hair, took one last look at herself in the mirror, and left him there.

***

"So what exactly seems to be the problem?" Dr. Greene regarded her, his hazel eyes gentle behind wire-rimmed glasses.

Lorelei shrugged. "I don't know. I just haven't been feeling well."

"Mentally or physically?"

"Both, I guess."

"Any theories?"

Her temper prickled. "I'm surrounded by vampires. I know all of two people here. One of them's all involved in—I don't know—saving the world or something, and the other can't think about anything but Nicky Nicky Nicky."

The doctor smiled. "You're lonely."

"I'm lonely, I'm depressed, I can't stand the smell of Julian's cigarettes. I never see him anymore. Nobody uses my name in front of me. It's always, 'The Senior's Woman,' or 'Julian's Woman.'" She stopped, feeling tears clog her throat. "Shall I go on?"

He regarded her soberly. "No. I think that's enough."

She sniffed, gathering herself. "So what's the verdict?"

"There are a few things I'd like to check. But honestly, I think you might need a vacation."

Five minutes later, though, they were both staring at a little plastic stick.

Lorelei could barely see straight. "This is impossible."

"Yeah," said Dr. Greene, which didn't make her feel any better.

She crossed her arms hard over her chest. "What the hell am I going to tell Julian?"

***

Julian was in his office, at the computer. Lorelei came in without knocking and sat down. He looked up at her with a smile.

"Good morning. Where have you been?"

She took a deep breath. "I went to see Dr. Greene."

His smile faded, his attention shifting fully from the computer to her. "What's wrong?"

"Nothing, really." Call that the understatement of the century. "I wasn't feeling well. I haven't been feeling right for a couple of weeks, and I wanted to know what was going on."

"So what is it? Are you okay?"

"I'm fine." She took another breath, deep and long enough to make her a little dizzy. "I'm pregnant."

Julian's eyes widened. "What?"

She spread her hands helplessly. "The test was positive. We did an ultrasound, found a heartbeat."

He just looked at her for a time, his face, as always, hard to read. She sat quietly. There was nothing to say, really.

He found something, though. "Whose is it?"

It was her turn to gape in shock. He'd said the words without anger, but that he'd said them at all . . .

"How can you ask me that?"

He shrugged. "We haven't been together all that long. Was there someone before?"

"No. There was nobody before. Not for a couple of years. This is your child, Julian."

His mouth tightened. "That's impossible."

"Apparently not."

Something stirred against her stomach, and she looked down to see her arms folded protectively across her abdomen. This was her child, born of herself and the not-quite-man she loved, and no one, not even its father, would be allowed to speak against it.

He leaned back in his desk chair, his dark, almost-Asian eyes riveted to her face. "You're serious. You're truly serious."

"I am."

"Then, oh my God and holy shit."

She blinked back tears of relief. "Yeah. Something like that."

Standing, he rounded the desk to stand next to her, setting the tips of his fingers against her shoulder. "You're sure you haven't been cheating on me?"

She pushed his hand away. "That is *so* not funny."

He smiled. "Then let's go see the doctor."

***

Dr. Greene looked up from his microscope. "They're motile, all right. See for yourself."

Julian looked into the microscope. "Oh my God and holy shit."

"Yep," Dr. Greene agreed. "They're some happy little swimmers."

Lorelei took her turn, mesmerized by the impossible sight of long-tailed sperm swimming randomly through the microscope's bright field of vision. They were silly-looking, and very beautiful.

"How is this possible?" Julian asked.

She forced herself to look up. When he decided to cloak his emotions it was impossible to tell what he might be thinking, and he had them cloaked now. The realization made her cold inside.

The doctor shrugged and continued, "It's really not much of a stretch, given everything else that's been going on here lately. After all, Lucien's fertile, and he's said you've become something closer to what he is. You don't need human blood anymore, you barely sleep, and you can go out in the daylight. How is motile sperm such a big surprise?"

"Well, when you put it that way." Sarcasm edged Julian's voice.

The doctor straightened, and when he spoke his voice was tight. "The thing you need to consider here is that there's a child on the way. The rest of it is just statistics."

Julian nodded. He looked at the floor, the wall. Not at Lorelei. Never at Lorelei. "This is no place to raise a child."

He walked out of the room, his shoulder barely brushing hers as he passed. She bit her lip and tried hard not to cry.

***

Julian left the doctor's office and kept walking. Down into the Underground, not sure where he went but letting his instincts guide him. There were places down here where no one had been in years. Decades, even. Maybe centuries. They all reeked of vampire. When he'd been one, he hadn't noticed the smell. Now it made him queasy.

Too many things had changed too fast. How was he supposed to assimilate them all? And how was he supposed to focus on the growth and birth of a child in the midst of all this? The vampire reek, the lurking dangers, not to mention the children already here, whom he'd pledged to protect in some way or another. The thought of Lorelei giving birth here was more than unsettling. It chilled his blood.

What was to be done, then? None of the possibilities appealed to him. And the only thing he was sure of was that he needed to apologize to Lorelei.

***

She was in their room, stuffing clothes into a duffel bag. He stood in the open door, staring a moment before it soaked in.

"Lorelei, no."

Her head jerked up to look at him. She'd been crying, but

she wasn't crying now. Her eyes were puffy, but bright and clear. Hard, even. Coolly, she looked away from him.

"I need to think."

"You can't think here?"

Her mouth thinned. "No. Not really."

"What I said . . . I didn't mean I don't want the baby. I only meant—"

"I know what you meant, and I agree. This isn't a suitable place to raise a child, or to give birth to one, for that matter. The place is lousy with vampires, and I get the impression there are bad guys on the way." She shoved a last pair of socks into the bag, then zipped it shut. "I need to think. I'll come back, if only to tell you what I've decided to do."

He swallowed, surprised at the intensity of his own pain. "Don't leave me."

She stilled, then straightened, lifting the bag from the bed. For a moment she stood there, resolve in the set of her body. Then she stepped toward him and brushed a hand down his cheek. "I hope not."

TWO

Standing in front of the once-familiar door to her apartment, Lorelei took a long breath. Nothing felt right anymore. Everything felt wrong. Smelled wrong. The smell of Julian's cigarettes had made her ill lately, but the absence of the same smell left a hollow feeling in her stomach.

She pushed the key into the lock and twisted it, pushed the door open.

Everything was exactly as she'd left it, but it seemed as if she'd never been here before in her life. The couch, the paintings, the stretch of bare floor where dying vampires had bled all over her favorite Oriental rugs—all of it was strange to her.

With a sigh, she tossed her duffel bag on the couch. She wasn't even sure what she expected to accomplish here, or to find. But she knew she had to be here, if only for a short time, to make the decisions she had to make.

She felt lost already. Empty without Julian, but she'd felt empty with him. She just didn't know where to go anymore.

Blinking back tears, which came far too easily of late, she went back out of the apartment. Maybe the boutique would feel more familiar.

***

Finally, downstairs in the boutique she'd nurtured to reasonable success, she found something that didn't seem to belong to someone else's life. Randy sat behind the counter, reading the *New York Times*. He grinned broadly when she came in, laying the paper aside and coming out from behind the counter to embrace her.

"Lor! It's so good to see you." He patted her back a few times, then let her go. "How was the vacation?"

It took her a few seconds to remember the story she'd told him to cover her extended absence. The vacation had

supposedly been to the Magic Kingdom, not Vampire Land.
"Not quite what I expected."
Randy studied her face. "Bummer. Didn't get to meet the Mouse?"
"No. No mouse." She folded her arms over her chest. "Look, Randy, I might be leaving in a few days. If I do, I'm not coming back."
"Ever?"
"No. Not ever."
"That's a bit of a bombshell."
"I know. I'm not sure yet it's going to happen, but if it does, I want you to take over the shop. Take my apartment, too, if you like."
"I don't understand."
"It's just . . . family stuff. I might have to, you know, move."
"I thought you didn't talk to your family."
"I haven't in a while. They're a bunch of freaks." The familiar words fell off her tongue, but they sounded ridiculous now, given the company she'd kept of late. "But they need me." In a way it hurt to realize it wasn't her flesh-and-blood family that needed her. Her mother had abandoned her years ago, her father before that. Aunts and uncles had made a mishmash of her childhood. And look where she was now. Carrying a vampire's illegitimate child. That was what happened when you got stuck with bad parenting.
"Well . . ." Randy seemed confused. "Let me know what happens, okay?"
"Okay." She took a step back, then stopped. "Look, Randy, I owe you more of an explanation than that. Can we get together tonight for dinner? My place?"
He smiled. "Sure."
"Great." Moving her hands helplessly, not sure what else to say, she backed toward the door. "The place looks great, by the way. Keep up the good work."
A less than graceful retreat, she supposed. The door chimed happily as it closed behind her. She took the outside stairs back to her apartment and stretched out on the couch. A good nap never hurt anybody.

***

Julian was moping, and he wasn't too proud to admit it. Concentrating on matters at hand was practically impossible, in spite of the seriousness of the situation.

"I've gathered as much information as I could over the past couple of weeks," Lucien was saying. "From what I've heard, it's hard to tell if the danger is immediate, but we definitely need to prepare."

"The e-mail didn't give a timeframe," Julian said, forgetting he'd said the same thing not ten minutes earlier.

Lucien tilted a brow at him. "No, it didn't. I've contacted my usual sources, and they gave me very little to work with. I believe their Senior is keeping things under tight wraps."

"I would, too, in his position." Julian rubbed his chin. He'd been clean-shaven when he'd died, and for the eight hundred years since. But with everything that had been happening to him lately, he wouldn't be surprised if one morning soon he woke up with stubble. What would Lorelei think of that? If she ever came back.

"Julian?"

His head jerked up. How long had he drifted that time? "I'm sorry. Go on."

Lucien shrugged. "Why bother? You're not listening."

"I'm sorry. I've got . . . things."

"Can I help?"

"I don't know." He took a long breath. "Lorelei left this morning."

"She'll be back."

"I don't know. Maybe not."

"I didn't mean that as a comforting platitude. I meant that as a fact."

"Whatever." Lucien had been getting on his nerves ever since he'd shown up in the Underground, and today was no different. "Let's just get back to this."

"All right." He pointed to the map laid out on the desk in front of them. "This group has been centered in Eastern Europe for centuries, but in the late eighteenth century an offshoot moved to northern Scotland—"

"Lorelei's pregnant."

For the first time since Julian had known him, Lucien looked surprised. His eyes widened a little. "You're serious."

"Yes."

"How did that happen?"

"The usual way, apparently."

"Huh. I wouldn't have expected her to cheat on you."

"She didn't."

Lucien leaned back in his chair. "Wow. You're sure about that?"

"We had a talk with Dr. Greene. My blood cells aren't the only thing that's gotten active over the past few weeks."

"Well, then. Congratulations."

"Yeah. And now she's gone."

"She'll be back."

"I hope so."

"And in the meantime you have to concentrate on this, or she might not have anything to come back to."

Lucien's voice had hardened, and Julian frowned. "I'm the Senior here, not you."

"Then act like it."

Clenching his teeth, Julian returned his attention to the map. "You say these Dark Children are the ones who originally destroyed the Book of Changing Blood?"

"Yes. And now they've gotten wind of our attempted reconstruction, they're probably gathering forces to stop it. They can be tremendously dangerous."

"Your spies. Are you sure they can be trusted?"

"Yes."

"Then we need to get as much information as we can from them."

"I'm working on that. I suggest we might want to send someone of our own out. A 'defector.' Do you know of anyone who could handle that?"

"I don't know. I'll have to give it some thought."

"Don't think for too long. This thing is going to blow up in our faces any minute."

"Okay. Point taken."

***

Lorelei woke two hours later, feeling like the world was an entirely different place. Refreshed, she felt ready to deal with the questions looming all around her. Ready, even, to have an almost-honest heart-to-heart with Randy. If she were making a bad decision, he'd tell her.

The apartment seemed more familiar now, as if its ambience had soaked in through her skin while she was sleeping. She walked around the room, studying her possessions, picking things up here and there and setting them on the coffee table. Part of the problem at Julian's, she realized, was that nothing there belonged to her.

Except him. But again, it just wasn't enough.

As she gathered items, she realized she wasn't making a decision about whether or not to go back. She was preparing to move. She stopped then, sat down on the couch, and looked at the assortment of knick-knacks and paperbacks scattered across the table.

Should she go back? If she did, it would be the end of everything she'd made here in the real world. She'd thought she'd been prepared to do that when she'd stayed with Julian in the first place, but now she wasn't so sure. It seemed a bigger step now that she wasn't the only person involved. She had to make the decision for two people now.

Tears rose suddenly, and she laid a hand over her stomach. How ancient was that reflex? As old as time. Older than Lucien, and Lucien was older than dirt.

She smiled a little. Lucien was good people. Or good vampire, or whatever the hell he was. So were Vivian, and William the accountant, and maybe even Nicky if you could overlook his recent murder spree. Dina had. Maybe it wouldn't be so bad for a kid down there, after all.

He—or she—wouldn't be the only child, after all. There were vampire children in the Underground, as well. Since his transformation and his healing of Nicholas, Julian had been working with Dr. Greene to find a way to reverse their vampirism. No one knew if it was possible, but Julian was convinced it was the right thing to do. She loved him for that.

She loved him. That was the single incontrovertible fact in this entire argument. Maybe if she thought about it long enough, that would be enough.

***

Randy came by at six. Lorelei had thrown together a non-gourmet dinner of spaghetti and root beer. Everything else in the house had spoiled or molded during her absence.

"I can't tell you how good it is to see you again," Randy said.

"Thanks." Lorelei turned down the heat on the pot of cooking spaghetti. "It's nice to be back."

"But you can't stay?" He sat down at the kitchen table, where Lorelei had put together two haphazard place settings.

"I'm not sure."

"So what's up, exactly?"

"It's family stuff," she said stiffly, sticking to the previous story. Then she took a long breath. She had to tell someone the truth, or at least a severely edited version. "It's not family. Not really. It's a guy."

A slow smile spread over Randy's face. "That's great, Lor."

"In a way it is and in a way it isn't." She checked the sauce. It was hot, so she took the pot off the stove and set it in the middle of the table, then followed suit with the spaghetti. "Sorry it's not fancy."

"It doesn't have to be." He transferred spaghetti from the bowl to his plate. "Do you love him?"

"I do." She could say that without hesitation. So why did the rest of the situation seem so difficult?

"Then do what you have to do."

She turned her attention to her meal, not sure what she should, or could, say next. Then, suddenly, she started to talk. "He's wonderful. He loves me. He would give his life for me, and I mean that literally, because he almost did."

Randy grinned. "Is he good in bed?"

"My God, you have no idea."

"Honey, if I could find a man who made me half as happy as you look right now, I'd hightail it out of this city in a minute."

She smiled. He was right. She poured Parmesan cheese

on what was left of her spaghetti. She'd made her decision. Except there'd never really been a question in the first place.

***

Two hours later, her heart considerably lighter, Lorelei bid Randy goodbye. The boutique would be in safe hands, she knew, unless Randy did find that man. Lorelei sincerely hoped he would.

From her closet, she retrieved a pair of suitcases, dragged them into the bedroom, and began to pack all the things she'd missed over the past several weeks. Lacy panties, practical cotton panties, the good bras with the comfortable underwires. Sachets and her favorite pale purple socks. She should have done this a long time ago. Maybe the doubt never would have surfaced if she'd had more familiar things around her.

Then her stomach roiled, suddenly and violently, and she ran for the bathroom. Maybe spaghetti hadn't been the best idea, after all. She rinsed her mouth out and, woozy, lay down in bed.

And woke to the smell of vampires.

THREE

It wasn't Julian's sweet, pleasant odor, either. It was a carrion odor, the smell of vampires who still very much subsisted on the taking of human blood.

She sat up straight in bed, staring out at darkness. Light oozed in through the blinds, painting stripes on the floor. She could hear nothing from the other room. Eyes and ears told her she was alone, but her nose said differently. So did the small hairs standing up on the back of her neck.

As silently as she could, she eased out of the bed. Her toes touched the floor, then her heels. She had no weapon she could think of. Barely breathing, she scanned the room, to see only darkness and the stripes of streetlight.

"You can't escape."

Lorelei gasped. The voice had come from right next to her, but she saw nothing, felt only a vague stirring of air against her arm. A woman's voice. Lorelei froze where she was, still perched on the edge of the bed, feet firmly against the floor, ready to run.

"I'm here to take you," the voice went on. It was a low alto, pleasant if not for the threat it held. Lorelei still saw nothing and no one.

"Take me where?" The words came out of her in a choked whisper. She was surprised she'd been able to make them at all.

"Away. Away from him."

"I don't understand."

"You don't have to understand. The battle begins here."

"What battle?"

Then she saw her. The vampire, barely illuminated by the light from outside. She was taller than Lorelei but waif-thin, long, nearly white hair cascading around an unlined, porcelain face. Her ghostly pale eyes met Lorelei's and held them.

That's how they take you, Lorelei thought. *With the eyes.* She knew the vampire was trying to hypnotize her into submission. The power emanating from her flowed along Lorelei's skin, cold and black. But even when Lorelei looked into the vampire's eyes, the power didn't move deeper than her skin.

The vampire's eyes widened, then narrowed. "Who are you?"

Lorelei clenched her teeth. "I'm the Senior's woman." She turned and ran.

In the living room, next to the fireplace, lay the same poker she'd shoved through another vampire's chest just a few weeks ago. It seemed like another life. In a way, it had been. She snatched up the tool and brandished it.

This vampire was smarter than that one had been, though, and showed no inclination to impale herself on the poker. Instead she walked easily—glided, almost—out of Lorelei's bedroom and stood clean and white next to the door.

"What has he taught you?"

"As much as he could."

The vampire sneered. "Julian is a disgrace to his kind."

"Julian is his own kind." Clenching her hands on the poker, she ran straight at her rival, wielding the makeshift weapon like a lance. The vampire smiled and moved her hand in front of her. Lorelei kept coming. The vampire stopped smiling.

Cold fury mixed with triumph in Lorelei's chest. Whatever tricks her opponent was trying, they obviously weren't working. She kept coming, as fast as she could given the limited distance between them, determined to plant the poker hard in between the white vampire's annoyingly perfect breasts.

At the last second, the vampire's hand came up and caught the end of the poker, flinging it aside, as well as Lorelei, who let go a half-second too late. Lorelei fell hard against the wall and lay still, looking up at her attacker.

"Who are you?" she managed.

The white vampire looked down at her, the thin smile back on her lips. "I am Lilith. I come on the orders of Ialdaboth, to take you away."

The eyes had her now, almost. Lorelei's skin went cold and clammy as her head spun. *Damned hormones*, she thought.

I could have taken that bitch . . .
Then everything went black.

***

Julian lay stretched out on the bed he'd once shared with Lorelei, looking at the maps Lucien had sketched for him. They lacked detail in some areas, but gave him a general idea of where they might start in their move against the Dark Children.

He'd never been to Eastern Europe. Somehow hanging out in the shadow of the Carpathians just seemed too cliché. These so-called Dark Children, though, seemed to have no such reservations. They had an enclave in Sarajevo, and another in Transylvania, for God's sake. Of all the ridiculous places for vampires to hang out en masse.

Then again, they could probably make a killing with the tourists. He frowned at the maps, noticing the location of the Transylvanian enclave—nestled in a sparsely occupied curve of the Carpathians. That story of Lucien's . . .

Lucien hadn't been able to tell them exactly where he and the other First Demons had been born. Geographical concepts hadn't been nearly as clear-cut twelve thousand years ago as they were now. But he'd thought it was somewhere in what was now Eastern Europe. Had these Dark Children maintained that ancient settlement? Many of the older vampires Julian knew, excluding himself, were creatures of habit, so it wasn't outside the realm of possibility that they might have maintained an enclave for twelve thousand years. But it begged the question: had they done it for reasons other than sentiment?

He circled the place on the map. Just a hunch, but someone would have to go there at some point. Back, perhaps, to the very beginning.

His head spun at the thought, strangely, then he realized it wasn't the thought that caused the sensation.

Lorelei.

He *felt* her then, inside his head, her presence steely but crying out for help.

Maps and papers spilled to the floor as he shot out of the bed, heading for the door. Her apartment was too far. He could never get there in time, even using every vampiric power he possessed.

But Lucien could.

He staggered for the door, reaching it just as it came open. Lucien pushed into the room, colliding with Julian. Julian grabbed at the bigger man for balance.

"Lorelei—" he started.

"I know," said Lucien. "Hang on."

Julian already had his fists clenched in Lucien's sweater. Lucien put an arm around his shoulders and drew him in closer. Julian had just enough time to be startled before the room disappeared.

An instant later they were in Lorelei's apartment. The bedroom, Julian noted. The place reeked of vampire. Julian put a hand over his nose as Lucien pushed him away, heading for the living room. Julian followed.

The room was ablaze with white light. Julian caught just a glimpse of Lorelei's black hair, and of another woman, slim and pale, before the light was gone.

He threw himself toward it, but ended up sliding across the floor on his chest, hands grasping at nothing. "Lorelei!"

"It's too late," Lucien's calm voice came from just behind him.

"Shit!" Julian came to his feet, looking wildly around the room. She had to be somewhere. She couldn't have just disappeared into thin air. "*Shit!*"

"They made the first move," said Lucien quietly. "We should have done it, but they beat us to it."

"What the hell could they possibly want with her?" He wanted to hit Lucien for his lack of response. He just stood there, his eyes on Julian's, as composed as if nothing had happened at all.

And he said, very calmly, "To get to you."

***

They went back. There didn't seem to be anything else to do. Julian detoured, though, before they reached his rooms in the Underground.

He kept his food in Vivian's house because she had a

refrigerator. He doubted Lucien would protest a visit to Vivian's. In her kitchen, he poured himself a tall glass of unpasteurized milk and threw a raw chicken breast on a plate. Standing over the sink, he tore into the meat viciously, not bothering to use a knife. He still had his fangs, though he didn't use them anymore. Except for this. It felt good to tear into something. He would have preferred to tear into the throat of the vampire who'd taken Lorelei.

"You all right?" Lucien asked after a time.

"I want her back. And I want whoever took her dead."

Lucien nodded. "We'll get her back." He sat at the kitchen table, folding his hands. "I sensed her strongly when they took her. She's not seriously hurt."

Julian spoke through half-chewed meat, feeling as feral as he had two centuries ago, when he'd still fed on human blood. "She's pregnant, dammit."

"I know."

Julian closed his eyes, calming the rage in his chest. "So what do we do?"

"We wait."

***

He left Lucien at Vivian's. She'd shown up not long after they arrived, and it hurt him to watch the way they looked at each other. It hurt to be in his room, as well, where he could smell Lorelei's skin on the blankets.

He couldn't sleep, anyway. He didn't need to. He sat at his desk and booted up the computer.

He should have paid more attention to the e-mails he'd gotten over the last few weeks. He'd shown Lucien the last one, but even together they hadn't been certain of its meaning. They were strange, though, stranger than the usual offerings. Verses from the Book, supposedly, speaking of the coming of Ialdaboth.

The name sounded so familiar, and not just because of its appearance in heretical Christian texts. No, there was more to it than that. Something to do with what had happened to Lorelei.

He put his head down on the desk, rolling the thoughts around in his head.

Ialdaboth.

And he saw a face. A long-boned, craggy face, with eyes as old even as Lucien's. The memory was clear and clean, burned into his mind.

It wasn't his memory.

It had happened to him before, on occasion, since the day he'd taken the life, the blood, and the memory of the previous Senior. He still wondered from time to time why the Senior had done it—why he'd so willingly given his life to Julian. Perhaps because of this: so Julian could have the memories, and the power to do something about them.

He lifted his head, suddenly groggy, as if he'd slept. The memories were valuable, but when they came to him they brought this weariness after them. He rubbed his eyes.

When he looked up, he was no longer alone.

A woman stood in front of his desk, slim and pale, with long, white hair and almost colorless eyes. Julian stiffened, recognizing her in a flash of realization. She'd taken Lorelei.

He lunged toward her, but she made a quick movement, then disappeared. Something fell on the desk in front of him. He looked down. A computer disk lay there, blue, unlabeled. He picked it up and popped it into the computer.

Five minutes later, teeth clenched so hard his head hurt, he went to find Lucien.

FOUR

When Lorelei's world returned she was stretched out on a mat on a hard floor. Carefully, head spinning, she sat up to examine her surroundings.

There was little to see. The room was small, dark, and damp, the floor and walls apparently of stone. It reminded her of places in the Underground, but it didn't feel the same. Whatever it was—smell, taste, aura—it didn't sit well with her. Her stomach lurched. She swallowed hard and closed her eyes until it settled.

"Welcome back."

Her head jerked toward the voice. The vampire—Lilith, she'd called herself—sat cross-legged on the floor against the opposite wall.

"Bitch," said Lorelei.

Lilith smiled. "Thank you."

"What's this about? Why me?"

"Your boyfriend. Lover. Husband?"

She shook her head.

"The father of your child, then." Lorelei jumped, eyes riveted to Lilith's too-pale face. "Which is an interesting trick, since every vampire I know is sterile."

"Julian isn't a vampire. Not anymore."

"So I'm given to understand. What is he, then?"

Lorelei shook her head. "Even if I knew, I wouldn't give you that."

Lilith pushed a long strand of white-blond hair back from her face. "So perhaps you're a little smarter than I was led to believe."

"What is this about?"

"War. If Julian responds as he should, it will all end here."

"I don't understand."

"He is an abomination, and he works to abominate all the rest of you. Of us. He has to be stopped."

"According to whom?"

"According to the Book. And according to my orders."

Lorelei closed her eyes, suddenly tired. Her body felt heavy and slow. So there were religious fanatics in the vampire world, too. Somehow that didn't surprise her.

"It won't work," she said, trying to convince herself. "He won't come." She knew Julian, though. If they asked him to trade his life for hers, he would do it. She would have done the same for him.

Lilith stood, smiling down at her. "Oh, he'll come. Have no doubt of that."

***

"You can't do this, Julian."

It was the third or fourth or eighth time Lucien had said it, and still Julian refused to hear. He had no choice.

"One life for two. It's a fair trade."

"Mathematics aside, we have to come up with another plan. This community is in no condition to lose you right now."

"And I'm in no condition to lose Lorelei. Or our baby."

"You don't understand the ramifications."

"I understand the facts."

He pulled the maps off the printer. The disk the pale vampiress had left on his desk had contained instructions for a trade, Julian for Lorelei, as well as maps and written directions to reach the exchange point. The instructions said Julian was to come alone.

"I'm going with you," Lucien said.

"No."

"If you go alone, it's all over."

"If you go with me, they'll kill her."

"Whoever she is, if she's alone, I can take her."

"What if she isn't alone?"

"Then I can take Ialdaboth, or die trying."

Julian closed his eyes. How could he make this decision when he wasn't sure what was on the line? Lucien hadn't made everything completely clear, mostly, Julian felt, because he didn't know how to, or didn't understand all the nuances of the situation himself.

"You know him? Ialdaboth?"

"He was one of the first. My brother."

"One of the First Demons?"

"Yes. Me, Aanu, Ialdaboth and Ruha. Aanu and I wrote the Book of Changing Blood. Ialdaboth and Ruha want to destroy it. That absolutely cannot happen, no matter what you or I have to sacrifice along the way."

Julian gave him a level look, a thick weight congealing in his chest. "What would you do if it were Vivian?"

"Exactly what I'm telling you to do."

"Can I believe that?"

"I've been telling the truth for twelve thousand years."

"You lied to Vivian."

"I withheld information. It's different."

Julian's laugh held little amusement. "If you withhold information from me in this, I'll rip your throat out."

"I don't think you could, but your point's taken." He took the maps out of Julian's hand and spread them across the desk. "This is what we need to do."

***

"I don't know. She's very strange, that one."

"Can we keep her alive until he comes? Or is she too much of a danger?"

"I'm not sure yet. Perhaps you should read her."

Lorelei drifted awake on the exchange of voices. Holding as still as she could, holding even her breath, she listened. They were talking about her. But as consciousness returned, the voices faded. Not as if the speakers had left the room, but as if her ability to hear them had simply gone away.

Puzzled, she sat up. The small room was empty except for herself and the few amenities they'd supplied her. So where had the voices come from?

Her neck ached and her back hurt from sleeping on the thin pallet on the floor. Carefully, she stretched, ligaments popping and cracking along her spine. Her stomach roiled. This kind of treatment didn't mix well with early pregnancy. The stench in the room, from the bedpan she'd pushed as far away from her as the small space would allow, didn't help.

"I could use some food!" she shouted, anger rising with her unsettled stomach. "Any of you sons of bitches want to bring me something to fucking *eat!*" She had to swallow the anger then, because if any more of it came out of her it would bring the meager contents of her stomach with it. She closed her eyes and breathed shallowly through her mouth, trying to regain control of her emotions, of her body.

The door opened, admitting the tall, pale vampiress. Lilith, Lorelei reminded herself. Her voice had been one of the two she'd heard earlier. In her head, she suddenly realized. What the hell was going on?

"Is there a problem?" Lilith asked through a thin smirk.

Lorelei wanted to claw the lips off her face. "Yes, there's a problem. I need food, and I need to be somewhere that doesn't smell like a goddamn outhouse."

Lilith glanced at the bedpan, lip curling in delicate distaste. "You shouldn't have filled it up so fast."

"I'm pregnant, you fucking moron. I have to pee a lot. And puke once in a while."

"You might want to moderate your language when your baby's born." She paused, with a hateful smile. "If it's born at all, after all this trauma."

Lorelei held back the urge to fly at her captor. She would have passed out after two steps, the way her head was reeling. But the anger sat hard and fiery just above her knotting, weaving belly. She concentrated on it, gathered strength from it. "You might want to get out of my sight before I rip the hair out of your head and make myself a pretty silver belt out of it." As she spoke, the anger seemed to come together in her solar plexus and shoot forward, an invisible laser beam of hatred.

Lilith blinked and took a step back. Her face seemed to grow paler, but it was hard to tell since it had started out nearly white anyway. She picked up the bedpan.

"I'll clean this for you." Was it Lorelei's imagination, or was Lilith's voice a shade weaker, less confident? "There'll be food in a few minutes."

She left the room. As the door closed behind her, a voice, like the earlier voices, sounded with bell-like clarity in Lorelei's head: *"What is she?"*

FIVE

"Are you sure this is the right direction?" Julian wiped dust from his forehead as Lucien helped him down from yet another narrow tunnel. This one had led them to a small open space, like a cave but obviously not made by nature.

"We're getting closer," Lucien replied. The last tunnel had barely been wide enough for his broad frame. In fact, Julian was relatively sure it hadn't been wide enough at all, by at least a few inches. But here was Lucien on the other side of it, though he looked a little hunched. "I can smell him."

"Who?"

"Ialdaboth."

"What does he smell like?" The question was more than a little facetious, and Lucien tilted an eyebrow at him.

"Like me, but evil."

Agitated as he was, Julian couldn't hold back a smile. "God, he must reek." He pushed his hands through his hair, sending a cascade of dirt and small rocks toward the ground. Coming out of that last tunnel had been like a birthing. "Vivian seemed to know quite a lot about these tunnels."

Lucien squared his shoulders with a disconcerting pop. Julian grimaced, realizing what had just happened. Lucien hadn't been hunched before—he'd dislocated both his shoulders to make it through the too-narrow tunnel. Now he tilted his head, eyes closed. "She helped map a large section of them for the former Senior shortly after she arrived in New York. That was about a hundred-and-fifty years ago." He looked up. "That way."

He pointed toward what looked like little more than a cleft in the opposite wall. "That's a way?" said Julian.

"I hope so." Lucien headed across the small room and stuck an arm into the cleft, his body following after a disconcerting moment during which Julian was relatively certain Lucien reconfigured half his ribcage.

Well, that was encouraging. Hoping he wouldn't have to follow Lucien's example and rearrange any parts of himself,

Julian followed.

***

"You're certain this is what happened?"

"She has some kind of power. I'm not certain she's aware of it, herself."

"What is your estimate of this power?"

"It's strong. Very strong."

"She was supposed to be human."

"If she was, she's not anymore."

Lorelei shifted on the thin pallet. She'd discovered over the last couple of hours that she could tune in to her captors' conversation. When it had happened earlier in the day, it had been an accident, brought on most likely by her sheer weariness. Now, if she closed her eyes and let herself drift into something approximating a meditative state—which wasn't too hard given how exhausted she was—she could listen in at will. The trick was keeping herself in the semi-meditative state without falling asleep.

She'd learned a great deal over the last two hours. First and foremost, Lilith was afraid of her. Ialdaboth was confused by her. He'd expected something different. Something wholly human, for starters. Her pregnancy had surprised him, as well. At first he'd seen it as an advantage. Lorelei's state would make her more malleable, Julian that much more willing to cooperate. Now it looked more like a liability.

"The pregnancy brings her power." This was Ialdaboth, his "voice" a dark, smoky sound, a black serpent slithering through her brain. *"She will do things she wouldn't normally do, to protect the child."*

Damn straight. At least they seemed to have a clue what they were messing with. Where before they'd dismissed her as weak and inferior, now they were taking her seriously. Best of all, they didn't seem to realize her "power" extended to eavesdropping on their conversations through a stone wall.

Lilith's voice sounded again, a paler snake of thought-sound. *"But he will, as well. He will come to save the child, if not to save her."*

Another sensation passed through Lorelei's inner hearing.

Like a long breath or a sigh, but black and reeking. She breathed slowly through her mouth to keep herself from flinching away. Then Ialdaboth spoke again. *"I must evaluate this before we proceed."*

Lorelei jumped, immediately breaking the connection. She'd felt Ialdaboth move forward, physically, toward the door to her chamber. Swallowing her fear, she drew herself up on her small pallet, putting as much confidence into her posture as she could muster.

Ialdaboth's exterior wasn't nearly as frightening as the voice she'd been hearing in her head. He reminded her of Lucien, in fact. Tall like Lucien, with similarly rough-etched features, as if he'd been made before God had quite figured out how to properly configure the human face. He had scars, too, like Lucien, threading all over his face, but his were darker, more recent.

The similarities ended, though, when she looked into his eyes. The eyes were ancient like Lucien's, but those thousands of years were full of hatred, pain—she hesitated at the word "evil," but perhaps it was the only word that fit.

"Lorelei Fletcher," he said. His voice thrummed, and she wondered if he were trying to put the vampire whammy on her. Nicholas had done it to her once, some time ago, but she'd changed since then. The rhythm of her heartbeat seemed to change a little, and her throat tightened.

"That's my name," she said evenly.

Ialdaboth took another long step into the room, letting Lilith come in behind him. He wore black, head to toe, with a little silver piping at his collar and a big, square, silver buckle on his black belt. No cape, though, so at least he'd stopped a few millimeters from pure melodrama.

"What are you?" he asked.

She shrugged. "How the hell should I know?"

He took a step closer, and she craned her neck up at him, still sitting serenely on the pallet, legs crossed, hands cupped one atop the other in her lap as if she were about to embark on a flight of Zen meditation. With effort, she kept her breathing long and slow, kept the ghost of a smile on her mouth. He stared down at her for a long moment, his eyes locked to hers. She stared back and realized his gaze had no effect on her. Was that normal?

Finally he squatted in front of her pallet. Silent, he continued to search her eyes, his mouth tightening as the seconds passed and Lorelei continued to smile placidly at him. She still wasn't sure what he was doing, but apparently it wasn't working.

Then she felt the little threads, mobile threads that worried their way down into her mind. Black threads, the same color as his shirt. He was, indeed, trying to put the vampire whammy on her.

So she thought about white. White light that filled her mind and ate the black threads as they tried to infringe. The threads dissolved in the onslaught, and she kept her Mona Lisa smile as she focused again on Ialdaboth's face.

And just for a moment she saw fear there.

If she could put fear in this creature's face, what else could she do? What had Julian made her into? She couldn't think about that now. Later.

Ialdaboth, rose, the scars on his face suddenly a shade redder than they had been before, took a step back, then turned and left the small, stinking room.

***

Julian leaned against the wall, puffing on a cigarette while Lucien stood staring into space. Per Lucien's earlier request, he blew the smoke back into the cleft from which they'd just emerged. Apparently when you were sniffing for evil, cigarette smoke interfered. But after that last tunnel, Julian had needed one rather desperately. He still hurt where he'd scraped half the skin off his back, though the wound had already healed. His shirt, however, would never recover.

"They're on the other side of this wall," Lucien announced suddenly.

Julian took a last drag on the cigarette and snubbed it out. He seemed to need fewer lately, to get the same effect. Maybe his body was naturally weaning itself. That would make Lorelei happy.

"So how do we get through the wall?"

Lucien looked back over his shoulder at Julian, frowning. "Well, that's the trick, isn't it?" He put his hands against the wall and closed his eyes.

Julian swallowed frustration. Lucien's methods didn't make much sense to him, and for the most part Lucien didn't bother to explain them, but they seemed to work. So, for the moment, it seemed wise just to let the big demon-spawn work.

"I think I can do this," he said finally, straightening.

"Do what?"

"Take us through this wall. There's an open space on the other side, part of a small complex of caves. Ialdaboth is in those caves, and another vampire, and someone else that must be Lorelei."

"A human?"

"No. Not human." He shook his head. "I'm pretty sure it's Lorelei, but she feels different than she did even as recently as the last time I saw her." He turned away from the wall. "Had you noticed that? That she was changing?"

Julian shook his head. "I don't have your sensitivity."

"But you Made her."

"I didn't Make her in the sense that I created another vampire. Whatever I did to her didn't cause the same kind of connection. I can sense things from her, but they're vague."

"Interesting. I wonder what exactly you did to her."

He said it matter-of-factly, but Julian couldn't help an inward cringe. He'd wondered the same thing, many times since the day he'd sent Lorelei off nearly to death and brought her back. But a number of factors had contributed to her transformation. He kept reminding himself of that, if only to alleviate his guilt.

"Or what we did to her," Lucien added, and Julian nodded. That felt more fair. Lucien rubbed his hands together thoughtfully. "So are you ready?"

"Ready for what?"

"To go through this wall."

"Are you sure you can do it?"

"We'll either make it through or end up embedded in granite for eternity."

Julian made a face. "That'd kill me, wouldn't it?"

"Probably. It wouldn't kill me, though, and that'd be a bitch." He gestured to Julian. "Let's go."

***

"It's not right."
"You question my judgement?"
"Yes, I do."
"I thought I trained you better than that."
"You trained me to obey without question."
"Then why are you not doing that?"
"Because this makes no sense."

Lorelei opened her eyes, easing the intensity of the thoughts she eavesdropped on. Some of the background emotions were so strong they physically hurt. The power of Ialdaboth's mind frightened her, yet he couldn't hear her intrusion. And Lilith—she lacked the power, but within her boiled conflict so violent Lorelei marveled she could even contain it.

I betray myself. I betray everything I have been taught, everything I have ever been. Instinctively, Lorelei knew these were Lilith's unvoiced thoughts. She seemed to burrow deeper into Lilith's mind with each session of contact.

You betray nothing, Lorelei thought, and wondered if Lilith could hear her. *The world is about to change forever. Choose your side. Side with the Eaters of Light.*

She wasn't even sure where some of that had come from. She was starting to sound like Lucien. And her head was starting to hurt from the intensity of what she did. She rubbed her belly in a slow, circular motion, half-convinced she could sense the growing child inside her.

"Hang on," she said aloud, softly. "Just hang on."

"Lorelei."

She sat up straight, shocked at the new voice. She knew it. "Julian."

But there was no answer, not right away, and then the door to her small chamber opened.

Ialdaboth's eyes were cold and hard. He stared down at Lorelei under a deeply beetled brow. Hatred rolled off him in hot, hurting waves. Lorelei flinched, but gathered herself quickly. Next to him, Lilith regarded her with pleading eyes, her hands twisting together.

"What did he do to you?" Ialdaboth demanded.

With a steadiness born either of courage or stupidity, or perhaps just from the fierceness of motherlove, Lorelei stared straight into his eyes. "He loved me."

The vampire or demon or whatever he was drew himself to his full height, towering over Lorelei where she sat on the floor, towering over the hunched and frightened, pale figure of Lilith. His eyes bored into Lorelei's, and she felt again the black intrusion of his mind. And again refused to let him in. He glared at her until his presence became a miasma around her, almost thick enough to smell. Then he snatched it away. Blinking, Lorelei could actually see it as it swarmed back into him through his eyes.

He turned and looked down at Lilith. "Kill her."

SIX

"No," said Lilith, her voice firm and thrumming in spite of her anguished face and wringing hands. Lorelei tensed. Someone was about to die, but who would it be?

"You defy me?" Ialdaboth's bellow filled the small room to bursting. Lilith flinched. Lorelei sat very still, knees under her chin.

And heard the voice again.

"Lorelei."

She closed her eyes. *"Julian."*

"You're there. I'm coming. Guide me in."

She had no idea how to do that, but held to the feeling of his voice inside her head, folding it within her. As she fought to keep his presence focused in her mind, she sensed more. Emotion—fear for her safety. Sensation—his arms locked around Lucien as they focused power. The taste of a recently smoked cigarette in his mouth—

"You will not defy me!"

The thunder of Ialdaboth's voice broke her concentration, and her sense of Julian fell from her mind. She fumbled after it as best she could, but the remnants slipped between the grasping fingers of her consciousness.

"I will," said Lilith, and Lorelei's focus shifted toward her. It felt strange to her. More than just turning her vision toward the other woman, she turned her mind and the new senses she had discovered within it. It was like rotating a column of power, or a huge-barreled gun.

"What you ask me to do is wrong," Lilith went on. "You would kill her for no more reason than that you do not understand her power."

"I do not need to understand her power." No longer bellowing, Ialdaboth's voice slithered now along the walls. Lilith cowered under it. "I need only to know that it is an abomination."

"According to whom?"

"According to everything we believe. Everything you have

been taught."

It amazed Lorelei that Lilith could hold up under the pressure of that voice. Ialdaboth had put no compulsion into it, but the slithering sound of it made Lorelei's skin ache. Had she been in Lilith's place she would have been tempted to do anything to make it stop.

Lilith drew herself up as straight and tall as possible, shaking her long, pale hair back from her face and shoulders. She looked so small, so breakable.

"What if everything I have been taught is wrong?"

Ialdaboth's glare transfixed her. Lorelei could see the power now—a sickening blackish-green cloud vomited from his eyes, falling onto Lilith's upturned face. He wove compulsion around her and within it Lilith turned slowly toward Lorelei, fighting vainly.

"You will kill her," said Ialdaboth. The words drifted through the cloud on ripples that broke against Lilith's face.

"No," said Lilith. The effort to speak brought blood to the corners of her eyes.

Rage filled Lorelei as the crimson tears wound down Lilith's alabaster face. Her fists clenched, and she turned toward Ialdaboth, fury a blinding red thing behind her eyes.

"No," she said, and flung the blood-red of her anger into the black-green of his compulsion.

It broke. The dark, ugly cloud separated in the middle and Lilith staggered backward, staring at Lorelei in amazement.

Lorelei was dumbfounded herself, but she didn't have time to indulge in shock. Instead she kept her focus steady on Ialdaboth, matching his black gaze, which changed as she stared from anger to shock to terror.

"If she doesn't want to kill me," Lorelei said calmly, "she doesn't have to."

For what seemed a very long time, Ialdaboth only stared at her, into her eyes, as if trying one last time to break the defenses she wielded against him. Then he lifted his hand, his fingers angled out toward her, their tips, in Lorelei's strangely enhanced vision, glowing brilliant red.

"No!"

Lilith's scream barely registered in Lorelei's hearing as she braced herself for Ialdaboth's attack, certain the flood of scarlet light would be the last thing she would ever see. But instead she saw Lilith's pale body arc in front of Ialdaboth, as the wave of red flooded from his fingers. She saw Lilith backlit in scarlet, saw the blood stream from her eyes down her face, saw her collapse onto the dirt floor like a broken doll.

And stood staring in the suspended moment as Ialdaboth also stared, as Lilith looked up at the ceiling and smiled, then closed her blood-filled eyes.

Then suddenly the room was filled with light. Lorelei took a step back away from it, smelling a puff of sulphur.

"Lorelei!"

Julian was there in front of her, Lucien next to him. She reached to him, too weak with shock to move, and he closed his arms tight around her. "Are you all right?"

"More or less." She peered at his companion. "About fucking time you got here."

Julian cradled her against him. "My dear, if the first word out of our child's mouth is 'fuck,' I'm going to be quite irritated." There were tears in his voice. She clung to him, reveling in his solidity. Then she straightened in his arms and turned toward Ialdaboth.

He stood with his eyes locked to Lucien's. In her new vision, Lorelei saw a blue-black, twisted cord of light connecting one gaze to the other. The blue and black strands writhed against each other, like pythons engaged in a deathmatch. Finally, simultaneously, both retreated. Ialdaboth gave Lucien a slow smile. "Belial," he said.

"Not for a long time," said Lucien.

"That's right. You and Samis abandoned the demon names."

"Because we're not demons."

"Yes, you are. We all are. To deny it is blasphemy."

Julian pushed Lorelei behind him, and she peered around his shoulder, annoyed by his insistence on protecting her. No more power passed from Lucien to Ialdaboth, but somehow she knew Lucien had the upper hand.

"Regardless," he said quietly, "you will leave now."

Ialdaboth held his gaze for a time, his fists clenching and unclenching, his mouth a thin line. Still, he sent forth no power. He looked at Lorelei, back at Lucien, then, in a sudden implosion of blue light, he disappeared.

A layer of tension fell from the room.

"That," Lorelei said, "is about the most annoying prick of a pre-vampire it's been my pleasure to meet." She stepped out from behind Julian, her attention focused now on Lilith, still and broken on the dirt floor.

"He was always my least favorite brother," said Lucien. He watched as Lorelei knelt next to Lilith. "Who's she?"

"She kidnapped me." She reached toward the pale, blood-sheeted face, hesitant, then let her fingers touch the curve of Lilith's cheek.

"Good riddance, then," said Julian.

"No." Lilith's skin was cold under Lorelei's fingers, but she wasn't sure if that indicated death, or simply reflected her vampiric status. "She saved my life, just before you popped in."

Julian knelt next to Lorelei. "Then I'll do what I can."

Lucien and Lorelei stepped back, leaving Julian to his work. He bent over Lilith, setting his hands against her forehead, her cheek. White light covered his hands, her face.

"Can you see that?" Lorelei mumbled.

"See what?" said Lucien.

"The light."

He quirked an eyebrow. "No."

She nodded. She'd expected as much. The light grew under Julian's hands and began to pulse, growing up his arms and down into Lilith's chest. Power moved along the pulsations, passing from him into her. If she listened closely in the suspended silence, Lorelei could actually hear it, thrumming with the rhythm of a heartbeat.

After a time the white light took on a pinkish tinge, then red, and finally Lilith stirred. Julian held on for a few more breaths, then sat back on his heels.

"I died," said Lilith, her voice weak and still hurting.

"Yes," said Julian. "But only for a few minutes." His smile

was gentle as he held a hand out to her and helped her to sit up. She wiped her eyes, stared at the blood on her fingers.

"Thank you," said Lorelei. Lilith looked up and smiled. Julian helped her to her feet.

"We should go," he said.

"I don't know how you came in," Lilith said, "but I know a quick way out."

Lucien made a sweeping gesture toward the door. "Lead on."

***

Lilith's way was quick, but it took them all the way out to an abandoned warehouse somewhere in Manhattan. Here, too, Lorelei could see the tendrils of power, the vampire "magic" that kept the warehouse abandoned, because no human being could quite see the building. Julian knew the way to the Underground from there, leading them through the nighttime streets to a back alley where the power appeared again. The tendrils were woven differently here, as if the camouflage had been constructed by a different vampire or group of vampires. The patterns of light and color fascinated her.

"What do you see?" Lucien asked, noticing her preoccupation.

"Colors. Lots of pretty colors."

Lucien nodded, but Julian looked at her as if he didn't know who she was. She swallowed hard. She hadn't expected this. Before Lilith had appeared in her apartment, she'd thought she'd made her decision. Now it seemed there were other factors to consider.

Finally their surroundings began to look familiar. Except for Lorelei's new layer of vision, which covered everything in the Underground with an aura of power. Once the corridors began to open into rooms, though, the power became sparser, paler, and finally disappeared. They passed through the rune-marked archway, the green-lit maze of crystal, then stopped outside the door to Julian's office.

"You'll need a place to sleep," he said to Lilith. "Lorelei, could you help her with that? Lucien, we need to talk."

And he went into the office and closed the door.

Lorelei, blinking back tears, looked at Lucien. "What the hell is his problem?"

Lucien shook his head. "I don't know. But if he doesn't get over it in the next five minutes, I'll slam him into the wall until he does."

That brought a faint smile to Lorelei's lips. "Thanks. I knew I could count on you." She took Lilith's hand and led her down the hallway. Julian was a moron. Lilith didn't need a place to sleep. What she needed was a doctor.

SEVEN

Julian fell into his office chair, sending it rolling across the floor. Absently, he braked with his foot against the desk.

He couldn't get the image out of his mind—Lorelei's odd, almost enraptured expression as she watched things around them no one else could see. And Ialdaboth, looking from her to Lucien before he'd disappeared, as if the two represented equal threats. It was too much to take in all at once. He turned toward the desk, put his head in his hands.

Behind him, the office door opened, then closed. He knew without looking Lucien had come in. "What did I do to her?" he said, a vague keen in his voice.

"Most recently, I'd say you pissed her off."

Julian turned to look at Lucien, surprised by the seemingly flip answer. But Lucien's expression was anything but amused.

"Get it together, Julian. She's been through enough without you going all apeshit about this."

"She's not even human anymore, and that's my fault."

"If it's anybody's fault, it's mine. I activated the marker in her, and I told her what that meant. It was her choice to give you her blood. I wonder if she's regretting that decision right now."

"I took away every chance she had of a normal life."

"She saved your life, and now she's carrying your child. You owe her, Julian. If you've decided you don't love her anymore, fine, but dammit, you owe her more than this."

"I never said I didn't love her."

"Then quit acting like an idiot. If there's one thing I can't stand, it's a whiny vampire."

He disappeared. No ceremony, no warning, just a soft implosion of the air where he'd stood. Julian stared, blinking.

Lucien was right. Julian owed Lorelei everything. But how could she ever forgive him for what he'd done to her?

In his eight hundred plus years, Julian had created only a handful of vampires. This was why. The guilt suffocated him when he saw them struggling to adjust to their new existence. He'd always given them a choice, made certain they wanted to be changed before he'd done the deed, but even then he'd accepted the burden of the responsibility. After all, he'd known exactly what they were getting into. They hadn't. Sometimes the price of immortality had been too much to take, and they'd broken under the strain. Those deaths weighed on his conscience as if he'd thrown them out into the sun with his own hands.

Lorelei had made her decision with eyes as open as it had been possible for them to be. Neither of them had known what the final results would be when she'd given Julian her genetically coded blood. Even now, the answers weren't completely clear. But she'd shouldered the burden of her change with courage far beyond anything Julian had ever seen. He loved her for that. He would always love her.

Still, it hurt to know he'd changed her. That she'd never be the same again, in any sense of the word.

Then again, none of them would. Nothing and no one in the vampire community would ever be what they'd been only a few weeks ago. Nothing could change that.

Julian lit a cigarette, sucking in the spicy smoke. He'd taken the first, irrevocable step toward this day when he'd smoked from the Sioux shaman's pipe over two hundred years ago. The path had seemed noble then. Now it was unfathomable.

And Lucien was right—whining wasn't going to change a thing.

He leaned back in his chair to enjoy the cigarette. When he was done, he'd go find Lorelei and tell her...something. Something lovely and deep that would warm her heart and make her want to be with him forever.

Something that didn't involve whining.

***

Lorelei watched from a chair by the door while Dr. Greene shone a penlight into Lilith's eyes. The pale vampiress sat motionless, moving her eyes when asked, saying nothing. She looked so fragile now, like white porcelain, that Lorelei found it hard to remember she'd been a threat only hours earlier.

The doctor lowered the penlight and touched Lilith's throat, searching for the vague, cold pulse that marked the movement of a vampire's borrowed blood. Then he brushed the back of his hand against her cheek and smiled. "I think you'll be all right."

Lilith began to shake. Lorelei rushed to her, taking her hand as she trembled, her whole body caught in tremors. The doctor cupped his hand around Lilith's face, his gaze steady on hers. "It's all right," he said gently. "It's okay."

Suddenly Lorelei felt she had no place there, with the woman who had almost killed her, then sacrificed her life to save her. She released Lilith's hand, and it moved to Dr. Greene's shoulder. When Lorelei closed the door behind her, the doctor had grabbed a handful of tissues from a box on the counter and was wiping tears and blood from Lilith's waxen face.

In the hallway, Lorelei leaned against the wall and crossed her arms over her stomach. How long before she could actually feel the life inside her? She knew next to nothing about things like that. There'd never been any need to know. She hoped it would be soon. Right now it seemed so unreal it was hard to believe she was pregnant at all.

In fact, right now the only thing that seemed real to her was the memory of Julian's face as he'd turned away from her.

He didn't want her. Whatever she'd become, it was as repulsive to him as it was frightening to Ialdaboth. She should go home, reclaim her old life, and forget him.

Strangely, she felt no sadness. No tears pricked her eyes, no lump rose into her throat. She just felt empty, numb. Too much had happened over the past hours. Too much for her to deal with all at once.

She walked slowly down the hallway away from Dr. Greene's office, her arms folded protectively over her abdomen. Once she would have gotten lost in the long corridors, but now she could see the growing patterns of light that showed her the way back to reality.

She could cry tomorrow.

***

As ready as he'd ever be, Julian knocked on the door to his and Lorelei's room. He had a peace offering in one hand, well thought-out and carefully wrapped.

There was no answer.

He tried again, then called her name. Still nothing. Finally he pushed open the door.

"Lorelei?"

The room was dark, Lorelei nowhere to be seen. Only a small, white square of paper on the nightstand next to the bed. Tamping down hard on his fear, he picked it up. It was written in a careful hand, and it occurred to him that he'd never seen Lorelei's handwriting before.

"Julian. I'm sorry for all that has happened. If this is too much for you, I understand. This is no place to raise a baby, anyway.

"With love, Lorelei."

Then below, in a much darker, stronger hand:

"Okay, no, I don't understand. I want to be with you, and you are a fucking asshole for driving me away. A baby should be with his parents. That includes his father. If you don't want to be with me, fine, go fuck yourself.

"With love, Lorelei."

Smiling, Julian folded the note and tucked it into his pocket.

***

"...so that's it. And now I'm back."

Lorelei sipped at her Coke, wishing she could drink something stronger. She wanted whiskey, to burn away the anger in the back of her throat.

Randy, sitting across from her on the couch in her living room, shook his head. "I'm sorry, Lor. Guys can be such jerks."

She shook her head. "I don't know if he's a jerk or not. I just know it's not working out the way I thought it would."

"You want me to go see the guy? Beat some sense into him?"

She smiled wanly. "I wish you could. But it really wouldn't be safe."

"He's a thug, or what?"

"No, he just has a lot of weird friends."

He nodded. "You be sure to let me know if you need anything, okay?"

"I will."

They sat in silence for a time while Lorelei sipped her Coke and wondered why she hadn't cried yet. Damn hormones. They made her want to cry when there was no reason to, but wouldn't let her cry now. It made no sense.

"Are you sure you'll be okay?"

She nodded at Randy's question, though she barely heard it. Someone was coming up the stairs, if her guess was right. She smiled and went to the door.

"Time for me to leave?" said Randy, his tone wavering between surprise and laughter.

"No. Not yet." She put her hand on the doorknob just as the knock fell. Randy's brows lifted.

Julian was standing in the hallway, as she'd known he would be. He had a hesitant smile on his face and a small, gold-wrapped box in his hand.

"May I come in?"

"I'm not sure."

"I got your note."

"Good."

They stood a moment regarding each other, until finally Julian looked over Lorelei's shoulder, into the room beyond. "Who's your friend?"

Lorelei half-turned into the room, looking at Randy. Julian took the opportunity to slide by her into the apartment.

"You've met Randy. He works with me at the boutique."

"Yes, I remember." He stepped toward the couch while Lorelei gently closed the door. "Nice to see you again, Randy. But you might want to go now."

Lorelei heard the faint edge of compulsion in his voice, then realized she could see it. Each word left a small blue haze of light behind it as its vibrations crossed the room.

"Don't," she said.

Julian quirked an eyebrow at her. "My apologies."

Randy stood, looking back and forth between them. He looked like he might be afraid, but Lorelei wasn't sure. In any case, his expression told her he'd realized he was out of his depth. "I'll head out now," he said. "I'll see you later, Lor."

"'Bye, Randy."

She saw Randy to the door. He paused in the hallway. "Damn, he's intense," he whispered.

"I know."

"Is he that focused in bed?"

"More."

Randy shook his head in admiration. "If I don't hear from you, I'll know why."

Lorelei smiled. "I'll call you and let you know what I'm going to do. He can't distract me that much."

"Damn, he could me."

"'Bye, Randy." She closed the door on his departing wave and turned around. Julian sat sprawled on her couch, regarding her with a look that made her skin prickle with heat.

She crossed her arms over her breasts, sure her nipples were giving her away. "So what do you want?"

He handed her the little gold-wrapped box.

"What's this?"

"Open it."

She sat in the chair opposite him and carefully untied the metallic ribbon. Inside was a small box. She opened it. Inside were a dozen or so of Julian's hand-rolled cigarettes.

"I don't get it."

"Consider it a peace offering. I smoked my last an hour ago."

"You're quitting?"

"Yes."

She put the lid back on the box. "You've been smoking for two hundred years."

"A little over, but yes. I don't need them anymore. It's just habit now. I can deal with that, especially if it's important to you."

"The smell was making me sick."

"I know. Because of the pregnancy. I quit using the tobacco a few days ago, and everything else is pretty harmless. I looked all the rest of the herbs up online. But the smell bothers you, so it's gone."

"This is a stupid gift." She said it through tears, as her recalcitrant hormones finally decided they were appropriate. "Next time I want chocolate."

"Come home with me, and I'll get you all the chocolate you want."

She put her nose in the box and sniffed carefully. The spicy clove scent of the cigarettes made her think of the first time they'd made love, here in this apartment. She would keep these. The smell didn't bother her so much when it wasn't coming from the smoke. Maybe they'd make a nice sachet. She could put them in her underwear drawer, and then all her panties would smell like sex with Julian.

Not a bad idea. She smiled up at him. "Okay, I'll come home. But that chocolate had better be Godiva."

He bent to kiss her, his hand gentle against her stomach where his child would soon make its presence known. She covered her hand with his and bent back, away from his kiss, to look into his eyes.

"We don't even know what we are yet," she said. "What will he be?"

Julian shook his head. "It doesn't matter. Not yet. But when we do find out, we'll do it together."